Dead Man Talking

Night of the Loving Dead

Tombs of Endearment

"[A] PI who is Stephanie Plum-meets-*Sex and the City*'s Carrie Bradshaw . . . It's fun, it's 'chick,' and appealing . . . [A] quick, effortless read with a dash of Bridget Jones–style romance."
—PopSyndicate.com

"With witty dialogue and an entertaining mystery, Ms. Daniels pens an irresistible tale of murder, greed, and a lesson in love. A well-paced storyline that's sure to have readers anticipating Pepper's next ghostly client."
—*Darque Reviews*

"Sassy, spicy . . . Pepper Martin, wearing her Moschino Cheap & Chic pink polka dot sling backs, will march right into your imagination."
—Shirley Damsgaard, author of *The Seventh Witch*

The Chick and the Dead

"Amusing with her breezy chick-lit style and sharp dialogue."
—*Publishers Weekly*

"Ms. Daniels has a hit series on her hands."
—*The Best Reviews*

"Ms. Daniels is definitely a hot new voice in paranormal mystery . . . Intriguing . . . Well-written . . . with a captivating storyline and tantalizing characters."
—*Darque Reviews*

"[F]un, flirtatious, and feisty . . . [A] fast-paced read, filled with likeable characters."
—Suite101.com

Don of the Dead

"Fabulous! One of the funniest books I've read this year."
—MaryJanice Davidson, *New York Times* bestselling author

Titles by Casey Daniels

DON OF THE DEAD
THE CHICK AND THE DEAD
TOMBS OF ENDEARMENT
NIGHT OF THE LOVING DEAD
DEAD MAN TALKING
TOMB WITH A VIEW
A HARD DAY'S FRIGHT

A Hard Day's Fright

CASEY DANIELS

BERKLEY PRIME CRIME, NEW YORK

THE BERKLEY PUBLISHING GROUP
Published by the Penguin Group
Penguin Group (USA) Inc.
375 Hudson Street, New York, New York 10014, USA

Penguin Group (Canada), 90 Eglinton Avenue East, Suite 700, Toronto, Ontario M4P 2Y3, Canada
(a division of Pearson Penguin Canada Inc.)
Penguin Books Ltd., 80 Strand, London WC2R 0RL, England
Penguin Group Ireland, 25 St. Stephen's Green, Dublin 2, Ireland (a division of Penguin Books Ltd.)
Penguin Group (Australia), 250 Camberwell Road, Camberwell, Victoria 3124, Australia
(a division of Pearson Australia Group Pty. Ltd.)
Penguin Books India Pvt. Ltd., 11 Community Centre, Panchsheel Park, New Delhi—110 017, India
Penguin Group (NZ), 67 Apollo Drive, Rosedale, North Shore 0632, New Zealand
(a division of Pearson New Zealand Ltd.)
Penguin Books (South Africa) (Pty.) Ltd., 24 Sturdee Avenue, Rosebank, Johannesburg 2196,
South Africa

Penguin Books Ltd., Registered Offices: 80 Strand, London WC2R 0RL, England

This is a work of fiction. Names, characters, places, and incidents either are the product of the author's imagination or are used fictitiously, and any resemblance to actual persons, living or dead, business establishments, events, or locales is entirely coincidental. The publisher does not have any control over and does not assume any responsibility for author or third-party websites or their content.

A HARD DAY'S FRIGHT

A Berkley Prime Crime Book / published by arrangement with the author

PRINTING HISTORY
Berkley Prime Crime mass-market edition / April 2011

ISBN: 978-0-425-24056-4

BERKLEY® PRIME CRIME
Berkley Prime Crime Books are published by The Berkley Publishing Group,
a division of Penguin Group (USA) Inc.,
375 Hudson Street, New York, New York 10014.
BERKLEY® PRIME CRIME and the PRIME CRIME logo are trademarks of Penguin Group (USA)
Inc.

PRINTED IN THE UNITED STATES OF AMERICA

10   9   8   7   6   5   4   3   2   1

For Leslie Wey,
as good a brainstormer as she is a friend.

Prologue

August 14, 1966

Here's the thing people didn't get about Lucy Pasternak, I mean people who never met her: Lucy sparkled.

Back when the rest of us Baby Boomers where white bread ordinary, Lucy was one of the beautiful people. Inside and out. She wasn't afraid to let it show, either. Lucy let her personality shine through, no matter what people said or thought about her. Like that time the kids in her sophomore class were picking on a newcomer simply because she was new, and Lucy stood up for the girl and welcomed her to her lunch table (which, because it was Lucy's, was *the* lunch table).

Or the night we went to the Beatles concert at Cleveland Municipal Stadium, and Lucy wore a miniskirt seven inches above her knees. Nobody was doing that then. I mean, *nobody* but the models in the fashion magazines. My mother practically choked when Lucy walked in to pick me up to go the concert. And me? I don't think the word *dork* had been coined yet, but I didn't need a word to explain how I felt standing next to tall, reed-thin Lucy in my turquoise and white plaid skirt, my blue blouse, my kneesocks, and the matching cardigan my mother insisted I wear in case it got chilly. Oh yeah, I was a dork, all right, and I could only pray that by the time three years passed and I was seventeen—as old and mature as Lucy—I'd be half as cool.

Yes, we did use the word *cool*.

I remember that distinctly, because I remember the first words Lucy spoke when we all piled onto the train (only, here in Cleveland, we call it the *rapid*) to head home after the concert.

"I am cool! I am brave! I am, my dear friends, groovy, neat, and really something else!"

Lucy flopped into the seat beside me. When most girls were still wearing their hair teased up into a beehive and hair sprayed to within an inch of its life, Lucy's sweet corn-colored hair was past her shoulders and as straight as she could get it with the help of her mom's iron and ironing board. She swung her head, and her hair gleamed. She was wearing golden lipstick and her nails glistened with gold polish, too, only Lucy called it "nail lacquer," the way the English girls we read about in *Seventeen* did.

Like I said, Lucy was cool.

And she was so hyped-up that night, she wasn't about to let anyone forget how cool.

Just before the train lurched forward, Lucy jumped out of her seat and squealed the news for all the world to hear. "I am the bravest person in the world! The bravest . . ." She heaved a sigh and touched one finger to her golden lips. "And the luckiest!"

When the old lady sitting across the aisle gave her a dirty

look, I signaled Lucy to sit down. "You're already in enough trouble for getting that F in your summer school poetry class," I reminded her, sure to keep my voice down. The kids we were with were Lucy's friends, and all of them were older than me. I didn't want them to think I was some kind of reject, or worse, a know-it-all. "You're lucky you got to go to the concert tonight. If your mom finds out you were acting up on the rapid—"

Lucy threw back her head and laughed, completely ignoring my warning.

"I kissed Paul," she told the woman sitting across from us, and I guess she figured it was all she needed to say, because she laughed again and turned away from the lady so she could tell us what she'd already told us a couple dozen times since we walked out of the concert. Not that I minded or anything. As far as I was concerned, Lucy could go right on telling the story forever. It was that amazing.

"I got out of my seat and ran onto the field and jumped up on stage and . . ." Her sigh heaved the pink blouse she was wearing with her khaki-colored mini. "I kissed Paul McCartney. Right on the mouth." Lucy giggled and I did, too. Before that night, there was no way I could ever have imagined anyone getting that close to one of the Beatles, much less my very favorite Beatle, and when the *anyone* in question was the girl who had once been my babysitter and now considered herself my friend . . .

A shiver of excitement raced up my spine just as Lucy crooned, "Oh yeah, I'm brave, all right. And I'll never let anything or anyone . . ." Lucy didn't look my way when she said this, but she did glance around at the other kids who were with us. She looked at Janice Sherwin and Bobby Gideon, in the seat in front of us, and then to the seat behind ours where Will Margolis and Darren Andrews sat side by side. "I kissed Paul McCartney! I'll never let anyone else's lips touch mine again. Ever."

"Get over yourself!" Bobby turned around and knelt on the seat so he could boff Lucy on the arm. "A couple thousand people stormed the stage at the concert. You weren't the only one."

"I was the only one who made it all the way up on the stage. I was the only one who kissed Paul. And . . ." Lucy knew a thing or two about pausing for dramatic effect. I'd tried it myself a couple times and always came off looking more like a goofball than dramatic and brooding like Lucy. "I was the only one of all of us who had the nerve to get out of my seat and dodge the cops out on the field." Lucy gave each of them another appraising glance, and yeah, she looked as superior as she was feeling. But then, she had every right. No way I could hold it against her, especially when she patted my knee to show she understood why I hadn't joined her when she took off running. Lucy knew my parents would have killed me if they found out I ever did anything that reckless. That—along with the fact that I was a born chicken—meant I'd never have the nerve, and Lucy knew it. But then, compared to Lucy and her friends, I was just a kid. "I didn't see any of you up there on stage with me and the Beatles," she told her friends.

"Thanks to you, the concert almost got canceled." The comment, just a little icy around the edges, came from Janice, and I wasn't surprised. Truth be told, Janice Sherwin terrified me, but then, Janice pretty much terrified everybody. In her tailored clothes and with her carefully bleached and ratted hair, Janice was a force to be reckoned with and not somebody who would tolerate the kind of chaos we'd all seen break out soon after the Beatles took the stage. The next day's paper would call it a *riot*, and they were pretty much right. In fact, the concert had been stopped for about half an hour. That is, until some man finally came out on stage and threatened to cancel it altogether if everybody didn't get back in their seats.

I was fourteen and more than a bit of an idol worshiper. I was convinced that if Lucy hadn't decided to sit back down, nobody else would have, either.

Silently, I thanked her for coming to her senses and allowing the show to go on so I could hear Paul sing "Yesterday" live and in person.

"If they hadn't let the Beatles come back on stage, I never would have forgiven you." This time, there wasn't just a tinge of ice in Janice's words, they were positively frozen. She tossed a look over her shoulder at Lucy that was just as cold. And twice as surprising. As the two most popular girls at Shaker Heights High School, Lucy and Janice had always been best friends, even though Lucy was going to be a senior that year, and Janice was a junior. I hadn't seen them together much over the past few months, but that wasn't all that unusual. Lucy worked a part-time summer job at the Shaker Heights Country Club, and Janice had spent a good part of June and July traveling in Europe with her parents. It wasn't my imagination, though—Janice was frosty but Lucy was just as cold right back.

Their icy clash put a chill on what had been, up until that moment, the most exciting night of all our young lives.

"Hey, but the show did go on, right? So everything's copacetic." I wasn't surprised that Will was the one who jumped in to smooth things over. Will was what the other kids called "sensitive." I was just going into my freshman year at Shaker and I didn't know much about boys, but I knew I liked the sensitive ones.

When I smiled at him over my shoulder and Will smiled

back, I turned around—fast—before everyone on the train could see that my cheeks had turned as red as a fire engine.

"Leave it to Lucy to go where angels fear to tread." It was safe for me to turn around again, because Darren said that, and I could look his way—and Will's—without looking too conspicuous. "Lucy is my hero."

If Darren Andrews had said something like that about me, I would have melted into a puddle of mush; he was that much of a dreamboat. Darren had sandy hair. It was a little long, and he'd have to get it cut before school started again in a few weeks, but for now, Darren's shaggy hair and his sparkling blue eyes made him look like the star of one of those surfer movies. That night, Darren was dressed just like a surfer, too. He was wearing shorts made out of that bleeding madras fabric that faded and ran a little every time it was washed, and a shirt that was open enough at the neck to reveal the Saint Andrew's medal that was his prized possession.

Yes, I know, I was only an almost-freshman, and Darren, who was going to be a senior, was way out of my league. But thanks to my friendship with Lucy, I knew things about the older kids, and I knew that Darren and his family liked to flaunt their connections to old Scottish royalty and that Saint Andrew, as the patron saint of Scotland, represented their blue-blooded roots. Who could blame him for showing off?

"You gonna tell your parents what you did tonight?" he asked Lucy.

Her jaw went rigid. But then, Lucy was always up for a challenge. "Maybe I will."

"Maybe you'll get grounded for life." Since he knew it wasn't nearly as likely that Lucy's hip mom and dad would punish her the way I knew my stodgy parents would have done, Bobby laughed. "Maybe we all will if our folks find out what you did and think we ran out on the field, too."

"Don't be ridiculous." Unlike the easygoing surfers in the movies, Darren had a way of lifting his chin and straightening his shoulders that pretty much said he was better than everybody else. From what I'd heard, it was true, so I didn't take it personally. "My parents know I'd never do anything like that," he snapped. "After all, people like us—"

"Don't mingle with folks from the lower classes." Bobby said this like it was a joke, but we all knew it was true. Maybe joking about it was what made it possible for Darren and these other kids to remain friends. Shaker was anything but a second-rate community, and none of our families was destitute. In fact, kids we met from other schools always assumed we were rich, just because of where we lived. But in the great scheme of things, none of us was in Darren's class. The fact that he hung out with us, anyway (or at least that he hung out with Lucy and the others—I was pretty much invisible in Darren's eyes) said a lot about Darren.

He fingered the gold medal around his neck. "You know I'd never say that about you peasants," he joked, and everyone laughed.

The train careened around a corner, and we all held on tight. Though it was summer and it stayed light until after nine, it was late and the streetlights were already on. The rapid pulled into its first stop and people shuffled off.

The moment the train started up again, Janice said, "You know it really was dumb of you." We didn't need to ask what she was talking about. We all knew the comment was aimed at Lucy's headlong dash across the baseball field to where the stage had been set up near second base. She turned to give Lucy a probing look. "You could have been hurt. You could have been trampled. None of us would have liked to see something bad happen to you."

"So kind of you, luv." Lucy added that last—very British—word and made it sound natural in a way I never could. "But there's no need to worry about me. I, after all, am the bravest woman in the universe!"

There were groans all around and Will piped up. "Brave, huh? Let's see how brave you are when you have that meeting with Mr. Wannamaker next week."

Lucy had a meeting scheduled with the school principal? This was news to me, and from the open-mouthed reactions Will got, I guess it was to everyone else, too. Apparently it was supposed to stay a secret, because Lucy shushed Will with a look.

"You mean I'm the only one who knows!" It's not like Will was rubbing it in; he was just used to being one of the gang instead of the center of attention.

"Will knows something we don't know," Bobby crowed, singsong. "Anybody want to bet that when it comes down to it, Lucy doesn't have the guts to face Wanny?"

"Nobody talks to Wanny one-on-one and lives to tell about it," Janice barked, and from what I'd heard about the principal, I knew it was true.

"Even you're not that brave, Lucy," Darren said, laying a hand on Lucy's shoulder. Maybe just being touched by Darren was enough to make any girl shiver, because she shrugged him off.

Darren leaned forward. "You're not really going to do it, are you? We'll miss you when you're gone!"

Lucy knew he wasn't serious. Me? I wasn't so sure. From what I'd heard about Wanny, anything was possible. Especially if Lucy wanted to see him to complain about a school policy. When it came to rules and regulations, Wanny was a die-hard. Lucy, of course, was a rebel. Oil and water didn't mix. I knew it, and I knew Lucy didn't care. It was the only reason I dared to pipe up. "You could get in trouble, Lucy, and—"

"Not to worry, Little One." I knew Lucy meant well, but I hated when she called me that in front of her friends. I didn't mention it. For one thing, there was no use calling any more attention to myself. For another, there was a tight muscle at the base of Lucy's jaw. I knew better than to push her when her mind was made up. "None of you need to worry," she added with another glance around at the group. "For I, Lucy Pasternak, am the coolest, the most daring, and the bravest—"

"Here we go again!" Janice moaned.

"No, here we really go!" Bobby jumped out of his seat. While we'd been busy talking, the rapid had arrived at a stop. Bobby, Darren, Will, and Janice lived near each other, and this was where they all got off.

"See you later, alligators," Bobby said.

Janice walked by without another word.

Will slid past Darren. He gave me a smile before he went to the door, and all I could do was hope he didn't hold being called *Little One* against me.

Darren lingered a little longer. But then, maybe a guy like Darren was used to things moving on his schedule, even rapid trains. "Come with us," he said. I didn't harbor any illusions; I knew he wasn't talking to me. "We're all going back to my house to listen to albums."

"I'll pass." Lucy's shoulders were stiff. They didn't relax, not even when Darren skimmed a finger along the back of her neck.

"I've got the latest album by the Stones," he said.

Lucy liked the Rolling Stones almost as much as she liked the Beatles.

"I said no, Darren." She had been looking his way, and now, Lucy turned to stare straight ahead of her.

Darren leaned over her shoulder and growled in her ear. "Come on, Lucy. We'll have fun."

Her mind was made up. "I can't," Lucy said, and thank goodness the rapid doors started to close and Darren had to get moving. I was afraid she was going to spill the beans and tell Darren that she'd promised my mother she'd walk me home. I didn't need any more embarrassment.

I didn't need to feel guilty for making Lucy miss out on all the fun because of me, either. But before I could tell her that and urge her to go with him, Darren mumbled something about how it was no skin off his nose if Lucy wanted to waste the rest of her night, and went to the door. It wasn't until the rapid started up again that some of the starch went out of Lucy's shoulders.

I knew I wasn't anywhere near as good when it came to people as Lucy was, but I thought she looked a little sad.

And that only made me feel worse.

"You should have gone with them," I said.

She waved away the thought with one hand.

"But it would have been fun. You could have gone to Darren's mansion and seen that room he always talks about, the one with all his stereo equipment in it. You could have heard the newest Rolling Stones album."

Another wave.

It took me a minute to figure out why Lucy wasn't saying anything. She looked like she was about to burst into tears.

I turned as much as I could in the cramped rapid seat. "I'm sorry, Lucy. If it wasn't for me, you could have gone with your friends."

She shook her head, and her hair gleamed like a golden waterfall. "This has nothing to do with you."

"But Darren wanted you to go to his house. And you could have. You don't have to walk me home. I could lie and tell my mom you did. I could tell her you dropped me off at the door, and it was late so you didn't want to come in and—"

Lucy sniffed. "This has nothing to do with me having to walk you home."

I scrunched up my nose, the better to try and figure it out. "Then why—"

Lucy gave me a watery smile. "It's no big deal," she said.

"It is a big deal. You're crying."

"Nah!" She swiped her hands over her cheeks and forced a smile. "Now that the concert's over, and the excitement's over . . . I'm just feeling a little melancholy, that's all. It's all because . . ." Lucy heaved a sigh of epic proportions. "Well, you know how it is. You've seen enough movies and read enough books. It's all about my lost love. And . . . you know . . . my broken heart."

I swear, my jaw hit the floor of the rapid. It was a shock to hear not only that Lucy had lost a love, but that she'd had one I didn't know about in the first place.

It was the most romantic thing I'd ever heard.

A moment of practicality short-circuited the fantasies brought on, no doubt, by reading *Wuthering Heights* too many times. "You're not talking about Paul, are you?" I asked her.

Lucy rolled her eyes. "Don't be silly! My thing with Paul, that was just a fleeting illusion. A moment in time where his essence and mine met and mingled and then . . ." She had been clutching her hands together on her lap, and now she threw them apart to demonstrate. "We were like ships passing in the night. Sure, Paul might go to bed to-night wondering who I am and how he can find me again but . . ." Another sigh. "It was never meant to be. No, I'm not talking about the kind of once-in-a-lifetime fairy-tale moment I had with Paul. I'm talking about a real love. In the real world."

"But you never told me—"

"Now, Little One." Lucy gave me the kind of look that reminded me of my mother right before she launched into a lecture, and a familiar prickle of annoyance skittered up my back.

"A girl's got to have some secrets, remember. And you're not exactly old enough to know everything."

"Am, too." I crossed my arms over my turquoise cardi-gan. "You told me about the first time Freddy Hawkins kissed you."

"That was freshman year." She tsk-ed away the thought as inconsequential. "We were both just babies, no offense intended."

"None taken," I said, even though it wasn't true. "I'm not that young," I reminded her. "You didn't think I was too young to go to the concert with you tonight."

"You're not. But concerts are a whole different thing. You know, different from undying love, and stolen kisses, and a broken heart. Someday when you're older, you'll under-stand."

I wanted to yell at her and tell her that I could under-stand, that I would, if she'd just explain what she was talk-ing about and give me a chance. But the rapid was getting close to my stop, and I didn't want to miss it. I stood and sidled between Lucy and the seat in front of us to get out into the aisle.

"Wait." She put a hand on my arm. "I'm coming with you."

"Don't bother." I shook her hand away.

"Come on, Little One, don't be so touchy. I promised your mom I'd walk you home. Besides, it's already dark, and you shouldn't be out alone."

"Why, because I'm too much of a baby?" I didn't wait. When Lucy made a move to get up, I just kept walking to the door. "I can find my own way home from the rapid stop." I tossed the comment over my shoulder. "Then maybe you'll see that I'm not such a little kid after all."

The doors slid open and I stepped outside. I half expected Lucy to be right behind me, but when the doors closed again, I saw that she was still right where I'd left her. As the train pulled out of the station, she turned in her seat, grinned, and waved good-bye.

I was so dead set on showing her that I was mature and independent, I never waved back.

I wish I had.

It was the last time I ever saw Lucy Pasternak alive.

Forty-five years later, same place, very different girl

The problem with public transportation is that it's public.

I was reminded of this sad but true fact too early one morning when the rapid stopped and a slew of people shuffled onto the already too-crowded-for-my-liking train. It had been a cool and rainy April and that day was no exception. Coats were wet. Umbrellas dripped. The windows of the train were fogged, and the air was heavy with a hodgepodge scent of damp, perfume, and people.

The old guy who plopped down next to me smelled like my Great Uncle Mort, and Mort was a legend in the Martin family. Weddings, funerals, picnics . . . it didn't matter. Mort always wore a brown suit. Even though I was a foot taller than him, he always pinched my cheek and called me honey bun. He always, always smelled like stale cigars.

I scooted closer to the window, and to pass the time, I

looked around, hoping to catch a spot of color or a hint of
style somewhere in the sea of gray raincoats and bent heads.
Unfortunately, the Midwest is pretty much a black-and-
white world from November until May. If it wasn't for the
middle-aged woman in the purple coat two seats ahead and
me in the leopard-print trench that looked pretty darned
spectacular with my fiery hair, I would have despaired of
the Cleveland fashion scene entirely.

Or maybe not . . .

A flash of color caught my eye, and at the same time I
wondered why I hadn't noticed her earlier, I saw a young
woman walk down the aisle.

Khaki-colored mini. Hot pink blouse.

So far, so good, as far as style was concerned, though
I did wonder how she could possibly be comfortable when
she was dressed for a summer evening rather than for a
damp spring morning.

She had long, straight flaxen hair and a complexion like
porcelain.

OK, I admit it, I was the tiniest bit envious. Not that Pepper Martin hadn't learned to make the most of the attributes
that she'd been blessed with, thanks to an unerring fashion
sense, Nature, and a good gene pool. Still, I had always
fantasized about not having to deal with riotous curls and a
sprinkling of freckles.

Rather than dwell on what couldn't be changed, I continued my assessment of the girl, ticking off the pros and cons.

The gold nail polish fell somewhere right in between.
Not a bad look for evening, but it was iffy at best on a Monday morning.

Then there was the gold lipstick.

Whatever style points I gave her went right down the

tubes with that fashion faux pas. Unless the girl was actually trying to look like a throwback to the flower power sixties.

Or if she was dead.

Dang! I gave myself a mental slap. I should have picked up on the whole dead thing right away. And not just because nothing says resting but not in peace like retro clothing and out-of-date makeup, but because the people standing in the aisle shivered when she passed. See, as anybody who's ever gotten too close knows, the dead are sort of their own little freeze machines. I should know. I've gotten too close. Too many times.

In my defense and just so a whole bunch of nasty rumors don't start about how the world's only private investigator for the dead is losing her edge, I had a perfectly good excuse for my supernatural radar being down: recently, my life had been quiet, and blissfully murder and murder victim free. In the months since I'd solved the last murder I was involved with, figured out what was going on with a gang of bad guys (and the gorgeous Brit who was their leader), and helped divert a national crisis in the name of a long-dead president, nobody had tried to shoot me, mug me, knife me, or kidnap me.

Oh, how I would have liked to keep it that way!

Yes, yes . . . I know this makes me sound like a prima donna detective. Not true! Fact is, when it's in the movies or on TV, this whole I-see-dead-people thing looks mysterious, and pretty darned glamorous. But in real life . . .

Well, in real life, being able to see and talk to the dead isn't all it's cracked up to be.

For one thing, they never just pop in to say hello or to give me the inside track on the winning lottery numbers or next fall's fashion trends. They always want something.

And since they can't touch things or communicate with any living person except little ol' me, the someone they expect to take care of those somethings is always me.

For another thing, the dead who are still hanging around have unfinished business here on earth. Sometimes there's someone they want to help—and I'm the one stuck doing that helping. Sometimes they've been wrongly accused of a crime—and I'm the one who has to put things right. Most of the time, they are victims. Need I say more? Each and every victim needs someone to stand up for them. Since I have been saddled with this Gift that is nonrefundable and nonre-turnable, I'm the one who does the standing.

And the investigating.

And the digging through sometimes decades-old information in order to get at any little kernel of truth that might be left behind.

And the grappling with the living, of course. That includes people who loved the dearly departed and are still dealing with their passing. And the people who hated them. The people who murdered them.

Truth be told, I actually don't hold any of this against the dead. It's not their fault I tripped in the historical cemetery where I work as a tour guide, knocked my head against a mausoleum, and woke up some sort of superhero detective.

I just wish they'd find better places to talk to me than crowded rapid trains.

And safer things for me to do than laying my life on the line again and again.

Unless this was my lucky day and gold lipstick was some sort of psychic flash into the fashion future?

I was cheered by the thought. But only for a moment. The next instant, I came to my senses. That fashion trend was as dead as the Golden Girl who had sidled up the aisle and was now standing next to my seat.

The old guy next to me shuddered. "Hey!" With barely a look, he snarled at me, "Close that window."

"It isn't open," I pointed out, though considering his attitude, I was tempted not to.

"Kids!" he snorted, right before he got up and tromped to the front of the train.

The ghost slipped into the seat next to me.

"Nicely done," I told her, edging even closer to the window to give her plenty of room, and grateful that so many people nearby were either on their cells, texting, or had iPod earbuds in, they'd never notice I was talking to myself. "I'm only on for a few more stops," I told her. "So make it quick. What do you want?"

"I haven't talked to a living person in forty-five years, and you start out by asking me what I want?" Now that she was close, I saw that she was no more than a kid. She sounded like a kid, too, all pert and perky and up for a fight, even though I hadn't intended to start one. Maybe she realized it, because she grinned. "Hey, how about asking how I am?"

"How are you?"

"Well . . ." Her smile dissolved, and she sighed the way only teenaged girls can. Like whatever was troubling her, it was the end of the world. And no one understood. Or cared. She gave me a mournful look, all sad-eyed and trembling lips, and pressed one hand to her nonbeating heart. "I *am* dead."

The girl dissolved into a fit of giggles. "I've been practicing that one for forty-five years," she said. "Good thing I finally found somebody who can see me and talk to me, huh?"

I think she would have elbowed me in the ribs, except she knew about the chill factor and stopped herself just in time. She wiggled in her seat. "So you want to hear my story, right?" she asked, and before I could tell her I really would rather not, she launched right in.

"My name is Lucy Pasternak, and I died on August 14, 1966." She leaned closer, her voice lowered in a way that was supposed to be spooky, even though this particular ghost was anything but. "I was murdered!"

"Of course." I figured I'd better set her straight before she thought that in the great scheme of my spectral visitors, she was somehow different or special. "Murders are—" I was afraid I'd said that too loud and that someone other than Lucy might have heard, so I lowered my voice, too. "Murders are my specialty."

Lucy nodded. "I heard that about you," she said and gave me a wink. "You know, over on the Other Side. People are talking, saying Pepper Martin is one cool chick."

After successfully solving six cases, I wasn't surprised to hear that I was the topic of gossip on the ghostly grapevine, or that the word was that I was good at what I do. After all, it was true.

"I haven't seen you before." She interrupted my thoughts. "You know, here on the rapid."

My smile was tight. A kid with that many years behind her should have picked up on the not-so-subtle differences between me and the other, more common-variety rapid rider.

"I'm more the I-own-a-car-so-I-don't-use-public-transportation type," I told her. It was important to make this clear right from the start. If we were going to work together (and once they showed up, it was impossible to get rid of ghosts, so I figured we were), it would be unfair to give her the wrong impression. "I wouldn't be here at all today except that my car got backed into in the parking lots outside of Saks. It's in getting repaired way over on the west side." She was apparently a local girl; I didn't need to elaborate.

Cleveland, see, is cut in half, north to south, by the Cuyahoga River. Over the years, a whole east side versus west side mentality has sprung up. The east side is where the old money has always been, and we east siders (yes, I'm one of them) like to think of ourselves as more educated, more discerning, and way more cultured and refined than our west side counterparts. West siders, so I've heard, wouldn't change places with us for all the gulls on Lake Erie, preferring the roots of the working class neighborhoods that have grown and spread into communities with malls every bit as chichi as ours and burbs that might rival ours for net worth, but will never (in my humble opinion) equal ours in pizzazz.

"I'm heading over to my boss's house," I explained. "Fortunately, she lives near the rapid line. She's going to give me a ride to work."

The train bumped to a stop and the doors swooshed open, letting in a blast of damp air, and letting out some of the passengers. With a bit more room to breathe, it would have been easier to relax if I wasn't so up close and personal with this golden wisp of funky sixties ectoplasm.

Too excited to sit still, Lucy scooted forward in her seat. "So you want to hear all about it, right? All about the murder and what happened and all? You're going to help me."

I would have liked to point out that my Gift didn't come with any guarantees. Lucy didn't give me the chance.

"I was here on the rapid that night," she said. "You know, coming home from the Beatles concert." She looked at me hard. "You do know who the Beatles are, right? I mean,

I know you're old and all, but you're not that hopelessly square, are you?"

One look, and she should have known. I, of course, though nowhere near old, was far too mature to get into that sort of one-upmanship so I simply pointed out, "Of course I've heard of the Beatles. My parents listened to them in the old days."

"Then you can imagine how groovy it was to see them in person." She shivered at the thought. "I kissed Paul, you know. He was the cute one."

"And then you got murdered."

"Not at the concert." Was I that hopelessly dense that I deserved an eye roll?

I thought not.

Lucy, apparently, had other ideas. She threw in a second eye roll, just for good measure. "It happened after the concert. After all my friends got off and went home. Then I got to my stop, and I got off the train and was walking home. It was dark. You know, the way a summer night can be." Again, she tried for the spooky voice. This time I was the one who rolled my eyes. Lucy didn't notice. She was on her own kind of roll.

"It was as if each and every shadow held a secret. The stars winked overhead." She fluttered her fingers, demonstrating. "Crickets chirped out a warning, but I didn't listen. I mean, I couldn't have known, could I? I was young and innocent. The world was fresh and held nothing but promise. I had just kissed Paul McCartney, and I knew that somewhere in that deep summer night, he dreamed about the mysterious girl with the golden hair and wondered, as only a star-crossed lover can, if I would ever—"

"Finish?"

Lucy made a face, but she wasn't about to let a little

thing like my sensible encouragement cut short her drama queen act. "I stepped off the rapid and took a careful look around." As if someone as intelligent as me wouldn't know what this meant, she glanced to her left and her right. "Even I couldn't have guessed what was lurking in the shadows as dark as ebony and as deep as the most profound abyss."

I cleared my throat.

She didn't get the message.

Lucy sat up like a shot, her story spilling out. "Somebody grabbed me from behind! He blindfolded me and threw me into the trunk of a car. It was dark in there."

"As dark as ebony and as deep as the most profound abyss?"

Leave it to a ghost not to pick up on my subtle sarcasm. Lucy nodded, and at the risk of sounding a little too much like my newest ghostly friend, I've got to admit, her hair shimmered like a golden shaft of sunlight. I am not in the habit of asking my dead clients for beauty tips, but I planned to do a little research on shampoos in the sixties.

Lucy went right on with her story. "It wasn't until later that the car stopped."

"How much later?" Yes, the detective side of me kicked in. It was bound to sooner or later, and besides, easing into my investigation was a better option than having to listen to another adjective-laden chapter of Lucy's story. "How long were you in the car?"

Thinking, she tipped her head. And shrugged. "I was awfully scared," she said. "Terrified. You know, like Allison MacKenzie in the second season of *Peyton Place*. When she got hit by that car."

I didn't know. I didn't care. Even at this early stage, I knew it would do me no good to point this out, so I simply stuck to trying to find out the facts. "If we knew how long you were in the car, we might know where this creep took you," I pointed out. "Unless you figured that out for yourself?"

She didn't even have to think about it. She shook her head. "All I know," Lucy continued, "is that it was a while before the car screeched to a halt. Through my tears and the sound of my heartbeat clattering against my ribs, I heard the whisper of trees overhead. A door opened. And then, the footsteps." Demonstrating, she stomped her feet against the floor of the rapid, but of course, they didn't make a sound. Too caught up in her own narrative to care, Lucy motioned, as if she were unlocking the trunk of a car, then opening it. "I felt the brush of fresh air against my face."

"And the kidnapper was there."

She didn't appreciate the interruption. Lucy threw me a sidelong look. "Well, who else would it be?" she asked. "It's not like I could see him or anything. I was blindfolded, remember."

"And your hands must have been tied, too. Otherwise, you would have taken the blindfold off while you were in the trunk."

Lucy's eyes flew open. They were as blue as the sky outside the rapid wasn't that morning. "You're right! I'd forgotten about that. He blindfolded me, and he tied my hands behind my back. But hey, it's not like I was a wimp or anything. I tried to get my hands untied. You know, when I was in the trunk. Even though I couldn't see. You know, on account of the blindfold. I groped around." She moved around in her seat, demonstrating, her hands behind her back. "And I felt something metal. Sharp. I wasn't sure what it was, but I didn't care. I got to work."

She showed me, sawing her wrists back and forth against

the invisible object. "When he opened the trunk, I was al-most free. And when he grabbed me—"

Lucy swung her hands out in front of her. "I was ready for him. I slapped him and I scratched him. I fought as hard as I could."

I had no doubt of it, but I wasn't thinking about that. My brain was still stuck on what Lucy had said earlier. "Which did he do first?" I asked.

"Do first? Oh, you mean the blindfold. Or the tying." Thinking, she wrinkled her nose. "Blindfolded. No, tied. No, blindfolded." Frustrated, she tossed her head. "I don't know. What difference does it make?"

This, I couldn't say for sure. Not this early in the game. "I just wondered if it was more important for him to keep you still or to keep you from seeing his face. If the blindfold was first, that tells me you might have known your murderer."

I didn't think those big blue eyes could get any bigger. Oh, how wrong I was. Lucy put the back of one hand to her forehead. "A friend who was really a foe? A lover who was really an enemy? Oh, the treachery!"

Oh, the drama of dealing with a teenaged girl.

I swallowed what I was going to say, not that I didn't think she deserved a good dose of common sense, but be-cause I remembered exactly how I would have reacted to a little constructive criticism when I was her age. I didn't need Lucy to tune me out and turn me off. What I needed was information, so I could solve the case—fast—and get this Little Miss Annoying out of my life.

"Then what happened?" I asked, bracing myself for her answer.

Big surprise, she didn't drag it out. Then again, I guess I couldn't blame her. It was obvious the story didn't have a happy ending.

"He put something over my face," Lucy said. "A pillow. Or a blanket. Something soft and squishy. I fought back." She looked at me as if she expected me to dispute this. "I wouldn't have just laid there like a lump, you know, even though I'm just a girl. I tried to fight him off, but he was too strong for me. He pressed the blanket over my face. He pressed it and pressed it and . . ." Her golden brows dipped low over eyes that were suddenly bright with tears.

"Yeah, I get it. Good for you for trying," I said, and because I couldn't leave it at that, I was sure to add, "But that *only a girl* thing? That doesn't hold much water anymore."

"Really?" Lucy sniffed. "Wow! Janice would love that. Janice Sherwin, she wanted to be president of the junior class in the worst way, only the school wouldn't let her. They said she was—"

"Only a girl."

We finished the sentence in unison, and I breathed a prayer of thanksgiving that, unlike Lucy, I hadn't grown up in the Stone Ages. We were nearing the stop closest to Ella's house, and I motioned Lucy to move so that I could step into the aisle.

I held on to the metal bar on the back of the seat. "You had enemies?" I asked her.

"Of course not." Like it was a stupid question, Lucy sloughed it off. "I had friends. Lots of them. I went to the concert with them that night, only they got off the rapid first, and they wanted me to go with them, and I didn't. I was just a kid. Nobody hated me."

As much as I didn't like it, I am often the one who has to point out the obvious. "Somebody did. And I need to find out who that somebody was so that you can rest in peace."

"I wish it was that easy."

Outside the rapid window, I recognized Ella's neighborhood. I stepped toward the door and said, "We'll talk," and I didn't doubt it for one minute. Once they find me, ghosts never give up. "You'll tell me more and we'll find out who did it."

"It was forty-five years ago." When I moved toward the doors, Lucy did, too. The rapid bumped to a stop. "It doesn't matter anymore who killed me," she said. "I don't care if you find out. That's not what I need you to do."

I had already stepped out of the rapid and onto the station platform. Lucy was still on the train.

"I can't rest in peace, Pepper," she said. "Not until you find my body and bury it."

I whirled around. "You mean you don't know where—"

She nodded. "I don't have a clue."

Call me psychic—or maybe I was just living up to my crackerjack detective reputation—in that one moment, I saw the pitfalls and the problems of launching into an investigation when I had pretty much nothing to go on. It was one thing searching for a murderer. People talked, witnesses remembered things they thought they'd forgotten long ago, there are police reports to read and follow, newspaper articles that contain tiny clues. Finding a murderer was a whole different thing from finding a body that had somehow stayed hidden for forty-five years.

"But you were in the trunk of a car," I reminded her, and myself, ticking off all the reasons I knew this wasn't going to work. "You don't know where the guy took you. And even if you did, that doesn't mean he left your body where he killed you. He could have left you right there, sure, but he could have driven somewhere else and dumped you. Your body, it could be anywhere."

There was that puppy dog look again. Like she actually thought I'd cave?

OK, I admit, I almost did. It was kind of hard not to when she wailed, "You've got to find my body. You've got to help me, Pepper!"

"But you can't give me anything to go on."

"You're right. I can't." She shrugged and sighed. Sighed and shrugged. She hung her head. "That's why I have to rely on your kindness, and your cleverness. You're the only one who can help."

Yeah, sure. But there was only so much even I could do. After all, I'm a detective, not a bloodhound.

It was a good thing the rapid doors slid shut right then. That way, I didn't have to disappoint the kid face-to-face when I mumbled, "No way, José!"

2

It was a short walk from the rapid station to Ella's house. Good thing. Though my peep-toe pumps were adorable, they were not meant for hoofing it.

By the time I arrived at her neat colonial complete with window boxes, daffodils popping up in the flower bed around the oak tree on the lawn, and the cheery wreath on the front door that was a riot of silk flowers and bows in bright spring colors, I was winded. I rang the bell.

There was no answer.

I knocked.

There was no response.

I stepped back and mumbled to myself, "This is odd."

Come to think of it, it wasn't the only odd thing that had happened that morning. And I am not talking about running into Lucy's ghost. In my world, that doesn't even begin to qualify as odd.

No, what was odd—and I thought about this as I pressed my nose to the glass on the front door—was that Ella hadn't called me that morning. I had been expecting her to. Oh, she'd pretend it would be just to say hello and how was your weekend and what's up, but I knew in my heart of hearts what Ella would really be doing, and what Ella would really be doing is checking up on me. She was the community relations director at Garden View Cemetery, where I worked, and she would remind me without actually coming right out and reminding me that a community relations director cannot afford to get to the office late.

Now that I thought about it, I was surprised she hadn't called more than once, just to make sure I hadn't overslept, and that I had made it over to the auto body shop in plenty of time, and that I was actually on the right rapid.

A mother of three teenaged girls can get carried away like that.

Frustrated that I couldn't see beyond the foyer and not as concerned as I was just baffled by a demonstration of irresponsibility that was more my style than Ella's, I pounded on the door. When there was still no answer, I tromped around to the back of the house and tried the door there. It wasn't locked. I went right in.

Just inside the kitchen with its black-and-white-tile floor, white cabinets, and the collection of kitschy cookie jars Ella kept out on the countertop, I stopped dead in my tracks.

I had been to Ella's house plenty of times before, and each and every one of those plenty of times, the house had been as neat, orderly, and clean as it's possible to get with three teenagers running around.

And now? Truth be told, even my single-girl-who's-so-busy-fighting-crime-she-doesn't-always-get-to-clean apartment never looked like this.

There were newspapers scattered over the kitchen table and mail piled on the floor. There were dirty dishes in the sink, and the dishwasher was open and empty. There was a pot of something that might have once upon a time been spaghetti sauce on the stove. It was crusted over and had turned an unappetizing rust color.

Call it detective's intuition or just the paranoid imaginings of a cemetery tour guide who deals with murder and mayhem far too often. I reached for my cell, not sure who I was going to call, but certain I wasn't going to wait a second longer to shout for help.

Before I could, the door to the half bath just off the kitchen swung open and Ella shuffled out.

At least I thought it was Ella.

I did a double take, used to seeing my closing-in-on-sixty, slightly plump boss in flowy skirts, matching tops, and sparkling beads. She also favored practical, clunky Earth Shoes, and an understated, spiky do that showed off both her red-tinted hair and the dangling earrings she loved to wear.

This creature had to be her evil twin.

She was as short as Ella, all right, and probably just as plump, too, though it was hard to tell considering she was wearing shapeless flannel lounge pants that looked like they'd been slept in and a ratty sweatshirt with a drawing of a knight on it right under the words SHAKER HEIGHTS HIGH SCHOOL RAIDERS. There was a smudge of spaghetti sauce across his helmet. One of the bad body double's shoes was an untied sneaker. The other was a fuzzy bunny slipper.

Her hair was flat and uncombed, and there were smudges of sleeplessness under her eyes. She stopped outside the bathroom door, took one look at me, and burst into tears.

"Oh, Pepper," she whimpered in a very Ella way. "I'm so happy to see you!"

Call me crazy. This did not look like happy to me. I told
Ella so, and approached carefully. Middle-aged woman gone
mad. It was not a pretty sight.

I put a hand on her arm and bent to look her in the eye.
This close, I could tell that this last bout of crying was just
one of many. Ella's eyes were swollen, and her nose was
red and raw. "What's going on?" I asked.

"Oh, nothing." There was a huge pottery mug on the sink
and Ella reached for it, took a swig, then clutched it in both
hands. "Would you like some tea? I have mint. And yerba
maté. It's a wonderful antioxidant, you know."

I might not know what was what when it came to herbal
tea, but I knew shock when I saw it. I plucked the ice-cold
cup of tea out of her hands and took her by the elbow to pilot
her over to the oak table in the middle of the room. There
was a stack of magazines on the nearest chair. I swept them
onto the floor and plunked Ella down.

I grabbed another chair. There was a bowl of half-eaten
Cheerios on it, long soggy and in milk that was quickly
morphing from liquid to chunky. As quickly as I could and
careful not to breathe, I took it to the sink. When I was done
consigning it to the nether regions of the disposal, I pulled
the chair over so that I was knee to knee with Ella and took
her hands in mine.

"What's going on?" I asked.

"Oh, Pepper!" Ella took a deep breath and let it go on the
end of a wobbling sigh. "It's been a very long weekend."

I wanted to say, *no duh!* but a detective is nothing if not
diplomatic. At least when she's dealing with someone she
actually likes.

Ella sniffled. "It all started on Friday," she said. "Friday
evening. You know, I worked late. I had to get the next issue

of the Garden View newsletter done, and I did, and I brought it home to proofread. I can get it for you if you'd like to look it over." She made to get up out of the chair and reach for the briefcase I saw near the back door.

I held her in place. "Newsletter, later," I said, keeping it short and simple, convinced it was all she could process. "Now, back to Friday night . . ."

"Oh, yes. Friday. I worked late." She nodded. "I got home just as Rachel and Sarah were headed out. They were going to the boys' varsity lacrosse game at school, and I wanted to make sure they ate something before they left, and they were running late, and their friends were here to pick them up and they were out in the driveway beeping the horn, and I needed to ask Rachel about that chemistry test she took Friday afternoon, of course, and Sarah had that paper for English, the one about *Romeo and Juliet*, and the phone rang and it was Jim from the office who had a question about the cost of our latest shipment of office supplies and—"

She blinked and sniffled.

"I guess I just wasn't paying attention. Oh, Pepper, I can't even bear to admit what a horrible, terrible, awful mother I am! It was so busy and so hectic, I never even thought about Ariel. What kind of mother does that? What kind of mother forgets one of her children?"

A fresh cascade of tears started, and I knew that this time she wouldn't be easily soothed. I went to the sink, dumped Ella's cold tea, filled the mug with water, and stuck it in the microwave. While it was nuking, I rummaged through the nearest cupboard, looking for an herbal tea that sounded wholesome. Indian gooseberry won. I figured anything with a name that goofy had to be good for something.

I didn't even bother to try and get through to Ella again

until I plunked the tea bag in the steaming water and added a squirt of honey from the plastic bear nearby. When I handed her the cup, she managed a watery smile.

"Once the girls were gone and the house was quiet," Ella continued, "that's when I thought about Ariel. I just assumed . . . Well, I mean, who wouldn't? I just assumed she'd gone with Rachel and Sarah. I made some dinner, watched some TV, took a bubble bath. But when the girls got home from the game . . . it was late, they'd gone to Geracci's for pizza and they even brought me a couple pieces." She glanced toward the countertop in back of me where the cardboard box still sat, a long string of mozzarella hardened on the side. "When they got home, that's when I realized Ariel wasn't with them. Rachel and Sarah, they said they hadn't seen her at the game. Or here at home. They had no idea where she was."

"Ariel." I nodded, confirming my worst fears to myself. On the whole, Ella's girls are good kids. At least two of them are. Rachel and Sarah are as respectful as teenagers can be, they get decent grades, and their sense of fashion, though certainly not inspired (they are related to Ella, after all), was coming around thanks to the years they'd known me.

Ariel was another story.

"She's not a bad kid," Ella said, and she must have been reading my mind, but obviously not clearly. Ariel was, indeed, a bad kid. Bad grades. Bad behavior. Bad hygiene. Bad manners. Bad taste.

Ariel was everything her mother was not. I suppose, in Ariel's fifteen-year-old mind, that was the whole point.

I had little patience for a kid who was that much of a mess. I sat back, and yeah, I was pissed. Then again, I remembered the time Ariel went joyriding with some kid she barely knew, who, it turned out, had been driving a stolen car. And the time Ariel pawned Rachel's watch so she'd have money to go see *Avatar.* And the time she stomped the family Nintendo—she claimed it was an accident, but we all knew better—just because Sarah was better at fighting Koopa Troopa paratroopers.

Not that any of this affected me personally. Which meant that in the great scheme of things, I really shouldn't/didn't care. But facts were facts, and fact is, I like Ella a whole bunch. She isn't just my boss. Ella is my friend, and yes, as corny as it sounds, she's family, too, especially since my mother lives in Florida and my dad is in prison (Medicare fraud . . . it's a long story). I'd seen the way Ariel's thoughtless behavior twisted Ella into painful knots of worry. No way was I about to forgive the kid for doing it again.

I didn't have to lie to Ella (well, except when it came to my love life and ghosts, but that doesn't count) so I didn't even try to hide my exasperation. "What did Ariel do this time?" I asked.

And really, was I surprised when the waterworks started up again?

"A . . . ri . . . el . . ." Ella blubbered. "Ariel ran away from home!"

This was not something I was expecting. Ariel was bad, but she wasn't stupid. At least I'd never thought so before.

"Oh, Pepper! I don't even know where to begin. You see, there's this boy, he's in Ariel's class, and he's nothing but trouble. I know, I shouldn't judge, but this isn't just opinion, it's a fact. Rachel and Sarah say so. All the other kids say so. They say he's . . . well, like a gangster or something. You know, all attitude and with his pants down around his ass."

I knew before that Ella was upset, but this proved it. Sweet little Ella never used words like *ass.* The fact that she didn't even blush when she said it solidified the seriousness of the situation.

"His name is Gonzalo, and I mean, really, who names their kid Gonzalo? No matter." She shook away her momentary lapse into political incorrectness as inconsequential. "What matters is that he's a bad influence on Ariel. And when I realized she wasn't with Sarah and Rachel, and she wasn't in her room, and nobody had seen her since Friday afternoon at school . . ." Ella pulled in a sharp breath, steeling herself. "I know you're not going to believe this, Pepper, but you might as well know the ugly truth right up front: I freaked."

One look at the state of the kitchen and I could have argued the point. I believed it, all right. Ella didn't give me a chance to mention it. She took a noisy slurp of Indian gooseberry and barreled right on.

"The first thing I thought was that something must have happened," she said, jumping around in her story the same way she was wiggling in her chair. "You know, the way most mothers would. I called every hospital in town, and I talked to every emergency room, every shift. I checked and rechecked my phone, too, just to make sure there weren't any messages. I had Rachel and Sarah call Ariel's friends, and none of them had seen her, either. Then of course, I thought of Gonzalo."

I could see where the story was headed, and while I didn't exactly approve, considering that Ariel was only fifteen, I had been a hormone-driven teenager myself once. I understood, and I nodded to prove it. "You know how that is, Ella, she's young and she's probably got this whole romantic notion about being in love. She was with her boyfriend, right?"

She shook her head and kept on shaking it. "But that's just it. I talked to his parents. I even made them get this Gonzalo character and put him on the phone. He hadn't seen Ariel, either."

Right about then, I wondered about the properties of Indian gooseberry for settling an upset stomach. I could have used it, because mine was suddenly jumping around like a SeaWorld dolphin with a fish dangling over the tank. My logical self gave me a not-so-gentle reminder that detectives shouldn't be prone to panic. I told it to shut up. Ella was my friend, and my friend was upset. I raised my voice. It was the only way I could hear myself over the sudden, staccato pumping of my heart.

"If she wasn't with Gonzalo—"

"Exactly what I thought." Ella slurped up another mouthful of gooseberry tea. "I mean, I guess I didn't know what I thought. My head was spinning and my stomach was turning. The girls and I, we stayed up all Friday night, making phone calls. I've never been so worried. And then Saturday, when we didn't hear anything, that's when we called the police."

"Why didn't you call me?"

OK, my voice was a little sharp, and that wasn't fair to a woman who was going through what Ella was going through. But honestly, how could I help myself?

I jumped out of my chair and paced the *Good Housekeeping* and *Time*–littered floor. "Ella, you know I would have come over. You know I would have helped you look. Why didn't you call?"

"I should have. Of course I should have. You've certainly proven yourself over and over again, Pepper. You have a way with mysteries. You should have been the first person

I asked for help. But really . . ." A fresh cascade of tears started, and Ella didn't even try to wipe them away. They trickled down her cheeks and plopped into her mug.

"I wasn't thinking straight," she admitted. "I was trying. Oh, I was trying so hard to be logical and unemotional and sensible. But when something like that happens to your baby . . ." she sobbed. "It took every ounce of strength I had just to make the call to Jeffrey."

As if I'd just gone one-on-one with a ghost, I froze. "Jeffrey?" I choked out the name. Jeffrey was Ella's ex, and though she tried her plump-little-sparkly-lady darndest to keep a stiff upper lip when his name came up, I am nobody's fool when it comes to love. I could read the subtext.

Jeffrey was a schmuck.

"I haven't talked to him in . . . oh, at least a year." Ella put down her mug and plucked at the newspapers on the table with nervous fingers. "There isn't much I have to say to Jeffrey, not anymore, not after he's pretty much ignored the girls all these years. What kind of man does that and calls himself a father?" Her voice brimmed with anger. "What kind of man walks out on his family when his girls are just little? Then never calls them on the phone? He can't even be bothered with birthday cards. And now . . ." Tears trailed down her cheeks and she burst into tears. "Now they know their mother is just as bad!"

"You're not. No way." I hurried over and sat back down again. At least if I kept looking Ella in the eye, it might help bring her back to reality. I did just that and said, "You've raised those girls all by yourself, all these years. You'd do anything in the world for them, Ella, and they know it. Just because you thought Ariel was with Rachel and Sarah, that doesn't mean you're a bad mother, it just means you're human. You're not anything like Jeffrey. What happened wasn't your fault. It was Ariel's fault. Ariel's decision. You can't blame yourself for that."

Big points for me, my strategy worked, at least a little. Ella sniffled and gulped. "You're right. Of course, you're right, Pepper. I'm sorry. I can't help but feel a little overdramatic. Worrying about Ariel, then dealing with Jeffrey . . . well, dealing with Jeffrey always does that to me. And when I finally got ahold of him, do you know what that idiot said to me?"

She didn't wait for me to answer. Her voice churning with anger, Ella went right on. "He told me he had an important meeting this morning. That I should call him at noon, Seattle time, that he'd be out of his meeting by then, and I could update him about the situation and then he could decide what to do. Decide?"

So much for keeping her grounded.

Ella hopped out of her seat, her cheeks bright with spots of color, her eyes blazing. "If I was in Seattle and someone told me my daughter was missing in Cleveland or any other place on earth, I'd be on the first plane, or the first Greyhound bus, or hell, Pepper, I'd walk if I had to! I'd walk all the hell the way to Ohio, because what the hell! I'd sure as hell want to know what the hell happened to my child!"

I stood, too, and fought to keep from getting caught up in the tidal wave of emotion surging through the kitchen. "Which proves it," I pointed out. "That proves you're a good mother. Right?"

She gave me a begrudging smile and a nod, right before all the starch went out of her shoulders.

I put a hand on her arm and pressed her back into the chair.

"So . . ." I didn't bother to sit, too. Sure, I'd been doing all I could to calm Ella down, but by this time, my stomach was flip-flopping and my head was spinning. I was already making mental notes about where we could look for Ariel and who we should talk to. Any other time, any other circumstance, I would have put flaming sticks under my fingernails rather than call Quinn Harrison, my former sweetie and a Cleveland Police detective. Yeah, things had ended that badly. For Ella, though? For Ella, I was willing to make an exception.

I went to grab my phone. I had erased Quinn's number, but no matter, I still remembered it. Damn it.

"I'm sure the Shaker Police are working as hard as they're able," I told Ella. "But we'll call in reinforcements. Quinn's got pull."

"Quinn?" Ella's eyes lit for an instant. But she was back to sobbing the next. "You'd do that? For me? Oh, Pepper!" I'd just started dialing the phone when she popped out of her chair and threw her arms around me. Maybe it was a good thing I didn't have a chance to connect the call, because the next moment, Ella said, "You don't need to do that, Pepper. I appreciate it, but really, you don't need to. Ariel came home last night. She went to school this morning."

I let go a long breath. That is, right after I disentangled myself from Ella's arms. That way, I could give her a better why-didn't-you-tell-me-that-sooner look when I blurted out, "Why didn't you tell me that sooner?"

She blinked like a surprised owl. "Oh, well . . . I guess I haven't been thinking straight. If I told you at the start—"

"I wouldn't have been worrying my fool head off!"

Ella smiled. She squeezed my hand. "Thank you," she said.

All the worry and emotion drained out of me, and I plunked back down in the chair.

"She was with a girl named Margot, a friend I don't

know," Ella said before adding quickly, "That doesn't forgive what she did, of course. What she put us all through. But it does explain why we couldn't find her. Even Rachel and Sarah, they didn't know Ariel was hanging out with Margot. Margot's parents were spending the weekend out at one of those indoor water parks in Sandusky. They invited Ariel along."

Anger rushed in to replace all the concern I'd been feeling only moments before. "And Ariel couldn't have called to tell you this?"

Ella shrugged. "She didn't think it was any big deal."

"I hope you grounded her for life."

Another shrug. "I told her we'd talk after school today." Ella sighed and her shoulders shook. "These last couple days have really taken the wind out of my sails. I called Jim this morning and told him I wouldn't be at work today. You can take my car and head to the office. I'll . . ." She looked around the kitchen. Her eyes filled with tears and her lower lip trembled. "I'll just stay here and get things straightened up."

"Wait until Ariel gets home and make her clean up the kitchen. And relax." I patted Ella's arm. "You don't need to worry anymore. Shouldn't you be jumping for joy?"

"Of course. I'm as happy as can be." Ella dissolved into tears, hiccupping out the rest of what she had to say. "I'm relieved that Ariel is OK. And grateful. It's just . . . It was like a terrible flashback. All the worry and the wondering and the waiting. It made it all so real again. So real and so horrible. You know, the whole thing about what happened to Lucy Pasternak."

S tammering is so not a good look for me!

 Good thing Ella and I were the only ones in the kitchen, and Ella was too busy blubbering to notice what I was up to.

Thinking about the ghost on the rapid, I stammered awhile longer before I finally blurted out, "Lucy Pasternak? What . . . What are you talking about?"

Ella snuffled. She got up, grabbed a paper towel, and wiped her eyes. "Lucy was a friend of mine," she explained. "She disappeared back in 1966. When Ariel was gone . . . well, can you blame me? I know it was a long time ago. I know I should be over it by now. I know that sometimes I let my imagination run away with me, but . . . Of course as soon as I realized Ariel was missing, I thought about Lucy. And Lucy . . ." She flopped back down into her chair. "After that night, no one ever saw Lucy again."

Technically not true, but this didn't seem the moment to point it out.

"Over the years," Ella said, "I've shown the girls old pictures and told them stories about Lucy. She was three years older than me, and we sort of grew up together. Lucy was an only child, and so was I. I guess it was natural that we were both looking for a sister. Lucy was everything I wanted to be. She was beautiful and popular. Her parents were really cool, not uptight and traditional like mine. They let Lucy go to parties, and her mom bought Lucy all the latest fashions. You know, miniskirts and knee-high boots and patterned tights. I idolized Lucy!" Troubled, Ella shook her head. "I would think after all these years and all the times that Ariel's heard about Lucy and how she disappeared, it would have sunk in. That she would be more responsible, more considerate. But maybe . . . maybe if she heard the story again? From you?"

This did not sound like a good idea to me, and the why is a no-brainer.

Putting me and Ariel in a room together is like wearing a fetching little White House Black Market black satin dress and finishing off the outfit with shoes from Kmart. I mean, who would, really? But think about it. At first glance, everything might look perfectly fine. But it wouldn't take long for anyone with half a discerning eye to see that cheap and ugly bring fetching down. Way down. In fact, they're bound to clash.

Kind of like what happens anytime I'm anywhere near Ariel.

She's rude and sloppy.

I am unforgiving.

She could actually be pretty if she'd give herself a chance, but she's so busy getting various bits and pieces of her body pierced (I shivered at the thought) and other, bigger bits and pieces of her body tattooed (a chill ran up my spine), there's no way anyone could possibly notice.

Oh yeah, Ariel's got cheap and ugly down pat.

Not that I held it against her or anything. I just cringed at the thought of all that lost potential.

I, of course, could not point this out. Not without putting Ella on the defensive, and Ella had been through enough already. While I was busy keeping my mouth shut, she was busy concocting what apparently sounded like a perfectly good plan to her. That would explain why for the first time since I had walked into the house, her eyes shone with excitement rather than with tears.

"If you could just sort of bring it up . . . you know, remind her about Lucy and how she disappeared and how we all worried for so long and how we've been wondering for so many years . . . and then you could mention . . . you know, just sort of in passing . . . you could mention how when Ariel doesn't keep in touch . . . well, like I said, I know it sounds crazy, but that's because you've never been through what I went through with Lucy. I mean, thank goodness. I wouldn't want anyone—not anyone—to ever have to endure the sleepless nights and the worry and all those times I went to see Lucy's mom to find out if she'd heard anything and had to face the haunted look in her eyes." Ella drew in a deep breath. I couldn't blame her. Just listening to her, I felt as if I needed a hit from an oxygen tank.

Refreshed, she launched right back in. "And then this whole thing with Ariel . . . I mean, really, Pepper, now that you know about Lucy, you can understand why I just sort of lost it. It brought all those old memories and feelings crashing in on me again. Maybe if Ariel got just a friendly little reminder . . . maybe if she heard it from you, Pepper, Ariel would listen. She admires you so!"

This wasn't the moment to quibble.

But it was the perfect time to do a little investigating. Yes, yes, I know I'd told Lucy I couldn't help her with this whole poor-me-my-body's-gone-missing scenario. But that was when she couldn't give me anything to go on, before I knew I might be able to get my hands on a lead.

I swallowed down my misgivings, and because there were so many of them, it took a while before I said, "I think that's a good idea, talking to Ariel, warning her that the world can be a big, bad place if she's not careful. I think it would be good if I told her more about Lucy, too. That is, if I knew more."

"I knew you wouldn't let me down!"

I hate it when Ella says that. It usually means I'm in for trouble, and I was afraid this time would be no exception. Rather than dwell on the pitfalls, I stuck to the possibilities.

"So what did happen to Lucy?" I asked Ella. "I mean, after she disappeared."

She shrugged. "Well, that's just the thing, no one ever found out. Not that there wasn't a big investigation. There was. The police interviewed everyone connected with Lucy. Her family. The teachers at school. The people at the country club where she worked that summer. And of course, they talked to all of us who were with Lucy that night. We went—"

"To the Beatles concert."

Ella's eyes flew open. "Yes! How did you know that? Well, I must have mentioned it before, and isn't it just like you to remember! A group of us went to the Beatles concert together. Oh, Pepper! It started out being the most wonderful night of my life. I adored the Beatles, and to actually get a chance to see them in person . . . well, it never would have happened if it wasn't for Lucy. My parents didn't want to let me go, you see. They said I wasn't old enough, and neither of them was willing to go with me. They said the Beatles weren't singers, that they just made a lot of noise. I pleaded and I cried, but my mom, she said a rock-and-roll concert was no place for a young girl. Then one day Lucy came over. And she said she had an extra ticket for the concert. It wasn't extra, of course. She'd bought it especially for me. That's just the kind of girl Lucy was. Then, when she swore she'd keep an eye on me, my parents relented. I was so happy, I thought I'd burst! And you know . . ." she added, almost as an afterthought, "that just proves how really cool Lucy's parents were. Lucy had taken a summer school class and she got a really bad grade. An F, I think it was, which was unusual for Lucy. She was a good student. And her parents, they realized the concert was a once-in-a-lifetime opportunity. They still let her go. They told her they'd worry about that F later."

Just remembering it, Ella smiled. At least for a moment. Her smile faded away on the end of a sigh. "Now when I think about that night, I don't even think about how happy I was, or how exciting it was to see the Beatles in person. Every time I hear 'Yesterday,' all I can think of is Lucy. About how she simply vanished."

I knew that part of the story. What I was trying to do was get some sense of what had happened after Lucy took that fateful step off the rapid. Something told me that what happened after the concert might have had something to do with what happened before it.

"Lucy had people who didn't like her?"

In answer to my question, Ella gurgled out a laugh. "That's just silly! Everyone loved Lucy. Everyone! I think that's what the police found so frustrating about the investigation. They never did find one single person who didn't speak highly of Lucy. Well, really, there was no way they could have. Lucy was perfect."

Perfectly irritating in a very teenaged girl way.

But this was not the time to bring that up, either.

Instead, I stuck to my questioning. "What about at the concert?" I asked Ella. "Did anything weird or unusual happen there?"

"Well, there was the riot, of course." She cocked her head, thinking. "Kids rushed the stage after the Beatles came on, and they wouldn't start the concert again until everybody got back in their seats." She looked at me out of the corner of her eye. "Lucy was one of the kids who ran across the field. I never told anyone that. I didn't want Lucy's parents to get angry at her when they heard she'd done something that crazy. But really, I don't think that had anything to do with her disappearance, do you?"

I didn't. But that didn't help me figure out how she'd ended up in the trunk of that car.

"The two of you went to the concert alone?" I asked.

Ella shook her head. "There was me, and Janice Sherwin, and Lucy, of course. I know it's hard to explain, but Lucy was the heart and soul of Shaker High. She was pretty and bubbly and funny. But there was more to her than that. She stood up for what she thought was right, but in a quiet, gentle way that made people see her side of things and think they'd thought of it themselves. Janice, she wasn't anything at all like Lucy, but they were still friends. Janice was pretty in her own way, too, but she was a mover and shaker—very intense, high-powered, and hard-driving. She owns some business here in town these days. Insurance, I think. Or real estate. Something like that. Then there was

Darren Andrews." She managed a laugh, threw back her shoulders, and lifted her chin. "Darren with his airs! Always acting superior to the rest of us. He always wore this gold medal of Saint Andrew because his parents claimed the family was descended from Scottish royalty. I know, I know . . ." Ella reached over and patted my arm.

"Talking about it now, it all sounds so silly, and you're thinking that we shouldn't have fallen for Darren's hoity-toity attitude. But Darren, he had a way about him. And he was very handsome!" She sighed. "Not that he ever would have noticed a kid like me," she added quickly. "He wasn't just out of my league, Darren was out of my universe. He had money and the prestige that went along with it. He's a highly successful businessman now. He owns tons of property around town. I saw him on the six o'clock news a couple weeks ago talking about some big development project downtown. He's still very handsome."

"So the four of you—"

"Oh no, there were six of us at the concert together. Bobby Gideon, he was there, too. I didn't know Bobby well. Well, really, I didn't know any of the kids well except for Lucy. They were all older than me, juniors and seniors, and I was just starting high school that year. I bet Lucy caught heck from them for bringing me along. But that was Lucy's way. Like I said, she didn't care what other people thought of her. And Bobby . . . I remember that Bobby was the one always making jokes. Always smiling and laughing and teasing. He's dead now . . ." Ella's voice trailed off.

"And number six?" I asked.

Ella had been lost in thought, but now she hopped out of her chair and scrambled around the table, sliding the newspapers into a neat pile, picking up the mail from the floor. "Number six was Will Margolis," she said.

I waited for more and didn't get it, but hey, I wasn't
going to let that stop me. If my experience as detective to
the dead had taught me nothing else, it was how to pounce
on an opportunity when I saw one. With any luck, the next
time I tripped over Lucy Pasternak's overly dramatic ectoplasm, I'd have the whole thing wrapped up.

"So . . ." Ella was so busy in cleanup mode that when I
spoke, she jumped. "What's the end of the story? What do
I tell Ariel? You know, to scare the pants off her. Where did
they end up finding Lucy's body?"

"Oh, Pepper, don't say things like that!" Ella pressed a
hand to her heart, the gesture very similar to the one I'd
recently seen Lucy use. "I didn't say Lucy was dead, I said
she'd disappeared. In fact . . ." She clutched a pile of papers
to her heaving chest. "I keep thinking that someday I'll be
walking down the street and it will be like something out
of a movie, that I'll see her there and she'll recognize me
and run up to me and give me a hug, that she'll have some
really good story about where she's been and what she's
been up to."

This, I doubted, and for good reason.

Of course, Ella didn't know Lucy was a ghost, or that I'd
recently talked to her and she'd told me she was murdered
the night of the concert. This was obviously a biggie, but
I'd deal with it later. For the moment, I wasn't as concerned
with Ella learning the ugly truth as I was with realizing
what her not knowing it meant to my investigation.

See, Ella's continued and unwavering belief in Lucy still
being found alive told me two things:

Number one: that no one knew where Lucy's body was,
and it wouldn't be easy to locate.

Number two: that I still had to try.

After all, Ella did say she and Lucy had considered themselves sisters.

"The police tried so hard to find out what happened to Lucy. They followed every lead." I snapped out of my thoughts to find Ella shaking her head sadly. "I suppose after all these years, all it is to them is just another cold case."

Cold?

She had no idea.

M y lucky stars were shining on me the next day. Not only was my car ready, but the call came telling me about it just as I finished proofreading the latest edition of Ella's Garden View newsletter. She was so pleased I'd pitched in and helped her out and her mood was so much better since Ariel hadn't caused her any new grief in the previous twenty-four hours, that she told me I could leave the office early and get my car.

Yes, it meant a trip in the other direction on the rapid. But by this time, that was one trip I was actually looking forward to. And not because I'd changed my mind about the so-called benefits of public transportation.

I didn't know where else to find Lucy.

Fortunately, Ella drove me to the station so there was no walking (or heaven forbid, riding a bus and transferring) involved. It was early, rush hour hadn't started yet, and the rapid wasn't anywhere near full. I settled myself in a seat that I didn't have to share with anyone who smelled like stale cigars, and took a good look around.

No flash of golden hair.

No glimmer of golden lipstick.

No Lucy.

This wasn't something I'd anticipated. After all, she was the one who'd come to me for help.

And I was the one who told her to take a hike.

My conscience prickled.

I told it to shut up and drummed my fingers against the empty seat next to me, considering my options. If Lucy were any other ghost, I would have gone to her grave and demanded an audience. It wasn't always an effective strategy, but when worse comes to worst (and when I investigate, it usually does), it's worth a try. Of course, since Lucy didn't have a grave . . .

Nobody was more surprised than me to realize that not finding Lucy ticked me off. It wasn't like I needed another ghostly investigation to keep me busy, thank you very much. My life was rich and full enough. It was exciting and more than satisfying. It was, in fact—

Duller than dirt.

It was sad, but true, and sitting there listening to the clickety-clack of the rapid on the rails, watching the scenery whiz by, and not having a ghostly client to talk to, I couldn't escape it. No matter how hard I tried.

Ever since my breakup with Quinn, my love life was a big ol' nothing. Yeah, I'd gone out with an FBI agent from Chicago a couple times, but let's face it, federal agents are all into their careers, and that eats up not only their business hours but most of their personal lives. There was the whole long-distance thing, too, putting a definite crimp in what Scott and I had of a relationship. Trust me when I say that by *relationship*, I do not mean we were sleeping together. We weren't. He was a buddy, a pal. A guy who was fun to be with. Once in a while.

Besides, what I had with Scott didn't even begin to fill the void Quinn had left behind. And I'm not just talking about the sex, though, when we were together, I thought that was the only thing Quinn and I had in common. Looking back on it, I guess there was more going on between us.

That would explain why I felt like there was still a hole in my chest where my heart used to be.

"Harrumph." That was me offering my opinion of all the Quinn memories—good and bad—tromping through my head. I crossed my arms over my chest and sat back to settle in and wallow in a little well-deserved self-pity just as the rapid lurched around a corner and under a bridge. The lights flickered and, for a second, went out altogether.

When they came back on again, Lucy was in the seat next to me.

"Geez oh Pete!" I jammed one hand against my chest. It was that or risk my heart slamming out of my ribs and going bumping down the aisle. "Can't you ghosts play some kind of spooky music or something before you show up? You know, like a warning?"

Lucy's face was as impassive as if it were carved of stone. Her golden lips were set in a thin, defiant line. She stared at the seat in front of ours when she said, "I figured you didn't need a warning. After all, you're the one who didn't want to be bothered with me." Her sigh was epic. "As I recall, you said you couldn't help me."

"Yeah, well, that was before."

Still refusing to look at me, she lifted her chin and pulled back her shoulders. "Before what?"

I hate it when the dead play hard to get.

But not nearly as much as I hate it when I actually care.

I set the thought aside, not as inconsequential, but as less important than a little revenge.

Lucy was chilly (I mean emotionally chilly; I've already established that, physically, she was way past that stage); I was just as chilly back. The better to catch her off guard when I nonchalantly threw out the comment, "Before I found out that you were friends with Ella."

The Ice Queen thawed in a nanosecond. Her mouth fell open and she turned in her seat. "You know Ella Bender?"

"Well, her name is Ella Silverman now," I told her. "And she's my boss at Garden View Cemetery."

Lucy's eyes sparkled. "Little Ella! I always wondered what happened to her. She's a boss, huh? I'm not surprised. The kid had brains. Of course, she didn't know it yet, not back then. She was just a kid. Now Ella, she's a boss." A huge smile revealed Lucy's sparkling white teeth. "Not bad for a girl."

We'd already had the I-am-woman-hear-me-roar talk. I wasn't going to go into it again. Besides, Lucy didn't give me the chance. She barreled right on.

"So you talked to Ella about me? She told you about what happened to me, right?"

"Not exactly. She told me you disappeared. Not that you're dead."

Lucy tipped her head, thinking this over. "You mean nobody knows I'm dead?"

"Nobody's been able to prove it. On account of how they've never found your body. I'm guessing that, unlike Ella, who's being the ultimate Queen of Denial, most people are smart enough to know that after forty-five years—"

Lucy sat up like a shot, a glint in her eyes as icy as her ectoplasm. "Are you saying Ella's not smart? You take that back! Right now. Ella's a great little kid."

I chose my words carefully, and not just because I couldn't imagine anyone, anywhere thinking of Ella as a little kid, but because I knew it would be easier to deal with Lucy if she wasn't angry at me. What I said now would determine if my investigation would go smoothly, or if it would be as full of bumps as a bowl of Ben & Jerry's Everything But the . . .

"Ella's very smart." This was true so it wasn't like I was pimping for my case. "She's raised three daughters, all on her own." (It should be noted that I did not add the word *successfully* to this statement.) "And she keeps things at Garden View running like clockwork. Only Ella . . ." I wrestled with the idea of glossing over the truth, or laying it on the line. A teenager deserved to have things sugarcoated. Especially a teenager who'd died too young. Then again, Lucy'd had forty-five years to come to grips with how tough the world could be. The way I figured it, she could deal.

"Ella's a believer," I told her. "It's one of the things that makes her an annoying boss. And a really good friend. She thinks that one of these days, she's actually going to find out that you're alive."

"Poor Little One!" Lucy shook her head. "Did you tell her?"

There wasn't any amusement in my laughter. "What? That I know for sure you're dead even though the police were never able to prove it? Or that I've been talking to your ghost? I may not be as smart as Ella, but I know that either way, admitting that would give whole new meaning to the term *ugly truth*. Believe me when I say this. I know. I once had a guy walk out on me because I told him the truth about how I talk to ghosts."

"Creep." Lucy grumbled the word. It was kinder than the ones I used when I thought about Quinn.

Rather than get into it, I stayed focused on my case.

"I think the only thing that will make Ella face the truth is if we find your body," I said.

Lucy's blue eyes lit. "You're going to help? You're going

to prop me up in my hour of need? Answer my call for help? Help lift me out of the darkness by shining a light on the truth? You're going to—"

It was cut her off or risk drowning in the sea of drama. "I'm going to look for your body," I told her. "But you're going to have to help."

Lucy's golden eyebrows dipped. "I'm not sure I can. I've told you everything I remember."

"Tell me again."

She did, start to finish, from running out on the field at the concert to those last terrifying moments in the trunk. And when she was done, she looked at me, hope gleaming in her eyes. "It makes more sense this time, right? You know what to do? Where to look?"

"Nope. And nope." The rapid was nearing a stop. Not mine, but a stop. I motioned Lucy aside and slid out of the seat. "But we're going to find out. And we're going to do it by starting at the beginning." I waved her to follow me to the door. "We'll get off here and take a rapid back in the other direction. That way, we can get off at the stop you got off at that night and walk through everything you did. It may not give us all the answers—"

"But it's a start." She nodded and grinned.

The train stopped, the doors swished open, and I stepped out on the platform. "It shouldn't take long for another train to come along in the other direction," I told Lucy, glancing over my shoulder to see that she was just about to step off the rapid. "We'll just—"

My words dissolved in the end of a gasp of surprise. But then, who wouldn't be surprised to see Lucy get as far as the door of the train and run into what looked like a wall of blinding white light?

She jumped back just as the train doors slid closed.

"What's going on?" I called out.

Her eyes filled with tears, she shrugged and sobbed. "I don't know. I've never tried to get off the train before. Oh, Pepper! I'm afraid . . ."

The rapid started up and Lucy stood there at the door, tears sliding down her face. Her last words echoed in my ears.

"I think I'm stuck here on the rapid. Forever."

4

There are only so many ways a detective can try and reason through things that are completely unreasonable.

Like the magic woo-woo that wouldn't allow Lucy to get off the train.

It's not like I didn't rack my brain to make sense of it. Believe me when I say I did. I spent the rest of that day and all of that night tossing the idea around in my head and got nowhere at all. I would have done just as much thinking (and probably just as much getting nowhere) the next day if my job didn't interfere.

It has a way of doing that.

Instead of trying to figure out a way to get Lucy off that train and onto my investigation, I spent that Wednesday morning dragging around Garden View Cemetery from angel sculpture to angel sculpture with the senior outreach group from Saint Basil's parish in tow.

And that was just before lunch.

It was spring, after all, the weather was finally improving, and (woe is me!) tour groups were coming out of the winter woodwork. That afternoon, it was the women's committee from the local Botanical Society. They weren't as interested in angels as they were in daffodils, so I trudged around Garden View from one spectacular spring planting to the next. They were, predictably, thrilled and went on and on (and on) about the differences between jonquils, daffodils, paperwhites, and narcissus.

Whatever.

By the time it was all over, I was glad to get back to the administration building, where I could put my feet up and get back to thinking about what happened to Lucy and, more important, where it had happened and where I could find her body.

I would have done it, too, if I hadn't walked into my office and found a . . .

Struggling for a word here, and since a polite one is not forthcoming, I'll go with—

Creature.

I found a creature in my office.

This particular creature was about as big as a minute. She was wearing black jeans that even I—always a believer in a girl making the most of her figure—wondered how she was able to move in, much less breathe in. The same applied for her Barbie-pink T-shirt with the name of some rock band on it that I'd never heard of. Not that she had anything to flaunt in that department. She was as flat as a pancake.

Her inky-dark hair hung well past her shoulders. A couple hefty hanks of it were dyed a hideous color somewhere between maroon and magenta. Her bangs had been trimmed with a lawn mower. They hung over her forehead, completely covering her right eye. I could see her left eye, though, and behind her heavy, dark-rimmed glasses, I saw that it was outlined with what looked like an entire stick of eyeliner. Her eye shadow matched her T-shirt.

We hadn't even exchanged two words, and already, I was exhausted by the encounter. Not to mention offended, appalled, and outraged in the name of fashion. I was tempted to mention that any woman who wants to be looked at as a woman and not as an alien from outer space pays more attention to her wardrobe, her makeup, and her grooming. In the name of peaceful coexistence, I controlled my opinions and my exasperation and marched to my desk. In an office as small as mine, it didn't take long to get there.

I dropped into my chair. "Hello, Ariel," I said.

Ariel flipped her hair. When she pouted, the silver stud in her lip poked out at me.

I averted my eyes. It was that or upchuck.

I pretended the papers I was shuffling around my desk were actually important, the better not to have to look at the girl. Now that I'd seen the lip piercing, I knew my sense of the bizarre would demand that my gaze automatically travel to her left eyebrow. And eyebrow piercings give me the heebie-jeebies.

"What are you doing here?" I asked her.

I heard her sigh, right before my guest chair creaked. When I dared to look up again, Ariel was draped in it, her head thrown back with one hand on her forehead. "I'm misunderstood," she said.

"Maybe that's because you don't explain yourself clearly enough. You know, like when someone asks you what you're doing here."

Another sigh, and she rearranged herself into another dramatic pose. "My mother . . ." She groaned these words.

"My mother says I have to come here to the cemetery every day after school. How stupid is that? How stifling to my inner life? Does she really expect me to give up my social life? To travel through the cold fog of my existence without the companionship of friends who understand how awful my life is? Spending my days in this place . . ." This time, she didn't stop at a sigh. She added a mournful groan. "It's going to turn my heart to stone."

I sort of got that. After all, I had to spend my days at Garden View, too.

Ariel was not a person I wanted to confide in, so rather than do that, I said, "It's your own fault. If you hadn't run away—"

"If I ran away, it wouldn't have been to Sandusky." As if that tiny body of hers actually weighed six hundred pounds, she hauled herself out of the chair. "I would have gone someplace mysterious, like the vast expanses of Canada, where I could be alone with my thoughts. Or the deepest, darkest rain forest of South America, where I could get in touch with my artistic side by communing with nature. That, at least, would have fed my soul."

"I guess you should have thought of that before you opted for Sandusky." Oh yeah, I smiled when I said this. Not that I was feeling particularly chipper, but according to Ella, Ariel was going through a phase that was all about angst. I knew nothing would mess with her head as much as smiling. "And now you're paying the price. The office every day after school, huh?" I nodded at the backpack that was tossed in the corner. "How about you go into the conference room and do your homework."

"My mother is in the conference room," she informed me. "She's with Jim, her boss. Your boss." Ariel looked at me through the curtain of her bangs, and in spite of the syrupy eye shadow and the black nail polish, she suddenly sounded very much like the little kid she was. "Wouldn't you love to know what they're meeting about?"

To prove how much I didn't care, I shrugged, and just in case Ariel didn't get it, I was quick to add, "Whatever it is, I'll find out soon enough."

"Oh, you will." She nodded as vigorously as a teenager can who's trying to pretend that every moment of her existence is unbearable. "But I know now. I saw a note from Jim. On my mother's desk."

"I suppose you looked through my desk, too." I actually wasn't as upset about this as I tried to sound. I had the newest issue of *Marie Claire* in my top desk drawer. With any luck, Ariel had found it, and had paid attention to the article called "Fifteen-Minute Hairstyles." Fifteen minutes, a bottle of shampoo, and a really good beautician . . . it could do wonders!

"Your desk is boring." This didn't stop Ariel from perching on the edge of it. "You don't have interesting notes on your desk. You know, like notes from Jim to my mother."

"Why don't you go back in her office and look around some more."

Ariel's shoulders dropped. "My mother . . ." There was that groan again. "She says I have to be with someone every single minute I'm here. She says someone has to watch me." She harrumphed like only a fifteen-year-old can. "Like I'm a little kid or something."

Far be it from me to take anybody under my wing. Especially when that *anybody* is a body as pathetically miserable and as miserably pathetic as Ariel. Still, I couldn't help but give it a try. Thanks to my soft spot for Ella, I was already dealing with one ghostly mystery I would rather have avoided. I wasn't about to sit here and listen to her daughter diss her. The least I could do—for Ella's sake and my own—was try to talk some sense into the girl.

"You want to stop being treated like a little kid, stop acting like one," I said, and I guess Ariel wasn't used to anyone laying it on the line so bluntly because she shot me a look. "Oh, come off it!" I rolled my eyes. Juvenile, yes, but warranted in this situation. She needed to know that she didn't have a lock on the melodrama. "You can't pretend that disappearing for the weekend wasn't dumb. It was. And it upset your mother. A lot. You know she had that friend who disappeared."

It was Ariel's turn to roll her eyes. "That was about a million years ago."

"That doesn't make it any easier for your mom to forget how painful it was."

OK, I'm not exactly warm and fuzzy when it comes to these sorts of situations, but I'm not a complete moron, either. I saw the way Ariel's shoulders stiffened just a little. I knew I'd hit a chord, and I went in for the kill.

"Your mom loves you," I pointed out, and then because I thought maybe that was too touchy-feely, both for Ariel and for me, I quickly added, "She's nuts about you. About all you girls. She'd do anything for you. She already has. She's raised you single-handedly, and she works hard here to make sure you have everything you need."

Ariel made a face. "She loves this stupid place."

"Not nearly as much as she loves you."

She crossed her stick arms over her chest. "My mother should know that I'm mature and responsible. She didn't need to spend the weekend worrying about me."

"I bet that's what Lucy would have said about her mother, too." This was, technically, not true. As far as I could tell, though Lucy was plenty annoying in her own drama queen way, she wasn't nearly as headstrong, unruly, or hygienically challenged as Ariel. But Ariel didn't know that. And I was trying to prove a point.

"But I bet Lucy's mother did worry. I don't know if the woman is still alive, but if she is, I bet she's still worrying. That's sort of what mothers do best."

"They shouldn't."

"Agreed."

"But—"

"Come on, Ariel. I know your mother, and I know she's told you about Lucy. You should have used your head and figured out that when you disappeared, your mother would be upset. But then maybe that was your plan, right? That's why you went away for the weekend and didn't call? You wanted to hurt her. You wanted her to freak. Well, congratulations, because you did a bang-up job of it."

She looked at me out of the corner of her eye, her voice no more than a whisper. "Did she? Freak, I mean?"

"Big-time."

"Really?" The silver stud in Ariel's lip wobbled. Of course, I wasn't supposed to notice. Of course, she wasn't going to take the chance that I might. She hopped off the desk and turned her back on me. She took a couple moments to compose herself, but hey, I'd been a teenaged girl once, too. Ariel might try to hide the tears in her voice, but I caught on. So the kid had a conscience after all! Who would have believed it?

I was shrewd enough not to point out what I'd discovered.

She was devious enough to still play the game.

"So now my mother's going to get even by making my life miserable?" Ariel wailed. "Just because I refuse to conform to her outmoded parenting paradigm? It isn't fair. It isn't." She spun around to face me, daring me to challenge her.

But hey, I'm the one who talks to the dead, whether I want to or not. Fair and I aren't exactly on a first-name basis.

Ariel mistook my silence for opposition. She threw her hands in the air. "What am I supposed to tell my friends? How am I supposed to explain it when, every day after school, I have to come over here? I could be back at school doing something. Or I could be hanging out and getting coffee with my friends after school. Or—"

"School." Sure, Ariel looked at me a little strange when I said this. But then, Ariel looked a little strange to begin with, so I wasn't going to let that stop me. I continued to think out loud. "What else does a seventeen-year-old have except school?" I asked, not looking for an answer. "I mean, her whole world would pretty much be school, wouldn't it, so if something happened to her . . ." I wasn't sure where this train of thought was heading, I just knew I wasn't ready to jump off yet.

I snapped my gaze to Ariel's. "If something happened to her, it would probably have to have something to do with school, right?"

She took a step back. Apparently, hanging around at Garden View was one thing. Dealing with the crazy tour guide who worked there wasn't part of the deal.

"What are you talking about?" she asked.

Ariel already knew the story, so for once in my ghostly-encounter investigations, I didn't have to make up a lie to cover my tracks.

I grabbed my purse out of my bottom desk drawer as I said, "Lucy. What happened to Lucy must have had something to do with school. It must have. School is pretty much all a kid has. So if I check out her school—"

"Why do you care what happened to Lucy?"

Who would have expected a kid that weird to be so perceptive?

I stopped in my tracks. Again, I thought about concocting a lie, and was grateful I didn't need to. "Your mom told me about Lucy. You know, after you disappeared. I care because she cares."

This satisfied her. And that might have been a good thing except that when I got moving again and got to the door, Ariel was right behind me clutching her backpack.

Nerve-wracking enough, because those piercings gave me the creeps. Worse, because I had a bad feeling about what it meant.

I was holding out hope when I asked, "When I leave, you're going back to your mother's office, right?"

Ariel shook her head. "You remember what my mom said. I can't be left alone."

"But—"

"There's nobody else for me to stay with. Jim and my mom are in a meeting. Jennine out at the front desk is helping some people pick out a plot for their grandma who just died. If you leave me alone—"

"Your mother will freak again."

Her expression brightened. It might have been because she liked the thought of Ella freaking, but I think it was more because of what she saw as a get out of jail pass. Excited and trying hard not to show it, Ariel shifted from black Converse to black Converse. "I've heard the stuff my mom says about you, Pepper, about how you help people out with all kinds of mysteries. That's what you're doing, isn't it?

You're trying to figure out what happened to Lucy. And now, we're going to investigate, right?"

"Right." I didn't like the self-satisfied look on her face, so I was quick to add, "Except for the *we* part. You're going to come along. And you're going to behave yourself. And you're going to stay out of my way." I looked at her hard. "Promise?"

A tiny smile sparkled around Ariel's mouth, and that darned lip stud winked at me. "Cross my heart," she purred.

I might have actually believed it.

If I thought the kid had a heart.

It was Ariel's idea to start out at the Shaker Heights Public Library.

This worried me, and not just because I was embarrassed that I hadn't thought of it myself. I figured we'd start at the high school. She pointed out that I'd never get past the security desk with my lame-ass story about how I was looking into the disappearance of a girl who'd gone to school there forty-five years earlier.

We didn't have security desks when I went to high school.

I felt old.

I shoved the thought aside, and in the library's reference room, I slid a stack of Shaker Heights High yearbooks—from 1966 to 1970—in front of me. Only five books, but to me, it looked a little too much like homework. And I was never very good at homework.

Unless I took advantage of my assistant?

I turned to where Ariel was sitting next to me. "Why don't you—"

She shushed me with a hand signal. She was texting a

mile a minute and never managed to break her stride. I was actually impressed.

I got to work without her.

I started with 1966 and flipped through the pages that featured the junior class. There was Lucy in all her golden glory, smiling like a beauty queen.

Of course, I knew I wouldn't find her with the senior class in the yearbook from 1967, but I looked, anyway. On the last of the pages dedicated to the seniors, there was that same picture of Lucy, along with the caption, *We miss you.*

"Somebody didn't," I grumbled.

Fingers flying, Ariel shot me a look.

I continued on, paging through the senior class, looking for the kids both Ella and Lucy had told me were at the concert with them the night Lucy died.

Darren Andrews was a cinch to find. Early in the alphabet, and with none of the nasty acne the other boys on his page were subject to.

Darren was a sandy-haired charmer, all right, I could tell that from the sparkle in his eyes. His hair was a little shaggy in a 1967-I'm-rebelling way, and he was wearing a turtleneck sweater and yup, just like Ella said, there was that gold medal he always wore. Except . . .

I took a closer look.

It was silver, and a crucifix.

So much for Ella's memory.

While I was at it, I checked out Bobby Gideon and Will Margolis, too—nondescript guys with teenaged goofy smiles and bad hair. In the junior class section, there was a picture of Janice. I could see why she terrified people. Janice had the hair and the makeup down pat. And the look . . . formidable, that was the word. Janice Sherwin was a force to be reckoned with.

Rather than stare into that face, I looked around for Ariel and discovered that while I had been busy researching, she'd disappeared.

Part of me was grateful.

That would be the part of me that didn't know I'd catch hell (a kindly phrased sort of hell, of course, and given to me with the utmost understanding and teary eyes, too) from Ella if she found out.

Exasperated, I pushed back my chair and went in search of her, and I really wasn't all that worried until I couldn't find Ariel anywhere. But then, I'd been a teenager, too, once, and I assumed if I followed the sounds of heavy breathing, I'd find her in the stacks either smoking or making out with a guy. With no panting noises to follow, I had to devise a Plan B. I was trying to figure out what that was going to be when I heard the murmur of a guy's voice. I did a U-turn in the stacks where I was searching, zipped past the encyclopedias, and rounded a corner.

Maybe I was getting old, because I was certainly surprised by what I found.

No lip-locks.

No nicotine.

In fact, Ariel was sitting cross-legged on the floor across from a kid who might have been her twin except that he was about thirty pounds heavier.

Same black jeans and sneakers. Thank goodness he wasn't wearing a pink T-shirt. His was black. So was his hair. Except for the streaks of color. My guess was he and Ariel had shared a bottle of dye. That would explain the magenta stripes.

He was reading to Ariel from a battered notebook.

"You must be Gonzalo."

I had the advantage. But then, a five-foot-eleven redhead usually does.

They both sucked in breaths of surprise and looked up at me. Ariel had tears in her eyes.

Damn my luck for getting drawn into lives—present and past—that really were none of my concern and certainly none of my business. I stepped forward, narrowed my eyes, and propped my fists on my hips.

"What's going on?" I asked, my gaze skimming from Ariel to Gonzalo and back to Ariel again. "Why are you crying?" I asked her. "And what . . ." I slid a laser look back to him. "What did you do to her?"

He hopped to his feet. But not nearly as fast as Ariel. "He didn't do anything," she said, her stance a mirror of mine. "He was reading to me. Beautiful, sensitive, wonderful . . ." She sniffed. "Poetry."

This, I wasn't expecting.

I was never very good at babysitting so I proceeded cautiously. I didn't need an all-out rebellion. I had enough to worry about.

"Poetry. Great!" I mustered as much enthusiasm as I could for a subject that had never made any sense to me in the first place. "When you're done . . ." I poked my thumb over my shoulder back toward the table. "I could use some help," I told Ariel. "I've never been very good at this research stuff."

"You're not serious?" When Ariel's lip curled, I looked away. "Looking stuff up, it's a piece of cake. It's the only thing about school that's really cool." She was sounding a little too much like she actually enjoyed one little piece of her life, and she caught herself and flipped her hair. "What I mean is that research is a chore. You know, like living. But if you really need the help . . ." Her shoulders drooping from the weight of her responsibilities, she dragged herself back to the table. Gonzalo came along. While Ariel and I looked through the rest of the yearbooks, he scribbled in his notebook, stopping now and again to sigh.

Ariel grabbed for the one marked 1970 and flipped the pages until she found a fresh-faced Ella Bender, her smile exactly as bright and sunny then as it was now. Her long, dark hair skimmed her shoulders, and Ella peered at the world through a pair of dark-rimmed glasses.

Ariel's eyes went wide. She slid off her glasses and tucked them in her backpack.

"Let's see what else is in here," I said, slipping the book in front of me. I wasn't sure what I was looking for, but if nothing else, I figured I could get a glimpse at what it was like to be a high school student back in the day. In the section about school activities there were three whole pages devoted to a visit from some poet named Patrick Monroe, jeans-clad, bearded, and with hair so long and straggly, it made Ariel look well groomed. At the end of the book was a picture of a kid I recognized, Bobby Gideon. Ella had told me he was dead. What she hadn't mentioned was that he'd been killed in action in Vietnam.

"So . . ." Ariel leaned closer, the better to hide her enthusiasm. "What does all this tell us? What did we find out?"

I didn't have the heart to put a damper on the kid's excitement, but the answers seemed pretty clear, at least to me.

I had a dead client.

And trying to find her body . . . well, I'd pretty much hit a dead end.

The next day, I didn't have any tours scheduled at the cemetery. This was good news for a couple different reasons:

1. It meant I didn't have to put up with senior citizens, flower lovers, or (worst of all) kids on school field trips who talked all at once, vying for attention, asking questions I couldn't answer and mostly just annoying me.

2. More important, it meant I didn't have to wear my standard-issue Garden View khakis and polo shirt. I was free to be fashion forward, and in the spirit of the season, I took full advantage. When I arrived at the cemetery that day, I was wearing an adorable new one-piece dress that looked like two. Let's hear it for the inventive genius who thought of pairing a solid-colored scoop neck top with short ruffled sleeves along with a curve-hugging tweed skirt shot through with metallic threads. All in a shade of olivey green

that was at once both a salute to spring and a complement to my hair.

Oh yeah, I looked good and I knew it, and I walked tall—literally and figuratively—in my suede pumps.

That is, until I rounded the corner from where I'd parked my car and realized that the entire cemetery administration staff was standing outside the building. My first thought was fire drill. Until I noticed the especially weird fact that every single one of them was clad in work clothes. I do not mean work-at-the-cemetery-administration-office attire. I mean grubby stuff.

I stopped short and stared just as Ella stepped forward. Her dangly earrings sparkled in the morning sun, the bright orange and yellow beads a stark contrast to her army green boots and gray sweatshirt.

She may have looked disappointed, but she didn't look surprised when she asked, "You didn't pick up your phone message from Jim last night, did you?"

I didn't want to dash all the misplaced confidence Ella had in me, so I didn't tell her that when I see the cemetery's number come up on my cell, I pretty much never do. "Battery is dead," I said, "and I couldn't find my charger." As if it would somehow prove it, I got my phone out of my purse and waved it under her nose. "What's up?"

She shushed me with a look, and like her short, round body had a snowball's chance in hell of actually concealing tall, thin me, she stepped in front of me just as Jim, the cemetery administrator, walked out the door of the building. He looked even more farmery than the rest of them. But then, in addition to his jeans and boots, he was wearing a wide-brimmed straw hat and a red-and-white-checked flannel shirt.

"Now that we're all here . . ." Jim slid me a look, and

honestly, since I wasn't more than a couple minutes late, that didn't exactly seem fair. "We can get to work. As I told you in my message last night, we'll be doing this once a week from now on." Another glance my way, and this time, he skimmed a look over my gorgeous new outfit, too. Was the man trying to tell me something? "Every Thursday, so be prepared. OK, everybody. Move out!"

They did. I didn't. Good thing Ella stayed put, too. I needed an interpreter.

"Cost-cutting measures," she said, like that was supposed to make some kind of sense, and she led me over to the entrance of the building, where there was one more pair of rubber boots waiting by the door.

My reaction was predictable. And automatic. I stepped back. "You don't expect me to—"

"Jim says everybody, and everybody means everybody." Ella crossed her arms over her ample chest. "You know I don't like to be tough on you, Pepper, but I'm sorry, I'm going to have to insist."

It was very un-Ella-like for her to be so firm. About anything. I guess that's what made me realize she was serious.

I sidled my way up to the unattractive boots, peering down into them just to make sure there were no surprises lurking inside. When I slid off my pumps and slipped on the boots, I made a face. "We're not some kind of cult now, are we?" I asked, and yeah, I knew it was close to impossible, but stranger things had been known to happen at Garden View. "We're not going to—"

"We're going to clean up the cemetery grounds."

I was bent over, adjusting the boot on my left foot, and I jumped up and would have twirled to face her with something like gracefulness if the boots weren't so big that my feet got tangled. I steadied myself, one hand against the stone administration building, and blurted out, "You're kidding me, right?"

Ella looped an arm through mine. "I'm not any happier about this than you are," she assured me.

She was wrong. There was no way she could be as unhappy as I was.

"I didn't sign on to do groundskeeper work," I wailed.

Ella's lips compressed into a thin line. "None of us did. But . . ." She released my arm and looked over her shoulder to make sure Jim wasn't anywhere near. He wasn't. He was across the parking lot near a memorial with an urn on top of it, poking the ground with a long, pointed stick to pick up a fast-food paper bag that had blown onto the grounds from the other side of the iron fence that bordered this part of the cemetery. She leaned closer and whispered, "We've got to save money, and Jim is convinced that one way to do it is to cut down on the groundskeepers' overtime hours. If everyone in administration helps out—"

"We won't get done all the work we need to get done and then we'll have overtime hours."

Her smile was fleeting. "Administration staff is salaried."

"So our overtime hours will essentially be a donation."

"It's not ideal."

"That's an understatement." I knew better than to speak too loud. Being Garden View's one and only full-time tour guide is not my idea of a job made in heaven. But it is a job. And my job paid my bills. Ella's, I knew, paid hers, too, and it would soon be putting Rachel, then Sarah, and maybe someday (if she wasn't in jail by then) Ariel through college. Neither one of us could afford to let Jim think we were planning a rebellion, so I tossed a look in his direction, too, and forced myself to keep my voice down.

Which doesn't mean I was ready to throw in the proverbial towel.

"I don't clean up litter," I said.

Ella's response shouldn't have been a smile. "Neither do I."

"But I look . . ." Just in case she missed it, I stepped back so she could get a gander at my new outfit. Thanks to the boots, it was suddenly not nearly so cute. Which didn't keep me from doing my best to preserve it. "This has got silk in it. It's dry clean only."

"Come on," she said, latching on and dragging me in the opposite direction from where Jim was working. "This week, I'll do the schlepp work." As we passed a pile of big fabric bags, she grabbed one and handed it to me. She took a pointy stick for herself. "Next week, you can do the poking and I'll do the carrying."

By the next week, I hoped to have some way out of what was looking a little too much like manual labor for my liking. For now, though . . .

Pouting, I clumped along at Ella's side, and when she stopped near the fence and got to work stabbing the trash there, I held the bag open so she could deposit it inside. Needless to say, I also held it far, far away. I wasn't going to take the chance of getting stains on my new dress. Dry clean only, remember.

"This is dumb." I could safely say this; Jim was nowhere near.

"Yes, it is." Ella stabbed and dumped. "But it's only for an hour. Every Thursday morning. We'll get some exercise, and we'll help the cemetery's bottom line. That's not such a bad thing." Leave it to her to find the silver lining, even in a cloud this dark.

I wasn't so sure. In fact, the only bright spot I could see was that I finally had an excuse to buy that pair of True Religion five-pocket bootcut jeans I'd had my eye on. I was just deciding if I'd do that over the weekend or wait until the next week, when Ella jabbed a page of newspaper, lifted it, and said, "Hey, look at this!"

I shook myself out of my pleasant, denim-clad thoughts to find that Ella had jammed the front page of that morning's paper two inches from my nose. I stepped back, the better to read the fat headlines that screamed across the top of the page. They were all about some deranged serial killer named Winston Churchill (I'm not making this up) who'd been apprehended overnight. The story was accompanied by a photograph of the accused, handcuffed and being marched into a waiting car by the cop who'd made the collar.

"Oh."

It goes without saying that had I been prepared, I would have said something far more clever than this. I wouldn't have stared, either. But let's face it, the last thing I expected to find behind a headstone in the cemetery was a photo of Quinn.

Stare I did, any ingenious comment I might have made caught up behind the sudden knot in my throat. The photo showed Quinn right behind the perp—cool, calm, and collected in spite of what he must have gone through to get his hands on the guy. As usual, he was as tempting as sin and looked like a million bucks in a suit he shouldn't have been able to afford on his detective's salary.

Like it or not—and believe me when I say I didn't like it at all—it was impossible to pull my eyes away. I grabbed the newspaper out of Ella's hands and stared awhile longer—at the dark hair, the impossibly green eyes, the complete and total deliciousness of Quinn.

"I shouldn't have pointed it out to you." Leave it to Ella to feel guilty. I dragged my gaze away from the picture to find her on the verge of tears. "I'm sorry, Pepper. I was just so surprised to see the picture, I reacted without thinking. I didn't mean to bring up bad memories."

And I was supposed to say . . . What?

Rather than say anything at all, I decided to demonstrate. I wadded the newspaper into a ball and stuffed it into my trash bag.

"Well . . . er . . . yes." Ella cleared her throat. She poked around the ground with her pointy stick. Her troubled expression cleared when she saw a way out of the awkward moment in the form of the Pepsi can over near the fence, and she scurried in that direction to retrieve it.

"We've been so busy, I forgot to tell you about Ariel," she said, dropping the can in my bag. Not exactly a subject that would take my mind off my Quinn troubles, but hey, any port in a storm. With a tight smile, I encouraged her to continue.

"She told me what you two did yesterday. How you took her to the library. Pepper, you're a genius."

This went without saying.

The only question remaining was what made Ella think so.

"She actually talked to me at dinner, Pepper!" Ella twinkled as bright as the daffodils (or were they jonquils?) blooming nearby. Still grinning, she did a sweep around the nearest headstones. Garden View's nearly three hundred acres are usually pristine, thanks to the groundskeepers, who would be royally pissed once they learned they'd no longer be getting overtime pay. But all things considered, Jim couldn't have picked a better day to begin his cost-cutting campaign. A brisk spring breeze had kicked up during the night, and debris from the surrounding neighborhood had snuck in through the fence and now littered the ground all around us. I was grateful not to have pointy-stick duty.

"Ariel told me how you two sat down and went through the old yearbooks," Ella said, practically crooning the words. "That's more sharing than she's done in as long as I can remember. We had a bonding moment, Pepper, a real bonding moment!"

I might have been as excited as Ella if only the library/yearbook exercise had gotten me anywhere in terms of my investigation.

When Ella ambled over to a clearing surrounded by the monuments to a family called Greenleigh, I galumphed along behind her, thinking all the while. "You know," I said, lying through my teeth without so much as a pang of guilt, partly because I was getting really used to lying and partly because, even as I said it, I realized it was a good idea. "I don't know if she mentioned it to you, but I asked Ariel to do some research for me. You know, about your friend Lucy. I thought if I put her in charge of a little project about Lucy—"

"It would help drive home my message about staying safe and keeping in touch. Yes!" Like an Olympic athlete, Ella poked a fist into the air. Right before she did a little dance step and spun around. I'm not sure how she managed since her boots were as clunky as mine. I can only think that a woman who habitually wears Earth Shoes is more used to making do when it comes to oh-so-unfashionable footwear. "I told you you're a genius. This proves it."

"Well, I could be more of one. If I knew more." I pinned Ella with a look. "Are you sure there isn't more you can tell me about Lucy? Anything that would help?"

"You mean help Ariel realize the dangers of being out in the world alone." Ella nodded. "Yes, I see." There was a teeny heap of fast-food wrappers piled against a headstone, and rather than risk damaging the stone with her metal-tipped poker, Ella bent and plucked the papers by hand. She dumped them in my bag and brushed her hands together, nodding all the while. "It does sound cruel when you come right out and say it, but this is all for Ariel's own good. We want to make this whole running away and being missing thing look as scary as possible. We've got to emphasize how it can have dire consequences. Even if Lucy really is still alive, Ariel doesn't have to know that."

The only way I could keep my mouth shut was to bite my lip. And keep my mind on my investigation.

"Is there anything you haven't told me about Lucy?" I asked her. "Anyone you think could have been involved in her mur . . . er . . . disappearance?"

"Well . . ." Ella jabbed her stick into the ground and leaned against it. By now, the sun was peeking over the trees and the air was quickly heating. She swiped one sleeve of her sweatshirt across her forehead. "There was Patrick Monroe, of course."

The name was vaguely familiar, but it took a second for the why of it to click in. When it did, I grinned. "You mean the poet? The one who visited your school."

"Senior year. That's right." Ella was pleased I'd noticed it in the yearbook. "Oh, he was something, all right. Patrick Monroe." She tipped her head back. "Every girl in school was madly in love with him."

This did not exactly scan with the pictures I'd seen in Ella's yearbook. I gave her an uncertain look. "Beard? Dirty jeans? Long scraggly hair?" I demonstrated, my hands raking over my own anything-but-scraggly locks. "Are we talking about the same Patrick Monroe?"

Ella laughed. "It was the sixties. And Mr. Monroe . . ."

She shook her head. "By the time he came back to Shaker for that assembly when I was a senior, Mr. Monroe was a world-famous poet. Come on, Pepper . . ." She poked me in the ribs. "You know how it is. There isn't a woman alive who can resist a poet."

I was pretty sure this woman could.

Rather than dwell on it, I glommed on to something else Ella said. "You said, when he came back to Shaker. Does that mean this Patrick Monroe guy—"

"He was a teacher at the school. Of course, you wouldn't know that if you hadn't run across his picture in one of the older yearbooks! Mr. Monroe was in the English department. He quit teaching when that poem of his was published. Oh, you must know it." Thinking, she snapped her fingers together, and when she finally gave up, she shook her head in disgust. "It's right on the tip of my tongue. I'll think of it. I'll bet it's a poem you studied when you were in high school. That's how famous it is."

She made her mistake there. *Studied* and *high school* in the same sentence.

"Anyway . . ." Ella stabbed up some more debris and put it in my bag. "Everybody else was taken in by him, but me . . . I always wondered if Mr. Monroe had something to do with Lucy's disappearance. Shaker wasn't his first teaching job, you know. The rumor going around school . . ." As if it hadn't happened forty-five years before, Ella leaned closer, sharing the confidence. "Rumor had it that he'd been asked to leave his first teaching job somewhere in New York. Because of . . . you know . . . an inappropriate relationship with one of the girl students."

Finally, something interesting connected with my case. Gross, but interesting. As for whether it had anything to do with Lucy, there was only one way to find out.

"Did Lucy ever say anything about Mr. Monroe coming on to her?"

"Oh, really, Pepper!" Ella fanned her face with one hand. "We weren't quite as blatant about discussing things like that back then as you young people are now. But no, there's no way." There was a fast-food burger wrapper across the road and Ella headed that way. She stabbed it and said, "If Mr. Monroe was doing something inappropriate, Lucy would have told me. And she would have reported him. She was that kind of girl. I told you, she didn't put up with any sort of unfairness and she didn't keep quiet in the face of what was wrong. She didn't—"

Ella's cheeks turned suddenly ashen. Her mouth fell open.

I put a hand on her arm.

"I just remembered," she said on the end of a breath. "That night of the concert, when we were on the rapid . . . I remember there was some talk about Lucy having an appointment with the principal. I can't remember . . . I don't know who mentioned it or if Lucy said it was true or not, but if it was . . ."

Interesting and more interesting!

"Did she say what she was going to see the principal about?"

Thinking hard, Ella squeezed her eyes shut. "She didn't. I'm sure of it. But I remember everyone seemed surprised."

"So she didn't confide in anyone?"

"Well, she certainly didn't tell me about the appointment. If there was really an appointment. In fact . . ." She thought some more. "Everyone was surprised to hear about it except Will. Apparently, Lucy mentioned it to him. But then, that wasn't anything new. Will was one of those guys the other kids confided in, a natural-born psychologist. From what I'd heard, any student brave enough to to see our principal needed some sort of therapy! Mr. Wannamaker didn't believe in being friends with his students. He was tough and he was strict. Not the sort of person you'd just stop in on to chat. If she really did make that appointment . . ." Ella sighed. "Lucy must have had a very good reason to want to talk to him."

"And do you think it might have had something to do with this Monroe character?"

She shook her head and my hopes plummeted. "Even if it did, the police investigated Mr. Monroe thoroughly after Lucy disappeared. I mean, everyone was talking about how he'd been let go from his last job. That was no secret. The police heard the stories, and of course, they checked out Mr. Monroe. Even after school started that fall, I remember seeing cops in the hall, and once, I saw them talking to Mr. Monroe. They apparently never really thought it was him, though. Or they never found a way to connect him to Lucy. Otherwise, I don't think they would have dropped it. Especially since Lucy took that summer school poetry class with Mr. Monroe."

This, too, was news, and I perked up, but apparently Ella didn't notice since she was busy poking and stabbing. I urged her on with a hopeful, "And . . ."

"Oh, the summer school class?" Like it was no big deal (and for all I knew, it wasn't), Ella shrugged. "That's the class Lucy got an F in and we thought she wouldn't be allowed to go to the Beatles concert, but her parents let her go, anyway." Her smile was bittersweet. "Fate is a funny thing, isn't it? Lucy almost didn't get to go to the concert. But she did go. And she had such a wonderful time! She even kissed Paul McCartney. And if she did die . . . I mean, I'm saying this theoretically, not because I believe it or anything . . . but if she did die that night, then the concert was her last happy memory." She sighed and got back to work.

And I got what looked an awful lot like an insight into why Lucy was stuck on that rapid. Her last happy memory, of course. Better she should be stuck there than in the horror of what happened after she got off the train.

I actually might have gotten all melancholy if Ella hadn't started talking again. "Then," she said, "when Lucy and I were on the train and she said that thing about how she had a secret boyfriend and a broken heart—"

"Whoa!" I put a hand on her arm to stop her. "You never told me that Lucy said anything about a secret boyfriend."

"Didn't I?" Ella is a lousy liar. When she tried to play it cool, I called her on it with a no-nonsense look. She was probably a lousy poker player, too, because she caved in an instant. "She told me in confidence. And I did tell the police about it when they questioned me. I mean, I didn't think the confidence extended that far. They obviously never thought anything of it."

"And you don't think it had anything to do with her disappearance?"

"It couldn't have." Ella was sure of herself. "Lucy told me they'd already broken up, so if it was over between them—"

"Then her boyfriend might have been plenty pissed."

"No, no." She dismissed the idea with a shake of her head. "Lucy was the one with the broken heart. That means he must have broke up with her."

"And she never said who it was?"

There was a paper lying on the ground and Ella stabbed and lifted it. "Not a word," she said.

"And do you think she might have been talking about Patrick Monroe?"

Ella was about to make another stab, and she stopped mid-stride. "I never thought of that."

"And when he came back to Shaker to talk to your senior class?"

She shrugged. "I never said a word to him. I mean, I wouldn't have dared. By then, Patrick Monroe was as famous as Dylan."

My blank look said it all.

"Bob Dylan," Ella said. "Patrick Monroe was living in Greenwich Village and writing these incredible, soulful poems about love and loss and longing."

"Longing for high school girls, you think?"

She twitched her shoulders. "Like I said, I always wondered if he had anything to do with Lucy's disappearance. Especially since I saw him talking to Lucy at the Beatles concert."

OK, that did it! I flung my trash bag on the ground and faced Ella down, my hands on my hips. I would have been more imposing in my suede pumps, but the green boots would have to do. "A little something else you might have mentioned?"

She wasn't as cowed as I expected. In fact, even in the face of my righteous indignation—and it was plenty righteous—Ella had the nerve to smile.

"Pepper!" She wagged a finger in my direction. "You're not just looking into Lucy's disappearance to help me out with Ariel. Now that you know Lucy's story, you're hooked. You're going to use your talent for figuring out mysteries and you're going to find out what really happened to her."

There was no use denying it. Especially since I wanted to hear about the concert. Right after I admitted my interest in Lucy had taken a very detective-like turn, I asked, "Monroe was there?"

"Oh, well, so were thousands of other people."

"But you saw him talking to Lucy?"

Ella nodded. "We went up to the ladies' room during intermission and I thought I got done first so I stepped into the hallway to wait for Lucy. Then I realized she was already out of the restroom. She was standing over near a refreshment stand, talking to Mr. Monroe."

"About her appointment with the principal?"

Ella shrugged.

"About that F in her poetry class?"

"I really can't say."

"Did they look really friendly?"

"I told the police all this," Ella said. "If they thought there was something between them—"

"So they did look friendly?"

"He had his hand on her arm."

"And she?"

There was nothing like loyalty that stood the test of time. Ella glanced away. "She didn't look like she wasn't enjoying it," she mumbled. "But really, Pepper, if something was going on between Lucy and Mr. Monroe, she would have told me. We were best friends. We were sisters. I thought he might have had something to do with Lucy's disappearance, that she might have run away with him or something. But that was just me being young and stupidly romantic. By the time Mr. Monroe came back for that assembly my senior year, I figured he couldn't have been involved. For one thing, Lucy wasn't cruel, she wouldn't have let her parents suffer that long if she could have told them she was OK. For another, if Mr. Monroe had anything to do with it, the cops would have found something out by then. And Mr. Monroe wouldn't have had the nerve to come back to Shaker. Not if he was responsible for Lucy . . . you know . . . going away."

Ella was probably right. I had no doubt the cops had done all they could to look into Lucy's vanishing, just like I had no doubt that it would take a guy who was either really twisted or really dumb to show up as guest of honor at the school his victim attended.

But then, who ever said killers were smart?

6

In terms of my investigation, the logical thing to do was to talk to Lucy about Patrick Monroe and that appointment she had with the principal.

I would have done it, too, except that over the next few days, things got a little out of hand. For one thing, I was so whooped from dragging myself around the cemetery carrying that disgusting trash bag, I didn't have the energy to get to the rapid, much less ride it. For another, when I finally regained my strength (thanks to a long bubble bath, a facial, and a well-deserved visit to Olga, a wizard with a file and a bottle of nail polish), and gave up my lunch hour on Friday in the name of my investigation, it was something of an effort in futility. I drove over to the rapid station and I was all set to hop on the train and question Lucy when I remembered the whole exact-change scenario, which, come to think of it, doesn't make any sense at all and really is nothing but a big ol' inconvenience.

Long story short, all I could do was stand there on the platform like some lost soul and watch the train whizz by. That, and wave to Lucy, who—speaking of lost souls—was sitting on the train with her nose pressed to the window, waving back.

And then there was the brawl, of course. The one in the biker bar.

But I'm getting ahead of myself.

After my wasted trip to the rapid station, I wasn't in the best of moods when I got back to the office. Finding Ariel sitting behind my desk didn't help.

"It's too early for you to be out of school." I dropped my Juicy Couture purse into my bottom desk drawer and stepped back, the better to allow her enough room to get her skinny little butt out of my chair.

"Early dismissal. Parent-teacher conferences."

I pitied the child for thinking I was that naive. That was right about the same time I gave her a probing look. "On a Friday afternoon?"

Oh, she was good. She never batted an eyelash. And believe me, I would have seen it if she had. She wasn't wearing her clunky dark glasses.

The silver stud was missing from her lip, too.

Surprised (not to mention grateful and not repulsed), I guess I must have smiled.

My mistake. She took it as a sign of weakness.

"You might not believe there are conferences this afternoon, but my mother does."

"If your mother actually believed there were parent-teacher conferences today, she'd be first in line to sign up."

Ariel grinned. "She went on Wednesday night. She thinks today's conferences are for the stay-at-home mothers."

Like this made sense, I nodded. But was I about to give up? Not a chance!

Since it didn't look like Ariel was going to move, I strolled around to the front of my desk. "Wow," I said, as casual as can be, "if I'd fooled my mom like that, I wouldn't be here at boring Garden View. I would have used the extra time to hang with Gonzalo."

"Gonzalo. Hmph!" Matchstick arms folded over flat chest, Ariel glared. The entire performance would have been more convincing if I hadn't used the same sort of posturing myself a time or two when I was trying to prove how much I didn't care about Quinn. Of course, Ariel's quivering bottom lip was a giveaway, too.

I dropped into my guest chair. "Fight, huh?"

"He's unreasonable."

"All men are."

"He's self-centered."

"Goes with the territory."

"He writes these incredibly intense poems . . ." She sighed in a very fifteen-year-old-girl way. "You know, poems full of pain and anguish, poems about this bleak, hopeless thing called life. And then . . ." She gritted her teeth. "And then I saw him over at Starbucks drinking a Caramel Frappuccino. How ordinary!"

I was about to point out that the boy's taste in drinks probably didn't really have any direct correlation to how miserable he found life, but Ariel didn't give me the chance. Now that she'd opened up about Gonzalo's middle-of-the-road tendencies, she was on a roll. She jumped out of the chair and threw her hands in the air. "With Tiffany Slater!"

Ah, the plot thickened!

"What's a woman supposed to do, Pepper?" Ariel asked, and it took me a moment to realize the woman she was talking about was her. "What do you do when a guy turns on you like that? When he breaks your heart into a million little pieces and betrays your very soul?"

I wasn't sure if this was some sort of rhetorical cosmic question, or if her *you* meant me personally. If it didn't, I would be better off just letting the whole subject slide. So would my ego. If it did . . . yeah, I'd have to swallow my pride, but it would give me a chance to impart a little hard-won wisdom. With the mood Ariel was in, she just might listen.

To up the odds, I leaned forward and pinned her with a look. "You know those million little pieces? That heart belongs to you and not to anyone else. So you pick up every one of those pieces and you move on."

She gulped. "I'm not sure I can."

"Then the only other thing you can do is stay in the same miserable place you are now."

Good advice. Now I just needed to remember it.

Before I could get into some uncomfortable soul-searching, I realized I'd made a mistake. *Miserable* wasn't going to scare Ariel away. *Miserable* and Ariel were best friends.

Big surprise, she actually nodded, swiped her nose, and smiled. "I needed that," she said. "A figurative slap in the face to remind me of the perfidy of the opposite sex. I must steel my heart." She slapped one hand over it. "I must keep my mind busy and occupied. That's why you do what you do, isn't it, Pepper? That's why you're always investigating. Somewhere back before you were so old, I'll bet your heart got broken and now you have to keep your brain from thinking about it too much."

Now that she mentioned it . . .

This was a little too much sharing, and rather than get caught in that trap, I U-turned. "You know," I said, "if you're looking for something that will take your mind off Gonzalo . . ."

Ariel's dark eyes sparked with what was nearly enthusiasm.

"There's this Patrick Monroe character, and he's supposed to be some kind of—"

"Some kind of god of poetry!" Ariel swooned and fell back into my chair. "Don't tell me you've never heard of Patrick Monroe. He used to teach at my school, but that's not why we study him in English. He's famous. He's more than famous. He writes the most fabulous, evocative, angst-ridden poetry. I mean, not all his stuff, of course. Some of it is just what Gonzalo thinks—" She caught herself and cleared her throat. "Some of it is what *I* think is just hackneyed drivel. But there's this one poem of his, 'Girl at Dawn' . . . that poem is perfection. Come on, Pepper, you must have read it. I mean, they must have taught it in English class, even back in the old days when you were in school."

It was the *old days* that stung. I rose above the insult and got down to some serious thinking. Now that she mentioned it, the title of the poem did sound familiar.

While I was thinking, Ariel began reciting:

> *Girl,*
> *Crimson and golden.*
> *Nymph*
> *Chick*

Babe.
Awake to the dawn,
Crimson and golden.
Alive to the pulse
The vibration
The beat.

She sighed softly. "It goes on from there, every line more brilliant than the last. Every emotion . . ." Another sigh, just for emphasis. "Every emotion is right out there for anybody reading the poem to feel and suffer. You don't need some English teacher to explain, not a word of it. That's how you know if a poem is good. You don't need some PhD or Cliffs-Notes to tell you what it's about. You can feel every single word down in your bones. That's where I feel 'Girl at Dawn.' I feel the ache of her adolescence, her yearning, her desire to fly free." She threw her arms out. "You must know the rest of the poem, Pepper. You must know how awesome it is. Everybody who's ever been in freshman English does."

Maybe everybody who'd ever paid attention in freshman English.

Since we were bonding, I figured this was not a good moment to point this out. Instead, I got back to the topic that had sidetracked us in the first place. "I could use some help," I told Ariel, "finding stuff out about Patrick Monroe."

"He's coming to town, you know."

This was news to me. I perked up.

Ariel nodded. "He's doing a poetry reading at Case Western Reserve. I have tickets. Two."

"Because you're taking Gonzalo."

"Who?" Ariel jumped out of my chair. "You can come with me if you want. Monroe is bound to read 'Girl at Dawn.' He closes all his readings with it, and I hear the audience goes nuts. You know, screaming and crying and all like that. So what do you need to know about Patrick Monroe?"

Ah, that was the question! "Everything, I guess," I told her. "See, your mom's friend, Lucy, took a summer school class with him."

"And got an F." So much for thinking I'd actually gotten Ariel on the right track. At the mention of her mother, she was right back to sounding like the Ariel of old. Attitude and sass. Not bad attributes when they're used judiciously (I should know). But not pretty in the hands of a teenaged girl. The upside? At least when she curled her lip, I didn't have to watch that silver stud jump. "So what you're not telling me is that this whole research thing, it was my mother's idea?"

I shook my head. "My idea. Because you're good at it. And I need help."

Her shoulders shot back and she stood a little taller. "Really? And it doesn't have anything to do with teaching me a lesson about running away and how Lucy's been missing like for a million years and nobody in the whole world still cares except my mother?"

"Not going to deny it." There didn't seem much point. "But first of all, your mom didn't know I was going to ask you to research Patrick Monroe for me. I didn't, either, until right now. Secondly . . . well, the research part would really help me out."

Ariel's eyes lit. "Because we're going to try to find Lucy?"

I was careful when choosing my words. I couldn't afford to string along a second Silverman woman. "We're going to try to find out what happened to her."

"So we're detectives?"

"Sort of."

She hustled to the door. "My mom's in a meeting with

Jim. I'll go use her computer and see what I can dig up about Patrick Monroe and everyone else who worked at the school at the time. That's what you're thinking, right? That Monroe might know something. He is brilliant, after all. I'll bet he saw plenty that the cops never noticed. You know, something that would point to the real perp."

Apparently in between being a runaway and a pain in the neck, Ariel watched TV. "We don't know that. Not for sure."

"But we think it's possible."

"Anything's possible."

"So you'll want information on any priors anybody might have. And Monroe's opinion of each of them. I'll bet there's stuff in his collected journals. They've been published, you know. I've got them at home, I just never actually thought to look for anything about Lucy in them." Her mouth dropped open. "You don't think Monroe knows who really did it, do you? That all these years, he's been protecting someone? Maybe someone he loves." She clutched her hands to her heart. "Leave it to Patrick Monroe to live the tortured life of an artist with a terrible secret."

She was way off base, but I had to give the kid points for imagination. I was used to that other Silverman woman and pulling the wool over her eyes. It looked like things wouldn't be so easy with her youngest daughter.

"Like I said, we're going to find out." That was all the incentive Ariel needed. The last I saw of her, she was heading to her mother's office, humming under her breath.

Mostly, Friday afternoons at the cemetery are pretty quiet.

This is good news because on Friday afternoons, I'm busy planning my weekend. That particular weekend, I was supposed to get together on Saturday night with some old friends: Absalom, Reggie, and Delmar, guys I'd worked with on a cemetery restoration project the summer before. Sure, they all had rap sheets. Not to mention trash-talking attitude galore.

It didn't mean we wouldn't have had a good time. As long as nobody decided to do anything that would violate their probation.

Unfortunately for me and my plans to spend a casual afternoon crafting an even more casual and nonfelonious weekend, cemetery work got in the way.

Remember what I said about the days getting out of hand? Perfect example. That afternoon I decided that almost three forty-five was just about as good as five o'clock in my book and I already had my purse in my hand and my car keys out. If anybody asked on Monday where I'd been, and if that anybody happened to be Ella (who was the only anybody who would notice, anyway), I would say I was out among the headstones, walking through a new tour. Too bad I wasn't quicker. Just as I was about to walk out of my office, Jennine, our receptionist, showed up to tell me Jim wanted to see the entire administration staff in the conference room.

Apparently he knew Friday afternoons were slow around there, too, because he took the opportunity to spend the next hour talking about watching our bottom line and then, believe it or not, he actually had us go through piles and piles of old memos and pull out staples so we could take the paper back to our offices and reuse in it our printers.

Really, I'm not kidding.

By the time it was over, my right hand ached, and my pristine manicure needed a touch-up. No wonder I was grumbling when I got back to my office.

I grumbled even more when Ariel showed up just as the clock was finally about to hit five. I had my purse out (again) and dreams of a staple-free weekend swimming through my head.

She, apparently, was thinking otherwise. She had a pile of papers in her arm. "Downloads from the computer," she said, waving them at me. "Stuff about Patrick Monroe."

"I hope you reused old paper."

She hadn't been in the meeting; she didn't get it. "I'm going to spend the weekend reading through it all," she said. "I've got highlighters at home. At the beginning of every school year, Mom always buys highlighters. She thinks they're going to help our brains expand, or something. I'll highlight all the interesting stuff I find. That way, you can review it easier on Monday. In the meantime, I'll see what I can dig up, then I'm thinking I could do a spreadsheet . . . you know, dates and places and a listing of Patrick Monroe's poems and what he wrote when. That way we can match it all up and see if he ever mentions Lucy. We can put it all together, too, and see what kind of pattern it forms. Like on the TV detective shows, you know?"

I didn't. Rather than point it out, I said, "I'm leaving. I'll just go down the hall and say good night to your mother and—"

"She's not here. She left the instant that meeting of yours was over."

For the second time in a week, an un-Ella-like action from a woman who was usually all about predictability. The odds were like, what, a million to one? Which is why I figured the kid didn't know what she was talking about. "I'll bet she's in with Jim," I said.

"No. She left."

"She never leaves this early, not even on Friday."

"She did today."

"But that's not possible."

"Her purse is gone and her car is gone, and she's gone, and she asked me to ask you to give me a ride home."

I was intrigued. Which says something about the patheticness of my existence.

"Did she say where she was going?"

"Nope."

"Did she say when she'd be back?"

"Just that she'd see me later."

"Did you see which way she turned when she drove out of the cemetery? That might at least tell us the direction she was headed."

"Didn't need to." Ariel lifted her chin. "I know where she went."

"You said—"

"I said she didn't say where she was going. That doesn't mean I don't know."

"Then where—"

Instead of telling me, Ariel grabbed on to my arm and dragged me down the hallway to her mother's office. Once we were inside, she looked up and down the hallway to be sure we were alone, then shut the door.

"I have a feeling she wouldn't want Jim to know about this," Ariel said, and she pointed to Ella's desk.

Now, here's the thing about Ella's desk: except for the girls' latest school pictures, a flowery tea mug, and a blue and white china saucer where Ella sets her reading glasses when she's not wearing them (and then can never find them), Ella's desk is always clean. I don't care how deep she is into a project, or what she's working on or how many balls she's juggling.

Ella's desk is speckless.

Except that day.

There were papers strewn all over the place, books open and left out, and the yellow pages perched precariously on top of it all.

Like anybody could blame me for jumping to the obvious conclusion?

"Did you do this?" I asked Ariel.

"Not a chance. Mom would get majorly crazy if I did. It was like this when I walked in. I swear. I didn't touch anything or move anything, I just sat in front of her computer and worked around the mess. I didn't even pay attention to what all this crap was. At least until Mom hotfooted it out of here like her shoes were rocket-propelled. Then I started looking through it all."

I'd already beat her to that. Carefully, I unstacked the stuff on Ella's desk, trying to get to the bottom of the mystery—literally and figuratively.

"It's an old Shaker yearbook," I said, lifting the book that had been the bedrock of the pile. "It's from 1967, the year Lucy would have graduated." The book was open to a two-page spread that featured senior boys, and automatically I looked for names I recognized. "No Darren Andrews," I said, and I didn't bother to explain. Since Ariel knew the Lucy story inside and out, something told me she knew exactly who was with her mom and Lucy the night of the concert. "No Will Margolis or Bobby Gideon, either. In fact . . ." Since I'm so much taller than her, I had to tip the book so Ariel could see it. "It's one of the last pages of seniors, and look, this guy's picture is circled."

The photo was of a kid named Chuck Zuggart. Last in the class, and something told me that wasn't just because of his name.

Chuck had a flat, broad face and a neck as wide as football field. No big surprise there since the paragraph about him below his picture said he played tackle on the varsity team. Chuck had beady eyes, a shaved head, and a scar that cut his left eyebrow exactly in half.

Of course, why Ella had bothered to ring his photo with red ink was still a mystery.

I set the yearbook aside and dug through the rest of the debris, hoping it would provide an answer. There were a couple of MapQuest printouts of towns in some mostly rural county to our west and a page from some website called hogfriendly.com. Then there was the phonebook. It was open to a section titled "Bars and Restaurants," and I looked it over and pointed.

"Here. She's circled something again."

Ariel had to stand on her tiptoes to see what I was talking about. She leaned in close and squinted. Maybe those clunky black glasses she used to wear were for more than just show.

"'Hog Wild,'" she read from the circled ad. "'Biker boys and their biker toys.' Yeah." She glanced up at me. "That's what I saw."

A funny, rat-a-tat rhythm started up in my chest, and when I set down the phonebook, my hands were shaking a little. "But that's just crazy. You don't think your mother actually went—"

"Kind of what I thought. Except it doesn't make a whole lot of sense. Unless Mom's got a dark side!" Ariel said this like it might actually be a good thing.

I was thinking not so much.

But there wasn't time to waste on thinking.

I grabbed Ariel and, keeping my promise to Ella, drove her home and made sure Rachel and Sarah were there to keep an eye on her. Then the moment I was back in the car,

I gave Reggie a call. Yeah, it was a day too early for our planned night out, but if there was one thing I'd learned in my years of being a detective to the dead, it was this: when it comes to places with names like Hog Wild, it never hurts to take along reinforcements.

7

Talk about a mismatched pair! Reggie Brinks is a hulk-ing thirtysomething bald guy with a rock-'em-sock-'em personality that matched both the pit bull tattooed smack in the middle of his forehead and a police record as long as my arm. Delmar Lui, on the other hand, is a slim Asian kid with spiky black hair. He was a first-year student at the Cleveland Institute of Art, a sensitive kid with a good eye and, back in the day, a tendency to express his creative side on the walls of buildings with a can of spray paint.

When they'd first met during my cemetery restoration project, they were both working off community service hours, and they couldn't stand each other. But hey, maybe it's the whole teamwork thing that worked its magic. Or maybe it's just that my team and I, we went through a lot together that summer, including becoming flash-in-the-pan reality TV stars and solving a murder. Whatever the reason,

Reggie and Delmar were now fast friends, and by the time I got to Reggie's downtown apartment building, they were both waiting outside for me.

I explained what was going on as best I could, but let's face it, in my world, even explanations come with a catch. For one, I couldn't tell them I'd gotten embroiled in trying to find the body of a woman who'd died forty-five years earlier. For another . . . well, the only thing I knew for sure was that I had a really bad feeling that Ella had headed off on her own to do something stupid.

That was good enough for Reggie and Delmar.

I was grateful. For their understanding and for the backup.

It didn't hurt that both the guys remembered Ella from the summer before. Reggie, especially. After all, she'd been the high bidder on him at a bachelor auction we'd sponsored to raise money for the renovation. Tough guy that he is, even Reggie admitted that Ella is funny and sweet. She's about twenty years older than him, and he said (I hope Ella never finds out; she has the secret hots for Reggie and she'd be devastated!) that the thought of an "elderly" lady like her doing something she shouldn't be doing and the people she shouldn't be doing it with taking advantage of her, or worse, putting her in danger . . . well, that just pissed him off. Big-time.

Neither of the guys had ever been to Hog Wild. That was no big surprise. The bar was on the outskirts of a little town called Wellington, about forty miles southwest of Cleveland.

The town itself was as charming as a picture book illustration, with cute little shops and Victorian houses heavy on the gingerbread. The outskirts? Not so much.

We pulled into a blacktopped parking lot in front of a cement block building with a lighted sign above the door that said HOG WILD, and I took a moment to look around. Away from the glare of the sign, the shadows that hugged the building were long and dark. The lot was filled with motorcycles of all shapes and sizes.

And one lone Honda Civic.

My hopes rose. So did my anxiety level. "She's here," I told the guys.

Delmar was sitting in the front passenger seat, and he put a hand on my arm. His black leather jacket was hand-painted with graffiti, and the silver studs in his lip, his eyebrow, and his nose reflected the glaring light and winked at me. "Maybe you should wait in the car."

He was a smart kid; he should have known better. I shook off his hand. "My friend is in there," I reminded him. "And I'm not going to let you two jokers go in and rescue her and get all the glory."

"And who's going to rescue you?"

This from Reggie, who leaned over the seat, studying me. I'd been in such a rush to figure out what Ella was up to and to get to her before she could do it, I hadn't changed clothes after work. I was wearing a cute little black denim skirt and a beige-y V-neck cami trimmed in lace. Back at the cemetery, I'd given in to the pressures of business over fashion and topped the whole thing off with a lightweight black cardigan, but it was a warm evening and I'd taken that off when I got in the car and tossed it in the backseat. I reached for it. "I'll just—"

"Don't bother." Reggie popped open the back door and swung out onto the blacktop. "It's gonna take more than a little sweater to keep the guys in a place like this off you."

This was not the encouraging rah-rah speech I needed.

I gulped and reconsidered taking Delmar's advice and staying put. Except that the thought of Ella in the Hog Wild doing I-don't-know-what made my stomach turn, and really, there was only one way to take care of that problem.

Reggie insisted on going first, and maybe that was a good thing, because just as we walked in, the country song wailing from the jukebox ended and a hush fell over the place. I guess most of the patrons were regulars because I heard a young guy in a corner booth growl the word "strangers," and one by one, heads swiveled and patrons looked our way.

Well, they looked Reggie's way.

Until they saw me.

Hog Wild was the size of a double garage, with a bar along one wall, booths along the other, and tables crammed everywhere in between except for the small empty square of floor that was used for dancing. Friday night, and the place was packed with men and women in jeans, black leather, bandanas, and what I suspected were more tattoos and piercings per square foot than in any other establishment in Wellington.

Every single one of the guys watched me walk over to the only empty table, and OK, I might have been a little standoffish, but hey, none of them was exactly my type. And I was preoccupied, remember. All that black leather. All those piercings. All those tattoos.

And no Ella.

Just to be sure, I took another look around. A guy with no teeth raised his beer bottle in my direction. A guy with a Mohawk winked. A couple others gave me looks that made shivers crawl up my spine. And I do not mean the good kind.

The bartender was a sixty-some-year-old guy as big as a house with a shaved head and a ring in his nose. He crossed his arms over a chest the size of a small European monarchy, and he and Reggie exchanged nods.

"Beers," Reggie said.

"I'd really rather have—" One look from Reggie stopped me before "apple martini" could cross my lips. "Beer will be just fine," I said, and took the nearest seat.

Our beers came in cans and were a brand I had never heard of. Reggie and Delmar sipped theirs, and while they did, I took the opportunity to take a second look around Hog Wild. Another song started up on the jukebox, and keeping an eye on us, the crowd went back to drinking and smoking. (By the way, the smoking part is illegal in restaurants and bars in Ohio, but I think it's safe to say I was not the good citizen who was going to point this out.)

"She's not here." I looked from Reggie to Delmar, and honestly, I don't know what I expected them to do. Nothing, maybe. Maybe just commiserate with the worry that was eating me from the inside out. "Something's wrong. Ella's car is here, but she isn't. We've got to talk to the people. We've got to—"

Reggie took a long gulp of beer. "We will," he said, swiping the back of one hand across his mouth. "But this isn't the kind of place you just waltz into and start asking questions. We've got to show that we're part of the crowd first, that we're just here for a good time."

I understood the wisdom of this approach, I just didn't like it. The blood thrumming in my ears, I forced myself to sip my beer, the better to fit in.

Which was, of course, next to impossible. It's a safe bet that I was the only woman there who knew anything about good grooming, color coordination, and the very bad fashion faux pas of squeezing a body full of lumps, bumps, and bulges into tight black leather. Honestly, could I help the look that must have crossed my face when a six-foot-tall, three-hundred-pound woman in silver-studded leather pants, a leather jacket, and a tiny leather bustier squeezed behind me on her way to the bar?

She jostled my chair, and my stomach slammed into the table.

I bit my tongue. Accidents happen, especially in crowded bars. I forced myself to ignore Leather Lady and keep my mind on my mission. "Can we talk to the bartender now?" I asked Reggie.

"Cool your jets." He finished his beer and signaled toward the bar for another round. "The way you're acting, you'd think we never investigated a murder before."

I was in mid-sip, and I looked at Reggie over the lip of my beer can. "Who said anything about murder?"

Delmar made a face. "Nobody needed to. Why else would you and that nice Ms. Silverman be in a place like this? And why do you think we wanted to come along? Heck, hangin' with you and solvin' those murders last summer, that's just about the coolest thing we've done in as long as we can remember."

"You don't think we came for the atmosphere, do you?" Reggie threw an arm over the back of the empty chair next to him, and as cool as ice, he looked around.

When he blanched, I sat up like a shot. "What? What's wrong?"

"It's nothin'." The beers arrived, and keeping one eye on the bar, Reggie handed the server a ten, waited for change, and popped the top on his beer. "Just a guy over there." He slid a look toward the far end of the bar. "Somebody I used to know."

I looked that way, too. It wasn't hard to pick out the guy Reggie knew. He was glaring at our table, and I swear I could just about feel the wall of anger that washed our way.

"Somebody who liked you, right?" Wishful thinking at its best. I actually might have fooled myself into believing it if Reggie didn't scoot his chair over, discreetly positioning it so that his back was toward the bar. "Please tell me it's not somebody who's gunning for you."

Delmar cringed. "Bad choice of words."

That thrumming in my ears picked up tempo. Keeping time with it, I drummed my fingers against the sticky table and took another look around hoping for some sign of Ella.

No luck.

"I don't like this," I said. "I'm going to walk around and check things out. Maybe—" I was already getting up when Leather Lady came back the other way, slammed into me, and knocked me back into my seat.

Like anybody could blame me for getting a little defensive?

I looked up at the mountain of flesh and leather, years of proper manners not forgotten, even in the face of so much ugly. "Excuse me?"

She was already past me, and she turned and stepped back to look me over. "Are you talking to me, bitch?"

Reggie put a hand on my left arm.

Delmar grabbed my right hand.

I twinkled like a beauty queen. "I'm sure you were trying to be careful where you were going, I just thought I'd point out that if you went around the other way . . ." I pointed one perfectly manicured finger (after the trash pickup incident, I'd gone for a well-deserved touch-up) toward the empty square of dance floor. "Well, there's more room over there."

"And you think I need more room, why?"

Oh, my! When faced with a question that blunt, how can a girl possibly lie?

I got to my feet. Sure, Leather Lady had a hundred pounds and more on me, but in my black-and-white cheetah print and patent leather sandals with their four-inch heels, I had the height advantage. I intended to use it for all it was worth—and I would have, too, if a flash of color on the other side of the bar hadn't caught my eye. I'd recognize that spiky red hair anywhere.

I didn't excuse myself. But then, I was over the whole polite thing. Too relieved and grateful to see Ella in one piece to question where she'd gotten a black leather jacket and how on earth she thought a woman her age could be seen in public in peg-leg jeans and a T-shirt with a picture of Ozzy Osbourne on it, I hurried over and intercepted her while she was standing outside the ladies' room, tentatively glancing around and looking more than a little lost. By the time I grabbed her hand and brought her back to the table, Leather Lady was gone.

"Oh, my." Ella glanced at me, at Delmar, at Reggie. Her cheeks got red, but then, it was warm in there. "What are you all doing here?"

"That's what Pepper wants to ask you." Delmar correctly figured that I wasn't going to drink the second beer Reggie ordered for me. He pushed the can in front of Ella. "We was worried."

"About me?" Ella tried for a sparkling smile, but when it comes to that sort of thing, she's just not in my league. She looked more flustered than feisty. "How did you know—"

"It doesn't matter. What does matter is what you're doing here. Ella . . ." She was playing with the can of beer, turning it in her hands and flicking the pop top, and I touched a hand to her arm to get her attention. "What are you up to?"

Ella shrugged. Her cheeks got a little redder. "I didn't think I'd have to explain myself. I mean, I never imagined I'd run into anyone I knew here. Now that it comes down to it . . ." Her gaze moved to the table and stayed there. "It's a little embarrassing."

I gulped. "You're not into leather. Or tattoos. Ella, you don't have some secret life as a biker babe, do you?"

She managed a laugh, and I let go the breath I was holding. With one finger, she made a figure eight on the table. "Actually, I was investigating."

This was just about as big a surprise as learning she might be a biker babe.

When I realized it was hanging open, I snapped my mouth shut. "Investigating because . . ."

"Well, it's all your fault, Pepper." Ella plumped back in her chair. "For a couple reasons. First of all, I've watched you all these years, and I've seen you find out information and help people and solve crimes. I'm embarrassed to admit it, but I figured, how hard could it be? Until I got here." When she looked around, the color in her cheeks drained. "I thought I was dressing the part." She looked down at her middle-aged-lady-imagines-biker-life outfit and shrugged. "I never thought I'd have to interact with people . . . well, you know . . . with people like this." She caught herself and realized she might have offended. "Not that I have anything against anyone who might possibly have a criminal background," she added for Delmar and Reggie's benefit. "They're just not—"

"Not in your class, Ms. Silverman," Delmar said.

"Not people you should be hanging with," Reggie added.

Ella nodded. "You make it look so easy," she told me. "But I got here and . . ." She fanned her face with one hand. "I got a little overwhelmed. I'm ashamed to admit that I was hiding in the ladies' room. I think I might have stayed in there all night if two girls hadn't come in and started comparing the tattoos they had on their—"

A rush of color left Ella looking like a ripe apple. She leaned closer and lowered her voice so the guys couldn't hear. "Their butts," she said. The message delivered, she was free to include Delmar and Reggie in the conversation again. "I had to get out of there, and I was going to give up on investigating altogether and head home. That's when I walked out of the ladies' room and you found me."

"Good thing we did." Two guys over in the corner were scuffling, and Reggie looked their way. "This is no place for either one of you."

"So what are you doing here?" I wailed. "Ella, what kind of investigating can you possibly do in a place like this?"

"It's all your fault." She plucked at the sleeve of her jacket. "Yours and Ariel's. It's not like I haven't thought about Lucy in all these years. Of course I have. I could never forget Lucy. But what with Ariel running away and then you asking all those questions about Lucy . . . well, it got me to thinking."

"Lucy?" Reggie leaned forward. "Is that whose murder we're investigating?"

"Nobody said she was dead," Ella snapped. "But nobody knows what happened to her, either. And thinking about it . . ." She ran a hand through her hair. In honor of the occasion, she'd added more gooey gel than usual to her do, and I swear, I heard it snap, crackle, and pop. "I was thinking about everything you asked the last time we talked about

Lucy, Pepper." She turned in her chair so that she was looking directly at me. "And that made me remember things. You know, about the night of the Beatles concert."

This simple statement made something blossom inside me. Something that felt like hope. I leaned forward, eager to hear more.

"Wanna dance?"

I was so focused on Ella, I didn't pay much attention to the voice behind me.

Until someone poked my shoulder. "I said, you wanna dance?"

By the time I registered that the question was meant for me and I turned to find a burly guy with a chew of tobacco in one cheek smiling down at me, Reggie was already on top of things. He ran a hand up and down my arm. "This is my old lady," he said.

Before I could object to either his choice of adjectives or the too familiar way he was touching me, Reggie shushed me with a look.

The burly guy eyed Reggie and decided I wasn't worth the fight.

I thanked Reggie by handing him money and telling him to get himself another beer, and once he walked up to the bar, I got back down to business.

"The night of the Beatles concert . . ." I pinned Ella with a look. "What about it?"

"Well, I told you I saw Lucy talking to Mr. Monroe. Patrick Monroe, he was an English teacher at our high school," she added for Delmar's benefit. "But the more I thought about it, the more I remembered about that night. Mr. Monroe wasn't the only one Lucy talked to at the concert."

Now she had my attention! I waited for more.

"You remember what I told you about that night, Pepper," Ella said. "I said we left our seats during the intermission, before the Beatles came on. I walked out of the ladies' room, and that's when I saw Lucy with Mr. Monroe. When they were done talking, Lucy told me to get in line and order a Coke for her, that she'd be right back. But when I got the Coke and went looking for her, I didn't see her anywhere. I finally found her with Darren."

It was my turn to supply Delmar with the running commentary. "Darren was a friend. He and Ella and Lucy, they all went to the concert together."

Ella nodded. "Which is why I never thought anything of it. Lucy and Darren were friends, only . . ." Ella worked over her lower lip with her teeth.

"You're not betraying a confidence," I said as a way of urging her on. "Lucy's secrets don't matter anymore."

"But she and Darren weren't dating or anything." As if the very idea was impossible, she clicked her tongue. "If they were, I would have known. Everyone would have. Girls who dated Darren considered themselves the luckiest girls at Shaker. Lucy never would have kept that a secret."

"Except . . ."

"Except just the way they were standing there together . . ." Thinking back, Ella narrowed her eyes and tipped her head. "Darren put a hand on Lucy's arm and I don't know, just something about it . . . it made me think that maybe there was something going on between them. Not that I think he had anything at all to do with Lucy's disappearance! Like I said, they were friends, and Darren is a prominent businessman. Don't get me wrong, Pepper. I'm not accusing him. I'm not accusing anyone. Like I said, I was just thinking. About everything that happened that night."

This still didn't explain Hog Wild. I waited for more.

"When Lucy and Darren were done talking, Lucy walked away," Ella continued, "and it was crowded so it was really hard for me to see where she went to. I was pretty short back then."

I bit my tongue.

"I wandered around for a while, and the next thing I knew, I saw Darren and Janice talking together. Janice Sherwin," she supplied the information to Delmar, who was looking more confused by the moment. "Janice came to the concert with us, too, and Janice and Darren had always been friends, but I'll tell you what, they didn't look friendly that night. Janice's cheeks were fiery and she pointed a finger in Darren's face." Ella demonstrated, using me as the target. "I tried to get closer to hear what they were talking about, but that's when I heard Lucy's voice behind me. She was telling somebody to get lost. I turned around, and that's when I saw . . ." As if she was almost afraid to look, Ella slowly turned toward the bar.

And the pieces fell into place.

"Chuck Zuggart." Now that I was thinking clearly, I could almost recognize the bartender from the picture in the yearbook Ariel and I had found on Ella's desk. "That's why you came here? To talk to him? You think he knows something about Lucy?"

Ella shook her head. "I don't know. It's not like I really saw anything. By the time I pushed through the crowd and made my way over to where Lucy was standing, Chuck had already walked away, and when I asked her about it . . ." She shrugged. "Guys were always flirting with Lucy. She knew how to handle them. She acted like it was no big deal. But what if it was, Pepper? What if there was something more to it than that? I never said anything to anyone about Chuck

Zuggart. I didn't even know his name. Remember, I wasn't at the high school then and I didn't know the kids everyone else knew. But then you got me to thinking about Lucy again, and I started looking through the old yearbooks. And there he was."

I, too, looked Chuck Zuggart's way. The way he was turned, it was the first I noticed the new scar that had been added to his pug-ugliness since high school. It snaked along his neck, down from his ear and all the way to the neckline of his T-shirt. He was not a man I would want to tangle with, that was for sure. But in the great scheme of things, I was more qualified to do it than Ella would ever be.

"I know you think I'm silly for coming to a place like this on my own, Pepper," Ella said, "but all I could think of was Lucy and how I owed her this. Lucy and Ariel. All I could think is that if something ever happened to Ariel, I'd want someone to stand up for her. That's all I wanted to do. So please don't think I'm a foolish old lady. After all this time, I just wanted to stand up for Lucy."

I squeezed her hand. "You did. And now it's time for the professional to take over."

And before I could convince myself not to, I sauntered up to the bar.

Zuggart was busy pouring out beers and shots and I waited until he was finished.

"Got any Beatles on the jukebox?" I asked.

He cocked an eyebrow at me. "A little young for the Beatles, aren't you?"

"Bet you are, too." Oh, yes, I can be shameless when the situation calls for it. Shamelessly, I slanted myself against the bar just enough to show a little cleavage. He was interested. It was creepy. I kept smiling. "My parents used to listen to them and . . . I dunno . . ." One well-timed shrug and his gaze traveled down to where the lace edging of my cami veed between my breasts. "I've always liked their music. Man, can you imagine what it must have been like to see them in concert?"

"Believe it or not, I think I did."

"No way!" He thought I was referring to the impossibility of him being old enough. He liked that. Good thing he didn't realize I was actually questioning the *think I did* in that sentence. "What, your babysitter took you?"

"Oh, you're good." He poured a shot and slid it in front of me. "On the house," he said.

I ran a finger around the rim of the glass. "Were they any good?"

"Hell if I know." He'd poured a shot for himself, too, and Zuggart chugged it down. "The only thing I remember about that night is being high as a kite. That and puking my guts out when I got home."

Colorful, yes, but not exactly an alibi.

"So you don't remember talking to Lucy Pasternak at the concert?"

It was on the tip of his tongue to say, "Who?" I knew, because of the way his brows dropped over his eyes for a second. The next second, though, they shot straight up. "Hey, I remember her. She was that chick who disappeared way back when I was in school." Now, he really was interested in me. But not for the same reasons he was interested before. "What do you care?"

"I'm a relative."

"Why do you think I know anything?"

"You talked to her at the concert."

"Who says?"

"It's true, isn't it?"

He wiped a rag over the bar. "I might have talked to her."

I slipped onto the nearest empty bar stool. "She told you to get lost."

"So you think I had something to do with her gettin' lost?" Zuggart pulled back his super-sized shoulders. "That ain't polite."

"Neither is murder."

He leaned over so he was right in my face. "Do I look like a man who would hurt a fly?" he purred.

"If I wanted to know about flies, I might care."

"Well, I didn't do nothin' to that stuck-up Lucy. And you'd better be careful if you're tellin' anybody I did."

"But you don't have an alibi."

He was holding a bottle of whiskey and he slammed it against the bar. "What are you, a cop?" His question boomed through Hog Wild and the results were predictable.

I was the center of attention again, only this time there wasn't as much lust in the eyes of the guys who looked me over as there was suspicion. Along with some anger and a whole bunch of hatred.

I glanced over at the table and tipped my head toward the door, signaling Ella and Delmar that it was time to high-tail it out of there. I slipped off the bar stool.

Only since Leather Lady was right behind me, I stepped on her foot.

"Sorry." I was. I liked these new sandals and didn't want anything to happen to them. "I didn't see you."

"I was saving that seat for a friend of mine." She stepped forward, and her elbow caught me in the ribs.

I'd tried to be polite, yes? But this was too much.

I didn't even try for a smile. "I doubt that. I'm pretty sure you don't have any friends."

I think she was about to say something clever like, "Oh, yeah?" but she never had the chance. Down at the other end of the bar, Reggie jumped to his feet. He smashed a beer bottle against the bar just as another guy—short, wiry, and looking like he was out for blood—tackled him.

8

"I love these shoes." I cradled one patent leather and
cheetah print sandal for a last moment, then, rather
than risk getting sloppy and sentimental, I kicked off its
mate, scooped them both up, and padded across Ella's
kitchen to toss them in the garbage can under the sink.

"Sorry." She was at the table, her head bent. And not just
because she was feeling guilty. Ella had an ice pack on the
back of her neck. It covered the purple bruise she'd gotten
thanks to the beer can Leather Lady threw.

"I'm the one who's sorry," I said. "That beer can was
meant for me."

"But you wouldn't have been there if it wasn't for me
thinking I could go out and investigate on my own." Ella's
shoulders heaved. "A bump on the back of the neck is a
small price to pay for what I put you all through."

"Good thing that beer can didn't hit you smack on the

head. It coulda done some real damage." Reggie got a fresh ice pack from the freezer, took away the one on Ella's neck, and replaced it, and she thanked him with a smile. He was looking at me over her head when he said, "Told you going to a place like that was a bad, bad idea."

"Which it wouldn't have been if you didn't start mixing it up with that buddy of yours down at the end of the bar," I reminded him.

Guilt wasn't Reggie's style. He poured himself a cup of coffee from the pot Ella (bruise or no bruise) had made the moment we walked in her back door. He blew on the hot coffee, sipped, and grinned. "I showed him a thing or two."

"And you sure showed that fat lady!" Delmar told me. His excited smile dissolved when he looked Ella's way and realized he might have offended.

"Get over it, kid." Without ever looking up, she brushed aside his worries. "You're not going to hurt my feelings. I'm way past stressing out about the size of my hips."

"You're not anywhere near the Shamu league," I reminded her, but of course, thinking big (really big) made me think about Leather Lady, and that soured the coffee I'd already poured into my own mug. I added an extra sprinkle of sweetener. "If it wasn't for that nasty, no good—"

Delmar whooped. "You gave as good as you got, Pepper, that's for sure. When she elbowed you, you showed her!"

I didn't need the reminder that I'd lost it. Childish, yes. But who could blame me? When Leather Lady came at me, I had to defend myself, and since I was no match for her incredible hulkness, I did the only thing I could do. I stomped her instep, so thrilled to watch her hop up and down and shriek, I hardly noticed that the impact of cute patent leather against meaty Big Foot broke my sandal.

That is, until Leather Lady stumbled into our table, and before he could get crushed, Delmar shoved her away.

And Leather Lady got really pissed and started flipping tables.

At the same time Reggie and his friend got into it and Reggie flew across the bar.

After that, the crowd at Hog Wild . . . well, they went hog wild.

The beer cans—and the fists—started flying, and it was time for a quick escape. That's when I realized my sandal was history—it's hard to run like hell in a broken shoe.

I propped my elbows on the table and dropped my chin into my hands. "I loved those shoes," I muttered.

"The hell with your shoes. We're lucky we got out of there with our heads." Reggie took the chair next to mine. The swollen skin around his right eye was quickly turning from a shade of sickly red to a vivid and even sicklier purple. He slanted me a look and I could tell his face hurt because he clenched his jaw. Tough guy that he is, Reggie had refused any first aid. Nice guy that he is (and he'd deny it in an instant), he said it was more important for Ella to use the ice packs. "You think it was worth it?"

"In terms of my shoe wardrobe, obviously not. As far as my investigation . . ." I'd been so busy staying alive, I hadn't had time to think about Chuck Zuggart. I shrugged. It was the only logical response. "He says he doesn't remember anything about the night of the concert."

Ella's head came up. Since she didn't have a tough-guy image to uphold, she winced for all she was worth. "But—"

"I know. You saw him talking to Lucy at the concert."

"And—"

"And it might mean something."

"But—"

"But it could mean nothing at all. Zuggart says he was high and he doesn't remember much of anything that happened that night."

"So he could have—"

"Sure. Or he could have been so drugged out Lucy could have fought him off with one hand tied behind her back." Considering that Lucy had told me she'd been tied up by her kidnapper, it was my turn to wince. Then again, since no one knew this bit of info but me, I didn't need to apologize.

"Except some drugs, they make you friggin' powerful!" At that moment, I'll bet Delmar wished he had some of them. He had a cut across his left cheek, his knuckles were raw, and one sleeve of his leather jacket was missing.

My sigh was echoed by the others around the table and I'll bet our thoughts meshed, too: Chuck Zuggart might have had nothing to do with Lucy's death. Or maybe he had.

And I was right back to where I started, except that now, my head was pounding, two of my fingernails were broken, and my newest favorite shoes . . .

I glanced toward the kitchen sink and the garbage can nestled beneath it, stretched my legs, and leaned back in the chair, the better to forget my problems.

While I tried, Ella dragged herself out of her chair and went to the cupboard for a package of Chips Ahoy. She grabbed three cookies for herself and put the bag on the table. After a long night of brawlin' at the biker bar, there was nothing like sugar. Reggie, Delmar, and I nearly started another brawl all reaching for the cookies at the same time.

"I've wasted everyone's time." Ella had a mouthful of cookie and crumbs on her chin. "I put everyone in danger, and for what?"

"Hey, it was no skin off my nose," Reggie said, and then

he chuckled because his nose was raw. He got up and sauntered over to the door. I'd offered to drive both Reggie and Delmar home, but they insisted they'd had enough of the Pepper Martin brand of excitement for one night and had called a friend to come get them. Out in the drive, a car honked. "That's more fun than I've had in I don't know how long. Who would have thought you two cemetery ladies would be so down and dirty. And the best part—"

"We didn't get nabbed." Delmar popped two cookies into his mouth at the same time, grabbed another one for the road, and followed Reggie to the door. "Which means no dings on our probation reports."

"I suppose that's all good," Ella mumbled once they were gone. "But it doesn't help with our investigation, does it?"

I was getting a little nervous about how everybody was suddenly calling this *our investigation*. But I wasn't about to argue the point with a woman who'd taken a whack from a beer can with my name on it. Now that I thought about the beer can incident, I actually smiled. Not because Ella got hurt! Believe me, it just about killed me to think what might have happened. I was grinning because if Leather Lady hit a short, round woman instead of the five-foot-eleven redhead she was targeting, it meant her aim was as nonexistent as her fashion sense.

That cheered me only as long as it took for me to realize that as far as the investigation went, Ella was right: we were no further along in explaining Lucy's disappearance then we were before we went to Hog Wild.

And that meant only one thing.

It was time for me to talk to my client again.

This time, I'd make sure I had exact change.

* * *

Since Lucy had already been dead for forty-five years, I figured another couple days wouldn't hurt anything one way or another. Besides, I was wiped out after our Friday night adventure. I canceled out on my Saturday night with Delmar, Reggie, and Absalom with the excuse that I'd already seen two of them the night before and I'd catch up with all three sometime soon. Then I spent the weekend in, napping and thinking, and while I was thinking, I was thinking how pathetic it was that a woman my age didn't have anything better to do.

I remedied that on Monday. OK, so talking to Lucy might not exactly qualify as something better to do, but it was, at least, something. And doing something in the name of my investigation was better than doing nothing.

I slipped into a seat on the rapid, sliding aside the morning's newspaper that someone had left there. No big surprise, the headlines were still all about that serial killer, Winston Churchill, and the front page promised more inside: photos of his childhood home, a look at his apartment, a one-on-one with a woman who'd actually survived one of his attacks. Too depressing. I scanned the articles briefly, all set to drop the paper onto the empty seat in front of me when something else caught my eye.

How predictable am I?

Of course, it was Quinn's name along with the words *arresting officer*. As always, he was a man of few words. This time they pretty much consisted of a snappy, "No comment."

At least there was no photo of Quinn accompanying the story. I got rid of the paper, sat back, and waited, avoiding the watchful eye of the transit cop lounging at the front of the car.

It didn't take Lucy long to show up.

"I thought you'd given up on me." Lucy put the back of

one hand to her forehead. "Abandoned. Again. It was as if
night had closed in around me, deep and impenetrable, and
I was separated from all earthly things."

"You pretty much are," I reminded her while at the same
time wondering if Lucy and Ella really weren't sisters. Lucy
and Ariel certainly shared the same drama gene. "I've been
busy," I told her.

"Investigating?"

It seemed simpler just to nod than to try to explain. "We
need to talk about Patrick Monroe," I told her.

"Oh." It wasn't my imagination. Lucy's cheeks flushed
a color that reminded me of fresh peaches.

My suspicion level rose. "He was your secret boyfriend."

"Oh my gosh, no!" It was hard not to believe someone
who went from flushed to sickly green in a heartbeat. "Ew.
Mr. Monroe? He was so old!"

I'd done my homework, and I pointed out that at the time
he taught at Shaker, Patrick Monroe was all of twenty-three.
"Not all that much older than the kids he taught."

"Maybe. But definitely not boyfriend material."

"Did he want to be?"

"My boyfriend?" She tried to make it sound like the
thought had never crossed her mind, but I am not easily
fooled.

I turned just enough in my seat to make it look natural to
the living around me, and clear to the dead that I wasn't
going to back down.

Lucy glanced away. "Yes," she said quietly. "I think Mr.
Monroe would have liked that."

I knew the value of a well-timed stall so I kept my mouth
shut.

Lucy squirmed in her seat. Sighed. Made a face. "He used
to write poetry for me," she said and grimaced. "Bad poetry.

I mean, really bad poetry. He'd slip the poems into my locker and sign them *Anonymous*. Like that was supposed to fool me? What high school boy would think to sign his poems *Anonymous*? The guys I knew couldn't even spell it."

"So did you tell Monroe you didn't appreciate his artistic efforts?"

"I told him I didn't think it was right when he tried to kiss me after class one day."

My stomach soured. "He didn't force you, did he?"

"It was nothing like that." Lucy pressed her lips together, no doubt coming to grips with exactly how she felt about the situation. "Hey, it was the sixties, and everyone was into free love and free thought. You know, all the groovy stuff. But I didn't think it was groovy. Not with an old guy like Mr. Monroe. He tried. I told him I wasn't interested. He backed off. That's pretty much all there was to it."

"But you decided to report him to the principal."

"What?" Lucy's mouth fell open. "No! I wouldn't have done that to Mr. Monroe. What he did was wrong, sure, but when I told him I wasn't interested, he didn't press it. And believe me, I kept my ear to the ground, and I told him if he tried it with any of the other girls, then I would go to the principal. I'd tell anyone who was willing to listen."

"Which means he might have been mad enough to kill you."

"I was actually mad enough to kill him." Getting her thoughts straight, Lucy shook her head and her golden hair shimmered around her shoulders. "He gave me an F in my summer school class."

"Because you weren't interested in him?"

"Well, that's not what he said. Mr. Monroe said it was because I hadn't turned in my final assignment. That's what I was going to see the principal about. To complain about my grade. And I wasn't going to squeal on Mr. Monroe or anything. I mean, not about how he tried to kiss me. I was just going to say that it wasn't fair for him to say I hadn't turned in my assignment because I had. I even had a copy of it so I could prove I'd turned it in. I never had a chance to show it to Mr. Wannamaker. I was murdered, remember."

Like I could forget?

I processed everything she'd said, then asked, "And when you talked to Monroe about your grade? I mean, you must have, right? You must have spoken to him first before you made that appointment with the principal."

She nodded. "Mr. Monroe said there was nothing he could do. That rules were rules, and the rules said that if the final project wasn't complete, I couldn't pass."

"So he deep-sixed your assignment, gave you an F, and got his revenge for you not being interested in him." This made sense in a sick and twisted way. "Killing you seems a little above and beyond. Unless . . ." I slid her a look. "You're not leaving something out, are you? Like that Monroe was your secret boyfriend?"

"Secret boyfriend?" For a moment, Lucy's golden brows dropped. Then her eyes flew open. "There's no way you could know about that. Not unless . . ." Again, she put the back of the hand to the forehead. The girl needed a new drama coach. "Oh, the treachery!" she groaned. "Little Ella spilled the beans. She must have. She was the only one who knew my secret."

"Only she didn't. Know the secret, that is. She only knew that you had one."

Lucy was silent.

And I had better things to do than sit there and watch her pout.

I threw my hands in the air, and then, because it attracted

the attention of that transit cop who was suddenly keeping a very close eye on the woman sitting by herself and talking up a storm, I grabbed my cell and pretended to be dialing, then talking.

"You and Ella are both dopes," I said into the phone.

Lucy's bottom lip protruded a little farther.

"You're keeping secrets that are, like, decades old. Both of you."

"So Little One didn't tell you?"

"She told me that you told her that you wouldn't tell except to tell . . ." Even I couldn't follow what I was saying. I grumbled at my phone. At least it didn't make me look as crazy as muttering in the direction of the empty seat next to me. "You told Ella that you had a secret boyfriend. And a broken heart."

"Which may or may not have been true." Lucy sat up straight and pulled back her shoulders. It was the lamest display of nonchalance that I'd seen since the time I tried the same thing in the mirror, just to practice how to look if I ever crossed paths with Quinn again.

"Who was he?"

Lucy glanced at me out of the corner of her eye. "It doesn't have anything to do with my murder."

"How do you know?"

"Because I know, that's all. He wouldn't have been my boyfriend in the first place if I thought he was a murderer."

"Yeah, that's what they all say." My editorial opinion delivered, I stared at her.

Lucy mumbled a reply.

"What was that?"

"Darren," she said.

"Darren Andrews?" This was big news, and hearing it, I was certain Ella wasn't holding out on me. She was so impressed by Darren and his big house and his bigger money, she never would have kept her mouth shut if she knew Lucy and Darren had been a couple. "And this is some big secret, why?"

"Because nobody knew about it. Isn't that what makes a secret a secret? Darren and I, we were keeping it all very hush-hush. You know, like the romance between Heathcliff and Catherine."

I wasn't sure when we started talking about whoever it was we were suddenly talking about. I didn't care. Heathcliff and Catherine weren't my problem. "Who broke it off?" I asked her.

With one finger, Lucy traced an invisible pattern over her knee. "Me. Mostly."

"Then if you broke up with Darren, he might have—"

"No!" The air around Lucy sparked. Just like her eyes. "Darren wouldn't have hurt me. He wasn't like that. Darren loved me."

"Then why did you break up with him?"

The sparks sizzled like a current of electricity. They were so bright, I had to turn my face away.

"He made some mistakes," Lucy said. "That doesn't mean—"

"You mean another girl." I chanced another look at her, squinting against the neon blue and icy white flickers that circled Lucy's head. It was worth it when I saw her flinch and knew I was right. "So that was what he was trying to talk to you about at the Beatles concert. Ella said he looked like he was trying to convince you of something. And then . . ." The truth dawned, and I grinned, not at Lucy's misfortune, but at my own brilliance. "And then Ella saw Darren and Janice and they were fighting. You were what they were fighting about."

Lucy crossed her arms over her chest. "He didn't love her."

"You're sure?"

"He didn't." She slapped her knee with one hand. "He didn't, he didn't, he didn't."

The sparks sizzled and flew. One of them landed on my leg and a puff of smoke poofed around me. I hurried to pat the spot before that transit cop could catch a whiff of smoldering raincoat, and while I was at it, I cursed my luck. So far, the only thing this investigation was any good for was destroying my spring wardrobe.

When the fire was out, I looked over at the seat beside me. It was empty.

And I was left with even more questions than I'd started with.

What was the deal with Darren Andrews? And Janice Sherwin, was she jealous of Lucy? Jealous enough to kill her?

And then, of course, there was still the big question mark that was Patrick Monroe. Like it or not, there was only one way to handle that.

It looked like I was going to a poetry reading.

Ariel and Gonzalo were still on the outs, and her mother had made it clear that if she couldn't find an adult to accompany her, Ariel was out of luck as far as Patrick Monroe's poetry reading was concerned. When I told her I'd go with her, the kid was so darned excited, it was clear—to me at least—that she needed a social life that included more than heart-wrenching poetry and boys with bad haircuts.

The heart-wrenching poetry I couldn't help. After all, that's exactly what we were headed to hear.

But I swore I'd do my best that evening to convince Ariel that she was better off without Gonzalo.

Since Ariel's love of bad poetry meshed just fine with my need to investigate, I made all the arrangements. She had to come to Garden View after school, anyway, so I told her it would be no big deal for the two of us just to go from there down to Case Western Reserve University together.

Of course, when I think things are going to be easy, that's when I should know they're not going to work out.

Ariel claimed there was no way she could be ready for something as wonderful as a reading by her favorite poet without a stop at home first. Rachel volunteered to drive her down to the university, and swore she wouldn't drop her off anywhere except right in front of the auditorium where the reading was being held and not leave her in the company of anyone except me.

I was waiting there the next evening, watching the time tick away on my cell phone and thinking that the girls had played both me and Ella for chumps. How Ariel had talked Rachel into something fishy, I didn't know, since Rachel was usually the sensible one, but the reading was about to start, and Ella was going to hang, draw, and quarter me when I had to call her and tell her there was no sign anywhere of Ariel.

"Hey, Pepper!"

I was looking right at the tiny redhead coming up the walk toward the building and I still didn't realize she was talking to me. In fact, it wasn't until she was three feet away that the voice and the face registered.

I bent for a closer look. "Ariel?"

She grinned and skimmed a hand over her hair. "I did it right before I left the house and I wasn't sure how it was going to look. What do you think?"

Since her hair was exactly the same shade of red as mine, it was impossible not to say it looked terrific.

"And the jeans?" She turned all around so I could see that her grungy black jeans were gone. They, too, were replaced with a pair that was sleek, stylish—and exactly like the ones I was wearing. Ariel was wearing sandals, too, and her toenails were painted a boisterous pink.

This was either the ultimate compliment or really disturbing, and I needed some time to sort it out.

Good thing I'd have a lot of time to think. Thinking was better than listening to poetry. "Come on," I told Ariel, "we need to get inside or we'll miss the start of the show."

Her laugh was light and airy. "It's not a show," she said, tossing her red locks in a manner that was, until that moment, all mine. "It's a reading. A poetry reading." She slipped an arm through mine. "And we, girlfriend, are going to have a crazy wonderful time."

I only nodded off twice.

This, I think, says something about my remarkable stamina in the face of the adversity that is an egomaniac poet (come on, Patrick Monroe was wearing a T-shirt with his own picture on it!) with a monotone voice reading a whole slew of unrhymed gobbledygook that ranged from the incomprehensible to the just plain weird.

I was about to slip into la-la land one more time when Ariel pounded on my thigh with her fist. I snapped to and saw that she was out of her chair, bouncing from foot to foot.

"Is it over? Already?" My head was a little fuzzy, but even that wasn't enough to keep me from pouncing on the opportunity to escape the blah-blah and get down to investigating. I grabbed my purse and the leather portfolio I'd brought along and whispered a silent prayer of thanksgiving that the torture was over. Poetry can kill you if you're not careful. "Boy, that sure went fast."

"It's not over yet, silly." Ariel grabbed my arm and did her skinny-little-girl best to drag me to my feet. "It can't be over. Not until he recites 'Girl at Dawn.'"

"Didn't he do that one already?"

The head toss she gave me told me she'd been practicing. It was that perfect.

Because I wasn't sure what the point was, I still wasn't standing, and Ariel gave me another tug. "He always reads it last," she said. "It's his encore. And when he does, everybody stands. You know, to honor him. Come on." She was more urgent than ever, and this time, it was give in or have my arm yanked off.

I gave in, and saw that all around us, the college students, academic types, and aging hippies who packed the reading were stomping their feet and clapping. Monroe had already exited the stage—I wasn't sure when that had happened since I wasn't paying attention—and when he walked back on, the roar was deafening.

He was my height maybe, a scraggly guy in jeans, wearing a sport coat that hung off his shoulders and looked as if it had been borrowed in honor of the occasion. It also looked as if it had been slept in. His hair was salt-and-pepper, thinning at the top, and long at the back and sides in a way that shouted *artiste*! He had a gold stud in his right earlobe, and wallowing in the applause, he never cracked a smile. But then, maybe poets never do. He bowed and pointed to his own face looking out from that T-shirt of his, all moody and glowering.

Ariel elbowed me. "You've got to clap," she mewled. "If everybody's not clapping, his artistic sensibilities get offended, and then he won't recite 'Girl at Dawn.'"

I clapped with as much enthusiasm as it was possible for me to muster. Apparently, Monroe had superhuman vision and spotted the last holdout finally cooperating there in the fifteenth row. He stepped up to the microphone.

"'Girl at Dawn,'" he moaned.

And the place went zooey.

Except for me. But then, I was busy sizing up the guy who just might be the guy I was looking for.

My powers were far from superhuman, but my imagination was pretty good. I did my best to visualize what Monroe might have looked like forty-five years earlier.

Just as scrawny, I was sure.

Just as self-centered.

I knew from seeing his picture in Ella's yearbook that his hair was even longer and scragglier back in his hippie days, and he'd had a beard, too, but I suspected that when he was teaching, he was all about clean-cut. Sans beard, his weak, pointy chin was evident. His eyes were little blue marbles. When he wrapped them around the microphone, I saw that his hands were small for a man and his fingers were long and thin.

I tried to picture those hands holding a blanket over Lucy's face. Pressing. Smothering.

I was so lost in thought, I nearly jumped out of my skin when Monroe cleared his throat. Looked like I was the only one in the audience who dared to move. As if all the oxygen had suddenly been sucked from the room, the crowd held its collective breath.

"Girl. Crimson and golden. Nymph. Chick. Babe."

He wiggled his silvery eyebrows. Ariel and all the rest of the Monroe-o-philes just about fainted on the spot.

"Awake to the dawn," he boomed. "Crimson and golden. A-l-ive . . ."

Who knew two syllables could get dragged out like that?
". . . to the pulse, the vibration, the beat."

From there, it went on and on. And on. And although I
heard the senior citizen hippie on my right purring the
words along with him and Ariel's tiny gulps of excitement,
I didn't listen. I was too busy trying to decide if a guy that
geeky could tie up a woman, kill her, and dump her body
somewhere where nobody would trip over it for nearly fifty
years.

Either I was having a horrible case of déjà vu, or the poem
ended the same way it began. Monroe, his hands poked into
the pockets of his jeans and his chin high, finished with a
flourish.

"Alive to the pulse." He strutted nearer the microphone
and lowered his voice to a growl. "The vibration." It wasn't
my imagination because, believe me, my imagination does
not go in such directions; when he said this, he actually
cocked his hips. "The beat."

I don't think a *t* on the end of a word has ever been drawn
out longer. The tiny ping of it hung in the air. One second.
Two. Three.

And then the crowd erupted.

"Come on." Ariel was out into the aisle before I had a
chance to shake away the weirdness. She had her hand boa-
constrictored around my arm again. "We've got to be first
in line for the meet and greet," she said. She was clutching
a copy of *The Collected Works of an American Master: Patrick Monroe* to her flat chest, and it was such a truly pathetic picture, I couldn't refuse.

But I had my own plans for the meet and greet, ones that
did not include being first in line.

I dawdled, shuffling my way along the back of the crowd
that surged toward a table where student volunteers were

selling Monroe's books as well as CDs of him reciting his poetry, those T-shirts with his picture on them, and an assortment of tote bags, bookmarks, and DVD recordings of readings like this. Ariel was impatient, but I was firm. With people pressing us to move forward, Monroe wouldn't have time to talk. But if we were last in line . . .

"This is going to take friggin' forever!" We'd already been in line for half an hour, and poetry lover or not, Ariel was a typical attention-deficient teenager. She groaned, bending at the waist to see down the line of people that still snaked ahead of us and toward the stage. "I told you we had to hurry if we were going to be first."

"You're young and impatient."

"I'm in love!" She clutched her book and crooned. "Even Gonzalo doesn't write poetry like that. Nobody in the whole history of the world has ever written anything as wonderful and as moving as 'Girl at Dawn.'"

I made a face.

"What?" Ariel could do offended like no one else. "You think just because I'm a kid—"

"I think you should pay more attention to what's going on around you."

She considered this, and yes, it took her a while, but maybe there was more going on behind that teenaged exterior of hers than I gave her credit for. After a couple minutes, her jaw went slack. "You've been asking about Mom's friend, Lucy, and you've been asking about Patrick Monroe. And Patrick Monroe was a teacher at Mom's school when Lucy went missing, and"—her eyes were suddenly as big as saucers—"you don't think that Patrick Monroe had anything to do with—"

I shushed her before she could say anything that would attract the attention of the people in front of us.

Lucky for me, besides having good taste in hair color, Ariel is a good sport. She swallowed whatever it was she might have said and her eyes sparkled. "We're investigating," she whispered.

"And we're going to be very subtle about it," I reminded her.

"But does that mean . . . ?" She sneered at the *Collected Works*. Right before her lower lip trembled. "I can't love his poetry. Not if he's a . . . you know . . ." She glanced all around to make sure no one was listening and mouthed the word *murderer*.

My instant and total dislike of Patrick Monroe aside, I tried to remain my usual objective self. "The jury's still out on that," I told Ariel. "But that's what we're here to find out."

By the time we got to the front of the line, Ariel looked more curious than starstruck. She slid her book in front of Patrick Monroe, stammered out that it was to be signed to her, and blushed sixteen shades of red when he squeezed her hand and offered what I think was supposed to be a sexy smile. I ignored my heebie-jeebies and made a mental note: he still liked 'em young.

With a little waving motion that urged me to take her place, Ariel stepped aside. I pulled back my shoulders and flipped open my portfolio. Then I stuck out my hand.

"Pepper Martin," I said by way of introduction. "Graduate student."

Monroe liked what he saw. But then, I was wearing a snug white T-shirt with my jeans, along with the cutest little sunset-colored shrug. Who says redheads can't get away with shades of pink? From the look in Monroe's eyes, I knew that as far as he was concerned, I could get away with anything.

I intended to try.

"I'm writing my thesis." Oh yes, I batted my eyelashes. "About you."

I wasn't sure which he liked better, the batted eyelashes or the academic adoration. Still holding on to my hand, Monroe stood. I was right; we were just about the same height. This close, I saw that his face looked as lived-in as his sport coat.

"I have a large body of work." His smile made it clear he wouldn't let go of my hand without a little encouragement, so I slipped it out of his grasp and got out a pen. I didn't have to pretend I was taking notes, because I wanted to remember everything he said. "What are you focusing on? My early poems? My eighties glam/punk stage? My newest works? Surely, you must have an opinion on 'Rock and a Hard Place,' the piece I premiered tonight? I think it's one of my best, but then, we'll have to wait and see what the critics say about that." He laughed, but call me a cynic, I could sense the desperation behind his nonchalance.

See, I knew from the research notes Ariel had provided for me that, these days, the critics were less than kind to the wonderboy of the sixties. There was talk about Monroe being washed-up, and more than a few of the essays Ariel had downloaded (believe me when I say I was grateful I didn't have to do it!) mentioned that he was no more than a one-hit wonder. After "Girl at Dawn" . . . well, a whole bunch of literary types claimed that it was all downhill from there.

Leave it to a poet to know how to talk a good game. As if his blatant self-promotion would actually convince me—and as if what I thought might actually matter—he whizzed right on.

"You're a graduate student. That means you must be a smart woman. No doubt you noticed the atypical meter in

'Rock,' the unusual rhyme scheme and the measured tempo . . . ah!" He tipped back his head, savoring the thought, so I guess all that atypical stuff was good. "This poem is going to turn heads," he said, and eyed me carefully. "But perhaps . . ." He wagged a finger in my direction. "Perhaps you're not as concerned about my new work as you are about something else?" He tried wiggling his eyebrows at me, and when I didn't melt like much of the audience had when he pulled that stunt during his reading, he turned down the volume on his attempts at sexy seduction. He did not, however, turn it off. A smile crinkled the corners of his mouth.

"I think," he said, "that perhaps you are one of those marvelous young women who cut her hormonal teeth on 'Girl at Dawn,' and you're going to concentrate on that poem exclusively in your thesis. Let me give you some friendly advice." He stepped closer, and I was glad there was a folding table between us. Lust gives off a pheromone all its own; advice wasn't the only thing Patrick Monroe wanted to give me.

I slid a look toward Ariel.

Even she wasn't fooled. She opened her mouth and pretended to poke a finger down her throat.

"Others have tried to concentrate exclusively on 'Girl,'" Monroe told me, and had I really cared, I might have appreciated his academic wisdom. "But remember, the piece cannot stand on its own. No poem can. Nothing is written in a vacuum. Surely you've discovered that for yourself in your studies."

"I surely have." My smile was sleek. "That's why I'm going to eschew the easy route." Yeah, yeah . . . I know . . . *eschew* is one lame word, and not one I normally toss around in everyday conversation. But I'd done my homework in preparation for meeting Monroe. I figured poets were all about words like *eschew*. I think it has something to do with the meter. Or maybe they like to use strange words to make their readers feel all woolly-headed. Four years of high school English and too many college lit courses, and I'm pretty sure that's what poetry is all about in the first place.

"Actually, I was going to concentrate on your early career," I told him. "Not your career as a poet. Your years as a teacher."

His face registered surprise, but I didn't give him time to think this over. I went right on. "I think I'm in an especially advantageous position," I said, pulling out all the stops and the last big word I knew. "I live in Shaker, and that's where you taught. It's like a sign from heaven. I'm destined to write about the time you spent here."

"Poets are big believers in destiny. After all, if it wasn't for destiny, I might be writing advertising jingles instead of speaking at prestigious universities to beautiful women like you." His smile never wavered, but I saw the way he looked past me, and the relief that swept over his face when he realized I was last in line. I was playing hard to get, and he wasn't used to having to trawl for women. I had to move quickly, or I was going to lose him to the groupies who were already collecting in tight knots near the front of the stage. No doubt, Monroe would soon be on the receiving end of who-knew-how-many dinner invitations.

"So much of the research I need is right here, all around me," I said, ignoring the *beautiful* comment as if I was modest, not grossed out. "I can talk to people at Shaker Heights High, and I imagine a lot of your students are still living here in the community. I'm so anxious to hear what they have to say about your brilliant classroom techniques. Especially the girls you taught."

His smile was gone in an instant. "What's that supposed to mean?"

Don't worry, I was prepared. As if I couldn't believe what a dummy I was, I laughed and blushed on command. "Oh my gosh! That came out all wrong. What I mean . . ." This time I pulled out all the stops and twinkled. "Come on, they all must have been in love with you."

He tried to keep his thunderous expression, but it melted in the warmth of my smile. When he laughed, the skin around his eyes crinkled into dozens of crow's-feet. "That's the problem with being a poet," he murmured.

"Oh, I don't know. I don't think it's a problem," I said right back.

Ariel coughed.

I ignored her.

"One of those girls was Lucy Pasternak, right?"

His smile froze, and before he could recover, I closed in for the kill. "I'm sure you remember her. She was in your summer school class. Right before she disappeared and was never seen again."

He scraped a hand through his hair. "Lucy. Of course. That girl who ran away."

"Did she?"

As if he didn't quite get it, he shook his head. "Did she . . . run away? Well, I don't know. I thought that's what happened. I left the area soon after, and it was a very long time ago." He signaled to his minions to get his books and CDs and tote bags all packed up.

"Which is why this opportunity to speak to you about that crucial summer is so perfect," I said, and when a couple college kids carefully moved the table out from between us, I stepped closer to Monroe. "I'm using the summer of 1966 as a focal point. The whole hippie movement was just beginning and that was starting to shape society. The Beatles were in Cleveland that summer. You were at the concert, weren't you?"

His look was as steady as a rock and just as soft. "You really have done your homework, haven't you?"

I took this as the compliment it was not meant to be and breezed right on. "You published 'Girl at Dawn' at the end of 1967, which means '66 must have been a crucial year for you. You know, as far as your artistic growth and development."

"It was . . ." He stepped aside as the kids folded the last table and carted it off. "It was an interesting time. So much of what we did and thought was influenced by the tidal waves of social change. There was the civil rights movement, of course, and the whole hippie subculture. There was the War in Vietnam—"

"And there was Lucy."

"Really, I don't see what she had to do with anything." With a shake of his shoulders, Monroe turned and walked away.

But I've got long legs, and I'm a redhead, which means I'm not easily put off. I caught up to him in a heartbeat. "Well, I don't know if her disappearance does have anything to do with your growth as an artist," I said, watching a muscle bunch at his jawline. "That's what I'm trying to find out. Between Lucy and that job you lost in New York—"

He spun to face me. "You'll never get anywhere academically if you listen to rumors and not the truth."

"And the truth is?"

"The truth is, there was never any truth to those allegations in New York. You can put that in your thesis. Tell them you got it right from the horse's mouth."

"And the truth about Lucy?"

He narrowed his eyes and looked me over. "The truth about Lucy is that I don't know anything about Lucy. She was here one day and gone the next. It was a long time ago and nobody cares anymore, anyway."

"My mom does."

I hadn't realized Ariel had followed us across the stage. Now I turned and saw that her shoulders were back and her head was high. "My mom," she said, "and Lucy were best friends."

"That's sweet. Really." He ruffled her hair. Ariel did not appreciate this. She stepped closer to me. Monroe pulled in a long breath. "Look . . . girls . . ." He took us both in with a look I imagined he'd used on freshman English students once upon a time. He might be a friendly guy, it said, but he was definitely superior, and that meant he wasn't about to put up with any crap. "There's really nothing I can tell you about Lucy. I hardly knew her. She may have taken a class or two with me. Honestly, I don't remember. It was a very long time ago. But other than that . . ." His shrug said it all.

And I knew when to back off. Or at least to make it look like I was backing off. I grabbed his hand and pumped it. "I can't thank you enough for taking the time to talk to me," I said. "Having your perspective on things helps so much."

"That's nice." His smile was tight. "Good night."

"There's just one more thing."

Since I had a death grip on his hand, it's not like he was able to go anywhere, anyway. His smile firmly in place, that muscle jumping at the base of his jaw, he gave me one more minute. I knew it would be the last.

"I hoped you could provide some insight into one little thing. It really would be a coup in terms of my thesis."

He'd had enough, but since I was standing between him

and the only exit off the stage, the only way he could get around me was to knock me down. Call me crazy, but I think he actually considered it. Lucky for me, instead he said, "I don't have much time. I have other engagements, other commitments."

"Of course. I understand." I took a step closer. "I was just wondering . . . about 'Girl at Dawn.' All that repressed sexuality. All that yearning and aching and vibrating. That girl was Lucy, wasn't it?"

He jerked his hand out of mine. "You think I had something to do with Lucy's disappearance? Think again. The police interviewed me after Lucy disappeared. Plenty of times. They never found a connection between us. Except for school, of course. If you did your research the way a graduate student is supposed to, you might have turned up the not-so-unimportant fact that there was someone else who was far more likely to have had something to do with Lucy vanishing."

He'd already turned to walk away when I grabbed his arm. "Who?"

He shook me off. "Research, darling," he purred. "Start with that friend of hers who died in Vietnam. From what I've heard, he walked right into a firefight, eyes wide open. Suicide by Nam, they called it. You know, like he was feeling really guilty about something."

10

"That's Lucy. Isn't she beautiful?"

Over my left shoulder, I heard Ella expel a breath and watched as she touched a finger to the faded color photograph she'd brought to the office at my request. I recognized Lucy at once, of course, but I couldn't let on. There she was in that cute little khaki mini, the pink top, the golden lipstick, and the waterfall hair. According to Ella, the photo was taken by her mom when the other kids came to pick Ella up for the concert. In it, Lucy was happy, smiling—and very much alive.

"She was always smiling like that," Ella said, her voice dreamy and faraway. "It wasn't just the concert she was excited about. Lucy was excited about life. About all the things she still had in store for her."

"If she only knew," I mumbled.

Ella moved down the row of bright-faced teenagers, left

to right. "And there's Bobby. You asked about him." Her voice dropped. "He was so young."

She wasn't kidding. Though I knew Bobby Gideon was going into his senior year and must have been seventeen or eighteen when the photo was taken, he didn't look a day over twelve, a grinning, goofy-looking kid with big ears.

"It wasn't more than eighteen months or so after this picture was taken," Ella said. "You know, when we heard he was dead."

"Did you hear how?"

"How he died?" She'd dragged my guest chair behind my desk and was sitting in it, and she sat back. "In Vietnam. In combat. That's pretty much all anyone ever knew."

Not anyone. Not if Patrick Monroe was to be believed. He'd painted an incomplete but tantalizing picture of the incident. Suicide by Nam, he'd called it. Like Bobby was feeling guilty about something.

For a while longer, I stared into the face of a kid who looked like the only thing he could possibly feel guilty about was filching treats from his mom's cookie jar, then I moved on. "This has got to be Janice," I said, pointing to a girl in a bright yellow sheath dress and a teased, beehive hairdo. Now that I knew about Lucy and Darren and suspected that Janice might have had something to do with their breakup, I took an especially close look at her. I remembered what Ella had said about seeing Darren and Janice talking at the concert, about how insistent Janice had seemed. Yeah, she looked the type. It was there in the way she stood, her head high and her shoulders back and her gaze aimed right at Mrs. Bender's camera in an in-your-face sort of way that wouldn't have been unusual for a teenaged girl these days, but back then, I imagined made quite the political statement.

"Janice was a pretty girl, too, in her own way." Ella slid the photo off my desk so she could take a closer look at it. "But she had a sort of harsh beauty, don't you think? Lots of makeup. Lots of ratting her hair. That sort of thing. It wasn't a natural prettiness like Lucy's." She set the picture back in front of me. "And there's Darren." When she pointed to a boy in madras shorts and an open-collared shirt, I gave him a careful once-over, too.

"Lucy's secret boyfriend," I murmured.

"Oh, no!" Ella was so sure of this, she boffed me on the arm for making fun. "Lucy and Darren? Don't be ridiculous. If Lucy was dating Darren, I would have known about it."

"Not if it was a secret," I reminded her.

She pooh-poohed the very idea. "I've seen you think your way through mysteries, Pepper, so I know you can logically work through a problem. Not this time, though. Look at that shaggy mop of hair of his! And those sparkling blue eyes. Back in the day, he sent shivers down the spine of every girl at Shaker."

Personally, I thought he was cute, but geeky. The fact that every girl at Shaker thought he was a gift from the gods made me wonder about the standards of the sixties.

"Besides," Ella added while I was still lost in thought, "if Lucy was dating Darren, she never would have broken up with him. I mean, who in their right mind would?"

And what detective in her right mind wouldn't ask why they had.

Then again, Lucy hadn't exactly given me the chance, not with the sizzling electric light show of hers.

I made the mental note and moved on.

"Will Margolis, right?" The nondescript kid was shorter than Darren and standing in front of him. He wasn't looking at the camera. His eyes were glued to the girl standing next to him, the one in the plaid skirt, Peter Pan collar shirt, and kneesocks.

"He liked you," I said.

Ella clicked her tongue. "Will was friendly, and not just to me, to everyone."

"And you were as cute as a button!" I had to look at her when I said this, because I wasn't going to take the chance of missing Ella blush. I was not disappointed. "Look at you in that adorable little skirt. I bet you had a matching sweater."

She slid the photo away. "The sweater was my mother's idea. And I . . ." She checked out the photo and cringed. "I looked like a complete and total loser."

"An adorable complete and total loser," I teased.

Ella tried to pretend she minded, but she couldn't control her smile.

While she was still in a good mood, I pounced for more information. "Tell me about Will."

Her smile was gone in an instant. "I really didn't know him well," she admitted. "He was a quiet, sensitive kid—an artist. He usually had a sketchbook with him, and he liked to show me his drawings. He wasn't as young as me, but he wasn't as old as the other kids. I think he and Bobby were neighbors; that's how he got to be part of the group."

"So what happened to him?"

She shrugged and looked at her watch. "Ariel should be here soon."

Too off the subject not to be conspicuous.

Since I'm far more subtle, I played it cool. "Did Lucy ever date Bobby?"

Ella laughed. "Bobby? You're kidding, right? I mean, I loved Bobby to death." Another shot of color heated her cheeks. "Bad choice of words, considering what happened to him, but you know what I mean. He was a great guy, but he was out of Lucy's league."

"Why? She liked them handsomer? Older?"

"Well, not older certainly." She made a face. "Not like Mr. Monroe. Handsomer? Maybe. She dated a guy her junior year who was really handsome. A chiseled chin, dark hair, eyes the color of oak leaves in spring."

She made him sound like Quinn's way older brother, and I batted the thought away before it could take root.

"Lucy liked guys with class, and that's not to say Bobby didn't have any. He was just . . . just a guy, just a buddy. He was always telling corny jokes and using puns so bad, they made us all groan. He was fun and funny. At least until . . ." Her expression clouded.

It didn't take a detective to catch on. "Let me guess. Until Lucy disappeared?"

Ella shook off the thought. "Well, that doesn't mean anything. We were all upset."

"But some of you were more upset than others. Like Bobby, for instance?"

She got up and fussed over putting the chair back where she'd found it. Since I was never all that worried about what my tiny office looked like, it wasn't a big deal to me, but Ella straightened and re-straightened, lining up the chair just right. When she was done, she stood behind it, her hands curled around the back. "Truth is, I can't tell you," she said, and call me psychic (I'm not, and believe me, it would come in handy more than this goofy Gift I did end up with), I knew Ella was embarrassed. And upset, too. Considering we were discussing something that had happened nearly fifty years earlier, this was odd. And interesting.

She turned away from me and walked to the far side of

my office, and since that took, like, maybe five seconds, she
flipped around and came back the other way, her hands
clutched where the waistband of her denim skirt met a
white peasant shirt embroidered at the neck and cuffs with
bright flowers. "Like I told you before, Pepper, I was never
really part of the group. I went to the concert with them that
night because Lucy invited me along. I was younger. I
didn't really fit in."

"What you're saying is that once Lucy was gone, the rest
of them dumped you."

"I wouldn't exactly put it that way," she said, but the look
of misery on her face told me otherwise. All these years,
and the rejection still hurt. "I was young, and probably too
sensitive. I really didn't expect them to somehow suddenly
welcome me into the group with open arms just because of
what happened to Lucy."

"But . . ."

"But after the night of the Beatles concert, they didn't
even acknowledge that I was alive. I'd see them in the hallways and say hello and be all set to ask how they were
coping, and they'd just walk right past me. It was like I
disappeared when Lucy did."

"And Will?"

"Will?" Her smile came and went. "After that night,
when I ran into Will . . . well, at least he wasn't as cold as
the rest of them, at least he'd say hello. But when I tried to
talk to him . . . you know, really talk? . . . it was like meeting
a brick wall. I was a kid, and I didn't know a thing about
psychology, but even I knew not talking about what happened to Lucy wasn't going to help any of us. After a couple
months of trying to get through to Will, I finally gave up.
And it wasn't like it was just me he was ignoring," she
added. She hurried around to the front of my guest chair

and sat down, suddenly looking tired. "Will cut everybody off. Even Darren and Janice and Bobby. He stopped drawing. He got into all kinds of trouble at school. There was talk of him drinking and doing drugs. I know it was all because of how worried he was about Lucy. If only he'd realized that talking about it might have helped."

There was a stack of old employee newsletters on my desk that I'd been asked to recycle by removing the staples and reusing the paper. Been there, done that, and I wasn't going to get conned into it again. With nervous fingers, Ella reached for the papers. I didn't stop her. Hey, if she was willing to do what I didn't want to, bless her!

"They closed ranks," she said, pulling out a staple, setting that newsletter aside, and reaching for another one. "That's as simple as it is. The kids who were with me at the concert that night closed me out and kept to themselves. Their relationships with Lucy were different than mine. To me, Lucy was the big sister I never had. To them, she was a friend. They handled her disappearance the only way they knew how."

"And the cops . . . did they see what was happening? Didn't they think Lucy's other friends were acting fishy?"

She stopped mid-pull and looked at me. "We didn't have such things as grief counselors then, Pepper. Not like they have at schools now when something terrible happens. Lucy disappeared, and her friends . . ." Ella got back to work. "Well, we were pretty much left on our own to deal with it. The teachers at school didn't talk about it, and I remember there was a big to-do when the yearbook editor insisted on putting that picture of Lucy in what would have been her senior yearbook. Like it was some kind of stain on the school's reputation to admit one of its students was missing." Still not understanding, she shook her head.

Finished with one pile of papers, Ella reached for another. "I was lucky," she said. "My mom and my dad were
great, especially my mom. She'd sit and listen to me cry, or
we'd talk for hours and come up with scenarios that would
explain what had happened to Lucy. I don't know if she
ever believed any of them. I think she was just trying to
make me feel better. The other kids . . ." Her shrug said it
all. "I have no idea what kind of support they got from their
parents. Maybe none. Maybe they were all each other's
support, and maybe the only way they could deal was to
lean on each other."

"But the cops did talk to them, right?"

"Of course." Ella was getting good at this recycling
stuff. Finished in no time flat, she tapped the papers into a
neat pile and set them back down where they came from.
"The police talked to all of us. When they found out Lucy
had been to the concert and who she went with, they brought
us all down to the station and talked to us separately and
then all together. We told them about the ride home on the
rapid." Since those old newsletters were in the most perfect
of perfect piles, they didn't need to be lined up again, but
that's exactly what Ella did. "I was the last one off the train.
Before Lucy, that is."

"And the other kids?"

Ella's thoughts had drifted off, and she snapped to. "They
told the police the truth, of course. Janice, Darren, Will, and
Bobby got off the rapid together and they went to Darren's
house. He lived in a big mansion and there was even a third-
floor ballroom. Can you imagine? That was where Darren
always took his friends. They all told the police the same
thing, that they were listening to record albums on Darren's
stereo."

"And the cops believed them?"

"Well, of course they did." Apparently, I was treading on thin ice by even suggesting that the kids knew anything. But though Ella's voice was edged with exasperation, she refused to meet my eyes. My detective senses tingled; there was something she wasn't telling me, and believe me, I intended to find out what it was. I settled back and waited for the right moment.

"And they had Mrs. Andrews's word to back up their story," Ella added while I was planning my strategy. "Mrs. Andrews said they all came home and trooped upstairs and she heard those albums playing and playing for hours. Besides . . ." She tugged at the cuffs of her blouse. "There was never any reason to think the other kids had any information that might have helped. They got off the train first. They were home listening to records by the time Lucy got off at her stop."

"They got off first. Then you got off the train."

My well-timed comment confirmed my suspicion. It was when she mentioned the train and how she'd gotten off before Lucy that Ella had gotten a little tweaky. Now, she tweaked some more. She stood up, then sat down again, her fingers laced together and her eyes bright.

"I've never told anyone," she said, her voice wobbly. "I suppose I never wanted to admit it."

I sat forward. "You saw what happened?"

"Oh my gosh, no!" She stood again, and sniffled. "It's just . . ." She paced over to the door and swallowed hard before she said, "Lucy wanted to get off the train when I did so she could walk me home."

Call me slow, I didn't get the connection. "So . . ."

A single tear snaked over Ella's cheek. "We'd been talking on the train, you see. About her secret boyfriend and about how she'd never told me about him because I wasn't old enough to know everything. So when my stop came up, I told her I didn't need her to walk me home."

"Because you were trying to prove how grown-up you were." The pieces chunked into place, and sure, it had happened long before I was born, but my heart squeezed in sympathy. "It wasn't your fault," I said.

Ella swiped her hands across her cheeks. "Of course it wasn't. I know that now. I think I knew it then, but—"

"But you felt guilty, anyway."

"If I had let her walk me home—"

"Then whatever happened to her that night would have just happened another time." I wasn't sure I believed this, but I said it to make Ella feel better. "You can't change the past."

Ella sniffled. "You can wonder how things might have been different."

"But you can't feel guilty. You were a kid."

"And she was my best friend."

"And you couldn't have known that she'd step off the rapid and get kidnapped."

Ella's head came up. "Did she? How would you—"

I was saved from answering when my office door banged open and Ariel sauntered in—in a sweet little denim miniskirt, a black cami, and three-inch heels.

While my mouth was still hanging open, she sashayed over to the desk, set down a leather portfolio, and slipped off her backpack. "I've been investigating," she said. "Pepper, darling, you never mentioned how tough it is for us detectives. Talking to people, retracing our steps, library research!" She could only maintain the blasé attitude so long before her face split with a grin. "This is the coolest job ever!"

"It's supposed to be my job."

As protests went, it wasn't much, but it didn't matter

since neither of them was listening to me. Ella was just about to burst, that's how happy she looked when she shot forward, wiped the last of the tears from her eyes, and beamed, "Did you hear that, Pepper? Ariel's been investigating. Isn't that interesting? She's been using her free time to do research."

"And boy, did I find plenty!" Ariel unzipped her backpack and pulled out a book. "Exhibit number one," she said, sounding like one of the characters in a courtroom TV show. "An autobiography of Patrick Monroe." She slapped it down on the desk. "I read it, cover to cover."

Something I never would have done, so I was actually impressed.

"Unfortunately . . ." Ariel lifted the book and dropped it on the desk with a splat. "He doesn't say anything about the night of the Beatles concert, and nothing about Lucy, either. Dead end there!" She tossed her head. "But not to worry, you know how we redheads are. We're not about to give up easily. I also talked to"—she flipped open the portfolio she'd left on my desk—"the six other teachers he worked with in the English department at Shaker."

Ella looked over Ariel's shoulder at the list, her head bobbing. "She made a list!" Ella was so impressed, her voice warbled. "That's a wonderful skill," she added. For Ariel's benefit, I hope, not mine. "It's the kind of time management technique that really pays off once you get to college. Don't you think so, Pepper?"

I had been known to make lists myself a time or two. Mostly of murder suspects. Or wardrobe essentials on my must-have list. Since they were so involved in this Ariel-as-detective lovefest, I didn't bother to point this out.

"Nobody liked Patrick Monroe," Ariel said. "Not one of them had anything good to say about the creep."

"Did they have anything to say about Lucy?"

When she looked at me, Ariel wrinkled her nose. "They say they always suspected Patrick Monroe had something to do with her disappearance. But . . ." She slapped the portfolio closed. "Close but no cigar. Nobody's talking, and if they are, they're not saying anything that will help us nail our perp."

There was that word again. *Our*. I had to tread carefully for fear of trampling on Ella's excitement or Ariel's ego, but tread I did. It was that or risk having my investigation whisked out from under me. I pulled back my shoulders. Even in her three-inch heels, I was taller than Ariel, and I intended to make the most of the advantage. "I really appreciate your help," I told her. "I really do. But it's probably time for me to just take over and—"

"Have you made lists about anything else?" Do I need to point out that the question came from Ella? Or that she wasn't talking to me? She looped her arm through her daughter's and they headed for the door. "You could try the same technique for homework assignments. You know, day of the week, what homework you have, when it's due. Then you could take that list and transfer it all to a master list and . . ."

They were still talking about it when they walked out into the hall.

And I was left—finally—to my own thoughts. It didn't take me long to put them in order because, let's face it, I hadn't learned much that was new.

Ella felt guilty for not allowing Lucy to walk her home. OK, I got that. But it had nothing to do with Lucy's murder.

And was it true that Bobby Gideon felt guilty, too? So guilty he allowed himself to be slaughtered in combat in

Vietnam? And if this was true, what was it that Bobby felt guilty about?

I didn't have the answers. But I intended to find out.

I t took me longer to find Dr. Sharon Gideon than it did for her to throw me out of her office.

But then, I suppose a dentist with patients waiting can't be expected to be all that excited about answering questions from a woman who wasn't even alive when her brother died in a jungle on the other side of the world. Especially when those questions involve suicide and a girl who disappeared so long ago Sharon barely remembered Lucy's name, much less the circumstances surrounding the mystery.

She was accommodating enough to ask where I'd even heard such bullshit (her word) about Bobby's death, and I was shameless enough to lie and tell her I was writing a book about local soldiers who had served in Nam and that I'd interviewed one of the guys in Bobby's platoon. He'd told me that Bobby walked into the middle of a firefight and never once tried to defend himself.

Sure, I was elaborating on the slim facts Patrick Monroe had provided me, but I could tell from the way Sharon flinched when I told my story that there was some kernel of truth in it. I took a chance and asked if Bobby might have had any reason to feel guilty about what happened to Lucy. That's when Dr. Gideon unceremoniously showed me to the door. With the caveat that I'd better not ever come back or she'd call the cops.

I may be persistent, but I am not stupid. I understand the meaning of the words *restraining order* and the concept of jail. I left and sat in my car out in the parking lot, thinking.

It was obvious that Sharon might know the truth about Bobby's death, but she was never going to talk.

It was just as obvious that when it came to Bobby, Ella couldn't help, either.

And that left me only one place to turn.

Well . . . let me correct that statement.

It left me with three places to turn.

It was time for me to track down Janice, Darren, and Will.

OK, I admit it, as places to live go, Cleveland often gets a bum rap. And some of that is well deserved. Our region's economy is in the dumps. Some of our public school systems are way less than stellar. Our river once caught on fire, but that was a long time ago, and it's been cleaned up since then so that doesn't actually count.

But there are good things about living in northeast Ohio, too. Sometimes the weather is spectacular. When it's not snowing, that is, or so humid it's like walking through a wet wall. We have great parks, fabulous museums—as a former art history major, I can say this with some authority even though I never go to them—and a sense of pride and history that is as appealing to some people as our relatively low cost of living.

People who are born here tend to stick around, and that's a real plus for me. It means that investigating in my home-

town is a tad easier than I imagine it would be in places like
New York or L.A. Yes, the shopping opportunities in those
cities would more than make up for the inconvenience, but
shopping aside, never let it be said that I don't look on the
bright side.

It took some digging, but remember, I had an assistant.
I put Ariel to work, and just like I found Bobby Gideon's
sister, she found Will Margolis's mother. When I went to
visit, I discovered a teeny, silver-haired woman with dark
eyes, and thank goodness, none of the attitude that made
Dr. Gideon so impossible.

Oh yeah, Will's mom wanted to talk. And talk. And talk.
She was just about ancient and a little fuzzy when it came
to reality. She thought I'd gone to school with Will. In spite
of the fact that I am about thirty years younger than him, I
didn't take this personally. In fact, I played it up for all it
was worth.

That old school connection I had with Will, that's what
got me his current address.

So there I was, just a couple days later in a part of Cleveland known as the Flats, the area immediately on either side
of the Cuyahoga River. Back in the day and thanks to easy
access to both the river and Lake Erie, this was where the
first pioneers settled. In later years, all that water meant
cheap and easy transportation, so the Flats became an in-
dustrial hub. That river fire I mentioned? It happened in the
Flats.

That incident was something of a wake-up call, and since
then, the Flats has undergone an ebb and flow of transforma-
tion, from nightclub central to gentrification, from down-
on-its-luck to hopping party town and back again. These
days, it's stuck somewhere right in between. There are still
some restaurants and bars down in the Flats, but there are

empty buildings, too, as well as newly built condos and a whole lake's worth of promises that never seem to get fulfilled. Developers are always itching to get their fingers into the pie that is the Flats, and from my research (OK, Ariel's research, but since I was in charge, it was like it was mine), Darren Andrews was one of them.

He was a problem for another day. That sunny Saturday at the end of April, I parked the Mustang and picked my way down a heaving sidewalk littered with beer cans and broken bottles, heading toward a relatively new and beautifully cared for complex called Stella Maris. It means Star of the Sea, which doesn't make any sense to me since the lake is right nearby and the sea isn't, but I'm not one to quibble. I stopped long enough to look over the two tidy redbrick buildings. One of them had an ultramodern rounded roofline and plenty of windows, and that's the one I went for. That's where I was told the Recovery Coffee House was located, and that's where I was going to meet Will Margolis.

The *Recovery* part of the name? Well, that was no big surprise. Stella Maris is a drug and alcohol treatment center, and according to his mom, it wasn't the first time Will had been a patient there. She'd talked about good intentions gone bad, and rehab that never quite stuck, and a treadmill that pretty much went round and round this way: promises, recovery, back to the bottle, and life on the streets. According to her, Will had been at Stella Maris for the last couple months and she was sure—this time—that rehab was going to work. As for Will, he'd seemed more than a little confused when I called to schedule this meeting, and more than a little unsure about why I wanted to talk to him in the first place. In answer to his questions, I had been less than forthcoming. But then, I've found that it's easier to get people to talk in person than it is over the phone. I didn't want to have him tell me to take a hike before I ever had the chance to meet him in person.

Hoping for the best, I pushed open the door to the coffeehouse and saw that, except for a woman in sweatpants and a hospital-type scrub top, it was empty.

My expectations had been running high, and they crashed and burned in an instant.

That is, until I looked around and saw that there was a man at a table on the outside patio. I pulled out that photo of Ella and her friends taken the night of the Beatles concert and took another look at the teenaged Will. He wasn't nearly as tall as Darren and had none of that surfer swagger, but in his own geeky not-quite-a-man way, Will was kind of cute. He had dark hair, and it was combed down over his forehead. In the photo, he was grinning at Ella. He was red-faced and very young, and call me a sucker, but the thought of finding him forty-five years later at a drug rehab center . . .

I pulled in a breath and told myself not to get caught in an undertow of emotion. I was a detective with a job to do, and I marched toward the patio, pushed open the door, and—

Stopped.

In spite of the pool of sunshine where he sat, the man at the table was muffled in a black cardigan and wearing a green stocking cap. He had a newspaper spread out in front of him, and as he read, he tapped the table with the fingers of his left hand, over and over, again and again. It didn't take long for the frantic rhythm to get to me. I doubted the young Will had a cough that made it sound like his lungs were filled with liquid. And the mustard yellow stains on his fingers? I'd bet anything that back when Ella knew him, he didn't have those, either. Even as I watched, the man lit a cigarette, sucked in a long breath, and closed his eyes, apparently enjoying the sensation of the smoke in his lungs and the nicotine clawing through his bloodstream. His hands were mottled with age spots. His fingers were as thin as claws.

I checked the photo again.

I looked back at the man.

The hair poking out of the back of his stocking cap was streaked with silver, but still mostly dark. His eyes were sunken, and the skin around them looked as if it had been smudged with gray eye shadow. But the cheekbones . . . Just to make sure, I checked the picture again. They were as high as the boy's in the photo, and since he was so thin, they were as well defined as a fashion model's. Though his chin sagged and was tweedy with a couple days' growth of stubble, it was just as round as that of the kid from long ago.

When I took a step closer, I made sure to clear my throat so I didn't catch Will Margolis off guard.

His dark eyes popped open. They were rimmed with red. Every movement stiff and painful, he dragged himself to his feet. "You gotta be Pepper Martin, the young lady who called me yesterday." He swept an arm toward the chair next to his. "You want to sit down?"

"Before I do . . ." I looked back toward the inside café. "You want a cup of coffee?"

"If you're getting one for yourself . . ." He poked a hand into the pocket of his worn jeans, but I was way ahead of him.

"My treat," I said, and I hurried inside. The last thing I needed was some uncomfortable *I'll get it, no I will* scene when I was trying to break the ice.

I was back outside in a couple minutes and I set a cup of coffee down next to the newspaper he'd folded up. While I was inside and since I didn't know how he took his coffee, I'd grabbed a bunch of little bags of sugar, a couple bags of sweetener for myself, and some of those tiny coffee creamers. I set those down, too, and when I did, the headline on the day's paper caught my eye.

"Oh!" I set down my own coffee cup and the leather portfolio I'd brought along so that I'd look official, and dropped into the chair Will had invited me to use earlier. I slid the newspaper closer so that I could skim the article. "It's about that serial killer who was captured a couple weeks ago," I said, tapping the paper with one finger. "He escaped."

"Read it." He tore open four packs of sugar with his teeth and sprinkled the contents into his coffee, then added three of those little creamers and stirred like there was no tomorrow. "Got away when they were supposed to be taking him to court. Hurt a deputy, too. Pushed the guy down and broke his leg." Will's gaze was glued to the newspaper, but the look in his eyes was unfocused. "His name is Winston Churchill. Weird, huh?"

"I know the cop who arrested him." I'm not sure why it seemed to matter that I mention this. Maybe it was part and parcel of that whole icebreaking thing. "I bet he's not happy."

Will's chuckle sounded like sandpaper on stone. "Bet he's plenty pissed."

It was unfortunate that the deputy had been hurt, and scary as hell to think this sicko killer was back out on the street, but I knew Will was right. I chuckled, too.

He darted a look in my direction. "You don't like him."

I knew we weren't talking about Winston Churchill. "I used to."

"I get it." He nodded, but luckily, Will didn't have much

of an attention span. He didn't press me for details. "Who are you?" he asked.

I knew he wasn't talking about my name. He'd already proved he remembered that so I just said, "I'm a friend of Ella's."

He pulled the newspaper closer. Fiddled with its pages. Pushed it away. By this time, his cigarette was nothing but a stub, and he slid another one from the pack on the table, lit it from the one still burning, and tugged in a stream of smoke.

"I don't know anybody named Ella."

"You used to."

The way his lips twitched wasn't exactly a smile. "I used to do and be a lot of things. I was an alcoholic. I was a drug addict. I've slept under bridges and in doorways and behind trash cans. Thanks to this place, I'm changing now. I'm cleaning up my act. I've been sober . . ." He glanced at his watch. Since it didn't have one of those calendar features, I didn't know why until he said, "I've been sober for forty-three days and six hours," he said. "This time, my recovery's for real."

"I know you can do it." Of course I didn't, but hey, what's a person supposed to say at a time like this? "I talked to your mother. She thinks you can do it, too. She's the one who told me where to find you."

"My mom's a saint." This time there was no mistaking the expression. That really was a smile that crossed Will's face. It looked as if it hurt. "She's put up with a lot from me over the years. But Mom's always there for me." He swigged down a sip of coffee, and when he was done, his left hand went back to tapping on the table. "How did you say you know my mom?"

"Well, I don't. Not really. But I wanted to find you and I didn't know how, and she's the one who helped me. I'm a friend of Ella's. Ella Bender."

He stopped tapping long enough to drag his stocking cap off his head. His hair was thinning on top and long past needing a good cut and style. He scraped a hand through it. "Told you I don't know anyone named Ella."

"She remembers you."

"Maybe. But that was a long time ago."

"I thought you said you didn't know her."

The tapping stopped for real this time, and honestly, I thought he was either going to tell me to get lost or he was going to get up and walk away. I'm pretty sure he considered both options. That would explain why it took so long before he said, "You're her daughter?"

"Ella's?" I guess it wasn't all that funny, but it was plenty strange, so I laughed. "I work with Ella at Garden View Cemetery." I was going to leave it at that, but figured it wouldn't hurt to try out a little experiment so I kept my eyes on Will when I added, "She does have three daughters, though."

His reaction told me nothing. But then, that's because there was no reaction. He took another drink of coffee. A long one. When he was done, he looked at me over the rim of the cup. "They look like her?"

I shook my head. "Not really."

"She was cute."

"She said the same thing about you."

His laugh dissolved into a cough. "I don't think anybody's called me cute in a long time. I hope she's happy with that guy who's the father of her children."

"He's a loser." I wasn't exactly betraying a confidence. Anyone who'd ever met him knew Jeffrey Silverman was the world's finest example of everything a man should not be. "They've been divorced for years. Ella, she's raised those girls herself. She's done a really great job, too." This wasn't a lie. Not exactly. Ella had done a great job. It wasn't her fault Ariel was a troublemaker. Besides, the kid seemed to be turning herself around. When I'd seen her at the cemetery the day before, her nails were manicured and polished, and not with black lacquer, either, but with a peachy color that just so happened to match the one I was wearing. Maybe there was hope for the kid after all. If nothing else, something told me Will knew all about hope.

"Glad the girls are nice," he said. "Sorry about the divorce. Ella deserves better than that."

"Don't we all." It was one of those general statements, but I guess even though I hadn't meant it, it was encouraging.

He flicked ashes into the aluminum ashtray on the table. "She's got a family. Not me. I lived on the streets for a lot of years. I lost myself in a bottle." He slid me a look. "Does that make me a loser, too?"

"It makes you a man with a problem and you realize it and you're dealing with it. That makes you kind of a hero."

Another laugh, and when it stuck in his throat, he pounded his chest. "Nobody's ever called me that. So tell me, Pepper Martin, why did you go looking for my mother so you could find me? Meaning no disrespect, but a pretty young woman has better things to do on a spring afternoon than sit here with me. You're not trying to save my soul, are you?" I would have thought he was teasing, but his expression was deadly serious. "If you are, you're wasting your time. It's too late for that."

"Souls are way out of my league." True, though spirits weren't. "But what I have to do . . . well, it involves you."

That wasn't as subtle as I'd planned on being, but there didn't seem to be much point in beating around the bush with a guy who'd seen as much of life as Will had. "You see, one of Ella's daughters, she ran away from home recently."

"I'm sorry to hear that."

"She's back, and she's fine, but the whole incident upset Ella. I mean, even more than it normally would."

He stubbed out his cigarette, but he didn't say a word so I was obligated to add, "Of course, that's only natural. Because of what happened to Lucy."

Will didn't say a thing. He didn't move a muscle, either. A truck rumbled by, and it was so quiet there outside the coffee shop, I could hear the table between us vibrate against the cement patio. When the quiet dragged on for another minute, I weighed the best way to approach the subject and decided on a direct assault. "You and Ella and Lucy, you went to the Beatles concert together the night Lucy disappeared."

Will scrubbed his hands over his face. "That was a real long time ago," he said. "I don't remember."

"You don't need to remember. Ella remembers every minute of that evening. She still has a picture." I pulled it out of my purse and set it on the table. "What happened to Lucy . . ." I touched a finger to her smiling, golden face. "A lot of people have been wondering about that for a very long time."

He never once glanced at the photo. "What happened to Lucy . . ." His gaze was vacant. The tapping started all over again. "Nobody ever found out what happened to Lucy."

"I know. But I think it's time, don't you?" Honestly, I thought of mentioning Lucy's ghost and the mission she'd given me. Something told me Will wouldn't find it so far-fetched. "I thought if I talked to everyone in the old group . . ."

Again, I gave the picture a pointed look. Again, Will ignored me. And it. "I thought if I talked to all of you, I might learn something."

He finished his coffee. It was the first I realized I hadn't touched mine. I added a little sweetener, stirred, and sipped. It was my turn to keep an eye on him over the rim of my cup.

What I saw was hardly helpful. Will pulled himself out of his chair, picked up his cup, and walking with stuttering steps, took it over to a nearby trash can. He deep-sixed it, then came back for the ashtray and emptied that, too. It would have taken him no effort at all to pivot away from the table and go inside, and I knew it. I think he did, too. A muscle twitched in the left side of his face when he stopped back at the table. "Nobody ever found out what happened to Lucy," he said again.

There seemed to be no point in repeating myself, so I didn't bother to mention that that's why I was there. Instead, I looked over the guy who was nearly lost in the folds of the bulky black sweater. "You were an artist. That's what Ella told me."

He sat back down. I breathed a sigh of relief.

He pulled the photo closer and his gaze darted over it, from Lucy to Darren to Bobby to Janice to Ella, to the young Will Margolis. "Haven't done any drawing for a real long time."

"You were good."

"Ella was easily impressed."

"She says after Lucy disappeared, you stopped drawing."

"Stopped doing a lot of things after Lucy disappeared. It's a shock, you know?" He looked up at me. "One day you're a kid and the whole world looks like fun and games. And then a friend of yours, she up and vanishes . . . That changes a kid."

"It changed you." I let the silence settled for a second or two. "It changed Bobby Gideon, too."

His fingers trembling, he reached for the photo again. This time, he picked it up and held it a couple inches in front of his nose. "Bobby and me were buddies." He set the photo back down and sat lost in thought.

"He died about eighteen months after Lucy disappeared," I reminded him, even though something told me I didn't have to.

Will didn't say a word.

I inched my chair a little closer to the table. "Somebody told me Bobby's death wasn't exactly an accident."

His gaze snapped to mine. "Who?"

"I don't remember."

"You're a bad liar, Miss Pepper Martin." He took out another cigarette, but this time, he didn't light it. He rapped it against the table, watching me the whole time. "Whoever told you that, they were wrong."

"So it wasn't suicide by Nam?"

"It wasn't anything but a good kid dying too young."

"Like Lucy."

His gaze traveled back to the photo. "She was a nice kid."

I sat forward. "Ella? Or Lucy?"

He flicked the photo away. "Both of them. Not Janice. She was a piranha."

"Did she steal Darren away from Lucy?"

"You're kidding me, right? I can't remember that kind of stupid teenager stuff. Honey, there are days I can barely remember my own name."

"And that all started after Lucy disappeared."

"The sixties were wild."

"Is that why you became an addict? The sixties made me do it?"

He sniffled. "Yeah, it was something like that."

"Is that why Bobby went and got himself killed? Did the sixties make him do that, too?"

Will's fingers moved in an invisible pattern over the table. He dug an orange plastic lighter out of his pocket and lit up. "Bobby was stupid."

"Somebody I talked to told me he wasn't as stupid as he was guilty."

He wiped his nose with the back of his hand. "About what?"

"That's what I was hoping you could tell me."

"The only thing Bobby had to feel guilty about was not asking Susie McNamara to the prom. We called her Speedy Sue. He missed a golden opportunity. He would have gotten her in the sack for sure."

"I thought you didn't remember any of that stupid teen-ager stuff."

"Speedy Sue is hard to forget."

"I'll bet Lucy is, too."

He tapped one sneaker against the cement and flashed me a look. "Why you?"

I knew he was asking why Lucy was my business. "Why not?"

"It was a long time ago."

"People still care."

"Like Ella?"

"Like Ella." I flattened my hands against the tabletop. "I'll bet Lucy's family does, too. I bet there's not a day that goes by that they don't think about her. And wonder. If I could help clear things up—"

"I can't help you. Wish I could." I actually might have believed him if he hadn't gotten up so fast that he knocked over his chair. Or if he wasn't so anxious to get away from me, he hurried inside.

He left me to pick up the chair.

And ask myself a whole bunch of new questions.

I t should come as no big surprise that I also wanted to talk
to Janice Sherwin and Darren Andrews. In fact, I tried to
make appointments to see both of them and found, much to
my dismay, that my wit and charm—usually so helpful in
situations like this—did nothing to thaw the iceberg that
was Darren's secretary. I even tried the same ol' song and
dance and told her I was writing that thesis about Patrick
Monroe, but she wasn't exactly impressed. In fact, she
wasn't impressed at all. She reminded me that Darren Andrews was an important man with commitments to his family and his community. He didn't see just anybody (yeah,
she said that in a way that made it clear I was one of those
anybodies who was really a nobody). And my suggestion
that I might get together with him sometime that weekend
to chat? Well, let's just say I'd never heard a sigh that was
quite so monumental.

Janice was, thankfully, another story. She owned an up-scale real estate company in one of the high-class suburbs to the east, and as everyone knows, real estate agents are all about working on the weekends.

And if I fudged the truth just a tad and told her I was dying to see the two-million-dollar, seven-bedroom house she had listed not far from where I grew up?

She'd find out soon enough that I was lying. With any luck, it wouldn't be before we discussed the good old days, her relationship with Darren, and how much she remembered about that fateful night Lucy never made it home.

As much as it pained me to do anything on a Sunday before the sun was high in the sky, I made that appointment for early in the morning. See, I figured once afternoon hit, there would be other realtors in and out of the office, and clients, too. And if there were people around, Janice might not have time to sit and reminisce. Early, I figured we'd have all the time in the world.

Which only goes to prove how wrong I can some-times be.

But I'm getting ahead of myself.

Sherwin Realty had its own building, a modern little number that featured lots of glass and walls that gleamed in the early morning light as if they'd been dipped in stainless steel. It was located on a chunk of prime real estate, a medi-cal building on one side and, on the other, a strip of stores built to look like a Parisian street and featuring a couple of chichi women's boutiques, a designer shoe shop, a day spa, and a wine store, and oh, how I was dying to check them out!

First things first.

Mine was only one of two cars in the parking lot. Since the other was a late-model two-seater Audi shined to within an inch of its life with a rag top and vanity plates that said

TOP SELLER, I knew two things: (1) Janice was a go-getter who would do anything for a sale, including getting up at an ungodly hour to beat her client to the office, and (2) the real estate business isn't nearly as down in the dumps as everyone says it is.

I parked far enough away from the door so that if I had to drag this interview out and we actually went to look at that two-million-dollar house, Janice would be forced to do the driving. Then I got down to business.

The front door was unlocked and I stepped into a sleek reception area with carpeting the color of the outside walls. The receptionist's desk (empty at this time of the day) was glass, and the chairs in the waiting area were plush wingbacks in a color a couple shades darker than the carpeting. The room was under the keen eye of the woman whose portrait hung on the far wall. Janice Sherwin hadn't changed all that much from the girl with the beehive hairdo. She was slim, elegant, and her hair, cut stylishly short, was still the same bleached blond it had been back in the day. What was it Ella had said about Janice? That she was a hard sort of pretty? She had that down pat. Janice Sherwin, with her firm chin and eyes that glinted fire, did not look like a woman who would stand to be crossed, in business or in her personal life.

I told myself not to forget it.

"Hello!" I called out, because I figured Janice the dynamo was probably already knee-deep in some project and would need the reminder that I was there. "I'm here to see Janice Sherwin."

There was no reply.

I moved through the reception area. There was a conference room on my left, its walls covered with pictures of expensive homes. Most of them had the words SOLD and JANICE plastered over them. Beyond that and past the recep-

tion desk was a long hallway, and I headed that way. The
doors on either side of me were closed, but the door to the
office at the end of the hallway was open. Sunlight spilled
through the windows and into the hallway, cut off now and
again by a long, thin shadow that swayed to and fro.

Kinetic sculpture, I told myself.

Leaves of a large plant.

Janice on the phone, waving her arms back and forth
while she was trying to make a point. And close a deal.

But like I said before, though it doesn't happen often,
there are times I can be dead wrong.

This was one of them.

That shadow was Janice Sherwin herself. Or at least it
was her body.

She was hanging from the ceiling fan above her desk.

I guess she wouldn't be showing me that two-million-
dollar house after all.

Of course I called the cops. Naturally, they hustled me
into that conference room, closed the door, and left
me there to think and wonder and try to see as much as I
possibly could out of the long thin window beside the door.
Which wasn't a whole lot.

When a middle-aged detective with a thin face and a
sharp eye finally came in to interview me an hour or so later,
he made it pretty clear he was convinced Janice had committed suicide.

Me? I wasn't so sure.

First Bobby, and now Janice? Two suicides in a group of
friends that also included a murder victim?

Call me crazy, but this was starting to sound a little too
coincidental.

And I am not a big believer in coincidences.

When the detective asked what I was doing there and I explained, I left out all the stuff about Lucy and the Beatles concert. Better he should believe I was a house hunter than to suspect I was some sort of busybody who had poked her nose into his case long before he knew he had one. Besides, I didn't want to advance any theories—with anyone—until I had a chance to come up with some that made at least a little bit of sense.

When I gave the cop all my contact information and finally got the OK to leave, I peeled rubber getting out of the parking lot of Sherwin Realty. Too bad it wasn't as easy to leave the memory behind . . . the one of Janice's body swinging gently back and forth in the current of the office AC, that pretty face of hers bloated, her tongue protruding, her skin blue and her bleached blond hair a mess.

There was only one way to deal with keeping that picture out of my head, and since shopping wasn't an option given the balance in my bank account and the fact that I had more pressing matters to attend to, I headed downtown. Sunday and no traffic. I got to Stella Maris in no time.

I smiled my brightest at the receptionist at the inpatient desk.

It was an expression that didn't last when in answer to my inquiry, she said, "Will Margolis is no longer a patient here."

"But I was just here yesterday," I said. Really, like that was going to make any difference? I took the whine out of my voice. "He said this time he was committed to making his rehab work. But he didn't tell me he was done with it. Don't you think he would have mentioned that?"

"Mr. Margolis checked himself out yesterday evening." The woman was young, heavyset, and trying to be as matter-of-fact about this as she was able, but considering I kept shaking my head and giving her *huh?* looks, I think I was throwing her off her game.

"He's cured?"

It was a reasonable question so she shouldn't have clicked her tongue. "An alcoholic is never cured," she said, the emphasis on that last word. "An alcoholic is always in recovery. Alcoholism is a disease, and the alcoholic—"

"Whatever." It wasn't like I didn't care, I just didn't have time for a lecture. "Did he say where he was going?"

It took her a moment to realize we were still talking about Will. She raised both her chins. "That information is confidential."

"But a friend of his just died, and he really needs to know about it. And I really need to talk to him about it."

"Like I said—"

"Confidential. Yeah. But if he mentioned where he was going—"

"Even if he did . . ."

"Which means he didn't." This was a pretty clever deduction on my part, so I didn't appreciate it when she rewarded me with a sneer. Still, I managed a smile. It was as stiff as Janice's hair in that old picture. "If you can't tell me where he went, then maybe you could tell me how to get in touch with Will."

"Like I said, even if I knew—"

"You wouldn't tell me. Right." Just like I don't believe in coincidences, I'm not a big fan of beating around the bush. I kept my tight smile in place as my own special way of saying thanks for nothing and headed for the door. Before I got there, I saw that there were a couple guys sitting out on the Recovery Coffee House patio. I grabbed a couple of bucks out of my purse in case anybody needed a cup of coffee and joined them.

"You all must know Will Margolis." There were three men seated at the table, and only one empty chair. I dropped into it like I'd been invited. "I hear he's gone."

"Will's been long gone since I met him." An African-American man with a hospital gauze patch over his left eye chuckled. Even with only one eye, he gave me a slow and careful once-over. "You don't look like Will's type."

"Who is his type? I mean, if he was going somewhere, who would he go with? Or go to?" I looked from man to man, and when nobody said a word and nobody looked like they were going to say a word, I asked, "Anybody need a cup of coffee?"

His face was as lived-in as a fleabag motel, but I could tell by his eyes that the man directly across from me wasn't much older than thirty-five. He kept his eyes on the dollars I put on the table. "Need a pack of smokes more than I need coffee," he said.

Subtle, but I got the message.

I wasn't sure how much cigarettes cost. I dug out a twenty and kept my hand on it when I looked from man to man. "Was Will ready to leave here? Did he finish his rehab?"

The man with the eye patch didn't so much shrug as he twitched away my question. "Been making good progress. That's just what I told Will yesterday when I saw him at lunchtime in the cafeteria. He's been tryin' hard and workin' hard, and I told him that, too. Told him this time, I thought he'd make it."

"But you don't think that anymore?"

This time, he did shrug. "Can't say. Will, he's the only one who knows that. But he never said anything to me about leavin', that's for sure. Then I go up to his room last night to ask him if he wants to step out and have a smoke, and he's gone."

I thought this over. "Did he leave alone?" I asked.

The men looked at each other. I dug back into my purse and came up with a ten.

"It's my last one," I said, slapping it on the table. "And payday isn't until Friday, so don't think you can hold out and get more. Did Will leave alone?"

"He got a call yesterday evening." This was from the one man who'd been silent. He was tall and as thin as a Giorgio Armani silk tie, and he tapped the table with nervous fingers, just like I'd seen Will do. "Next thing I knew, he said he was outta here. Said a friend was coming by for him."

"Did he say who the friend was?"

The man shook his head.

I tried another approach. "Did any of you see him leave?"

Apparently, this was asking too much. All three men stared at me, speechless.

And I knew a losing cause when I saw one.

I got up from the table.

And left the money there.

I was already at the door and on my way out when the man with the eye patch stopped me.

"We've been talkin'," he said, glancing over his shoulder toward his buddies. "And . . . well . . . if it's your last one, you'd better just keep it." He thrust the ten into my hands.

I actually might have argued with him if he didn't turn around and walk away, and if my attention wasn't caught by a flash of color across the street.

Green. The same shade as a familiar stocking cap.

I hurried out of the café and picked my way down the

sidewalk and across the street, heading toward the alley where I'd seen the movement.

There was nobody there.

There was nobody around anywhere.

In fact, the only sign of life on that deserted street was an empty bottle of Seagram's VO on the sidewalk.

I didn't want to wait until Monday to talk to Darren Andrews, but it's not like I had a whole lot of choice. Guys like Andrews aren't exactly listed on the Internet phonebook sites, and girls like me do not hang out at places where we are likely to cross paths. Yeah, I used to. In the old days. These days, the country club set and I aren't exactly on speaking terms.

With all that in mind, I waited semipatiently for the workweek to roll around. When it finally did, I went through the Monday-morning-motions over at Garden View. (That week, these included doing my best to console Ella as I watched her weep into her teacup when she talked about Janice and the old days.) I took an early lunch hour, headed out, and arrived at Darren's downtown office building full of determination, even if I didn't have much of a plan about how I was going to get in to see him.

I was in luck.

Maybe.

When I pulled into the lot next to the gleaming high-rise with the words ANDREWS ENTERPRISES etched into the granite facade, I saw that there was something going on right outside the front doors.

TV cameras. Reporters. Sound trucks.

For one gut-twisting moment, I was sure Darren Andrews

was dead, too, and the media was all over the event, and I kicked myself for not being pushier with his secretary. If the guy bit the big one before I ever had a chance to talk to him, I'd be at another dead end. Literally.

And I'd had my fill.

I grabbed my leather portfolio off the passenger seat, hopped out of my car, and took my place at the edge of the crowd. I saw that at least part of my thinking had been correct: Darren Andrews was the center of all that attention, all right. Lucky for me, it wasn't because he was dead. In fact, he was in the middle of a news conference.

Glaring cameras, microphones, reporters . . . any normal guy would break out in a sweat, or at least look a little humbled by all that attention. Darren Andrews? Not so much.

He was still as golden as he was back in his high school days. Smooth and shiny and as well dressed as my dad used to be before he exchanged his Versace suits for prison issue. Darren smiled at the cameras, pointed to reporters, and fielded their questions, and I did my best to stay out of the way so I could get a sense of the man behind the legend just as a young woman in an ill-fitting gray jacket raised her hand and asked, "Are you saying, Mr. Andrews, that you don't think new construction would be good for the Flats?"

Of course, I was coming in right in the middle of things, and I had no idea what was going on. That didn't keep me from seeing the momentary flash of annoyance in Darren's baby blues. *Momentary* being the operative word here. The next second, he was as smooth as the glass doors behind him. Too bad he wasn't as transparent. I would have loved to know what was going on behind that unruffled exterior.

"It's like this, Taylor . . ." He turned a thousand-watt smile on the reporter. She was young, and she blushed like all get-out. "Of course I believe that the Flats is a viable site for revitalization. In fact, I'm committed to making that happen. I see the area as being a hub for entertainment and transportation and I'm as excited as anybody else that developers are talking about condos and cluster homes and retail space. But . . ." He glanced at the reporters gathered all around him. "That doesn't mean we throw the baby out with the bath water. There are plenty of solid buildings down in the Flats already. We don't have to knock them down and start rebuilding. They've got artistic value, historic value. We can build on the foundation we've already established."

"Including that building on Main Street? The one you own?"

This came from a male reporter in a rumpled denim shirt, and looking his way, Darren nodded.

"Yes, I'm certainly talking about the Andrews Building. Like dozens of others the city has improperly acquired through eminent domain, that building is safe and sturdy. Like those dozens of others, it never should have been targeted, and the courts never should have let the city take possession of them. The mayor talks about the good of the people and the rights of citizens to live and work in a modern, thriving community, but let's face it . . ." Here he looked directly at the cameras, delivering a personal message to each and every person who would be watching the evening news. "This is all about greed. It's all about the mayor trying to make himself look good. When he's doing it at the expense of the people he's supposed to be working for . . . well, that's just not right."

"Is that why you're considering running for mayor in the fall?" a bald guy asked.

Andrews raised a hand, distancing himself from the question. "That's a topic for another day. What we need to do now is focus, the way this city administration is not focusing. We need to address one pressing issue at a time. That's why I invited you here today. I want you and all the property owners in Cleveland, who are in fear of their rights being slapped out from under them, to know that I'm going to move heaven and earth to get an injunction against the city's eminent domain decree. I'll go all the way to the U.S. Supreme Court if I have to. And you know me, folks . . ." He turned a smile on the reporters, one so bright, I had no doubt that everybody who'd be watching at home would feel its warmth. "I don't give up. And I don't back down. I never have, and I never will."

"Let's put it all on the line here, Darren . . ." A middle-aged woman with big hips and a pointy chin stepped forward. It was clear—at least to me—that the two of them had sparred over this subject before. But then, maybe I was the only one who saw that flash erupt again in Darren's eyes.

Or maybe that reporter saw it, too. Maybe she just didn't care. "What we need to know," she said, "is if you're really looking after the good of the people, or if you're just mad that the city didn't give you as much for that building as you could have gotten from one of the developers."

Darren swiveled to face her. "Come on, Mary Linda, you know me better than that. You know that's not a fair assessment. If the city had legitimate reasons to seize property— any property, even mine—I'd be the first to support their efforts. But *legitimate* . . . that's the key here. Revitalization or no revitalization, I'm going to use every legal means to make sure the city isn't overstepping its legal bounds. That's the democratic way. It's the American way. And now . . ." When he backstopped toward the doors, it was clear the interview was over.

I couldn't wait until the reporters shuffled away. When

Darren pushed through the doors and stepped into the lobby, I was right behind him.

Good thing I'd pulled out all the stops and my best black suit. One look at the smile on Darren's face when he spotted me, and I knew he appreciated nothing but the best. But then, my skirt was short, my heels were high, and the V-neck cami I wore under my nip-waisted jacket was a golden color that was sure to put a spark in any guy's eyes.

"You're not one of the reporters I've met before. You must be new in town." Darren stuck out his hand.

I moved my leather portfolio from my right hand to my left, shook his, and offered a smile that was polite enough for business and personal enough to make him sit up and take notice. Not that I was coming on to him or anything. Yikes, the guy was like sixty years old! No matter, old or young, guys were guys, and as I'd learned in a lifetime of getting my way, guys who were busy looking into a woman's eyes (or at her boobs) were far more likely to cooperate. No matter what she wanted.

I kept my smile in place. "I'm not a reporter. My name is Pepper Martin, and I'd like a couple minutes to talk to you."

He glanced over my shoulder toward the sidewalk, where the reporters were still taking their good ol' time to pack up and get out of there. "If you're not a reporter . . ." His gaze swung back in my direction. "What do you want?"

"Did you hear about Janice Sherwin?"

Oh yeah, I was bold enough to pull that out of thin air. No small talk. No niceties. Then again, I was hoping to study his reaction.

Too bad he didn't give me much of one.

"A shame," he said. Since his brows dipped and he shook his head, I guess it meant any hopes I'd had that he'd confess that he'd strung Janice up (honestly, I didn't, but a girl can dream) were dashed. "Janice was an old and dear friend and a successful and capable woman. She forged her way in a man's profession long before that was common." He looked to my closed portfolio. "If you were taking notes, I'd tell you to quote me on that."

I smiled as if this was terribly clever. (See above and my theory about how to get a guy talking. You'd think they'd be clever enough to see the difference between honest admiration and blatant flattery. Then again, the longer they didn't, the longer I would be able to bluff my way through my investigations.)

"Like I said, I'm not a reporter. I am, however, looking for information."

He pursed his lips, waiting to hear more, and in the interest of getting back to the element of surprise, I didn't waste any time. "Have you seen Will Margolis?"

"I can't say I have. At least not for forty-five years or so."

So much for surprise. Andrews was as coolheaded as . . . well, as if he was expecting someone to come around and ask about Will.

I thought this over at the same time I wondered how a man as busy and important as Andrews didn't even have to scramble to remember a kid from so long ago. Since there didn't seem to be much point in trying to figure it out, I clutched my portfolio to my chest and said, "You're not surprised that I asked about Will."

"Should I be? First you mention Janice, then Will. The next thing I know, you're going to ask me about—"

"Lucy Pasternak?"

He stood as still as a statue. I swear, he didn't even breathe. I knew this for a fact because his red-and-gray-striped tie never budged. In fact, it took like what seemed forever before he twitched his shoulders, shaking away his surprise. "I thought for sure you were going to say Bobby. Bobby Gideon, he was another of my old high school friends."

"Yeah, I know. Do you think he committed suicide?"

Now that he'd had a chance to get used to the fact that there was more to me than eye candy, he was as poised as he'd been outside in front of the cameras. He pursed his lips, thinking. "Is there someone who says he did?" he asked.

"Did Janice commit suicide?"

When Darren laughed, the skin around his eyes crinkled. I recognized the signs; he spent lots of time on sunny golf courses. "You're full of questions, but you should know the answer to that one. The coroner's ruling isn't in yet. That was mentioned in this morning's paper. You'd think a person as curious as you would be thorough, too." Another glance outside, and I saw a look very much like relief sweep his expression. I looked, too.

The reporters were gone, and a young guy in a navy suit was just getting out of the aquamarine convertible he'd left idling in front of the building in a spot clearly marked NO PARKING.

"'Sixty-five Mustang. In Tropical Turquoise!" This was the stuff dreams were made of, and I practically swooned.

It was apparently the first thing I'd done that actually impressed Darren. He gave me another once-over, this time with admiration in his eyes. "You know your cars."

I wasn't actually trying to come across as cute, but I guess when I shrugged and my suit jacket rode up and my cami tugged tight over my breasts, I couldn't help it. "I've got a newer Mustang," I said, leaving out the model year since it wasn't old enough to be a classic but not new enough to be hot. "Mine's not a convertible."

"Maybe someday you'll join me for a ride."

I guess this wasn't the day. He started outside but seemed to sense that I was right behind him, because his shoulders went rigid.

"So there's nothing you can tell me." I figured it wouldn't hurt to remind him what we were talking about in the first place. "Nothing about Janice? Or Will? Or Bobby? Or Lucy?"

He paused, the fingers of his right hand tented and perched against the hood of the Mustang. "You weren't even born when I knew those people. Why do you want to know about them?"

I stepped closer. "I could tell you I was writing my thesis about Patrick Monroe," I said.

"The poet." He'd apparently missed that subtle *could*, and I didn't point it out.

"Yeah, the one who used to teach at Shaker."

"Of course, you came across Lucy's name in relation to that hippie nutcase." He nodded, confirming the information to himself. "There are people who think Monroe had something to do with Lucy's disappearance, you know."

"Do you?"

"I always wondered. And that . . ." He shook a finger at me. "That is not for the record, and if I see it in print anywhere, you're going to be sued for libel so fast, your head will spin."

"No print," I told him. "No quotes. I'm just looking for opinions. Impressions."

"And you want to know more about Lucy. I understand. How much do you know already?"

"I know you two were dating."

He moved around to the other side of the car. "True or

not," he said, "I'm not sure why that's relevant forty-five years after the fact."

"Neither am I," I admitted. "But I figured you were the kind of person who would appreciate knowing what I know."

"And you know . . ."

"Not a whole lot more than that." I hated having to admit it. "Is there anything you can tell me about Lucy's murder?"

"Murdered? Was she? If you're trying to get your facts in order . . . and really, you should . . . you're going to have to go back to square one. Lucy Pasternak disappeared. She was never seen or heard from again. No one ever determined that she was murdered."

"Yeah, see . . . that's where I'm kind of stuck. That's why I thought maybe you could help."

"Really, I don't see how I can." He opened the driver's door. "In fact, I'm a little confused about why you thought I could."

And I knew a brush-off when I saw it. I scrambled to say anything that might keep him there. "You were with Lucy. At the Beatles concert that night."

"And with my friends for hours and hours after."

"And now three of them are dead. And one of them is missing."

"You mean Lucy."

"I mean Will."

The top was down on the car so I could hear him perfectly even after he got in. His voice purred. Just like the Mustang's engine. "Then I guess I'll need to be careful nothing happens to me."

By the time I got home from work the next day then went out to grab a bite to eat at the closest greasy spoon, it was all over the news.

No, not the stuff about me striking out in the information department with Darren Andrews on Monday afternoon.

The stuff about how Winston Churchill had been spotted in one of the neighborhoods near downtown and how the police were closing in on him.

I lived in one of those neighborhoods near downtown, so this was not necessarily good news for me. Then again, when I got home that evening, there weren't any cop cars around. No SWAT teams, either.

That should have been encouraging. It was. At least when it came to Winston Churchill.

Then again, the absence of police meant that nobody saw anything, and nobody came to take a report (not for hours and hours, anyway) when I arrived home and found that my door had been bashed in and my apartment had been ransacked.

L eave it to Ella to be the one and only person I knew who could bustle around a cemetery trash can sorting recyclables from throwaway-ables and still take the time to be concerned about me. "You must have been terrified!"

"I was surprised." Understatement. When I realized that someone had broken into my apartment, I was more like flabbergasted. At least in the nanosecond before I was royally pissed. "Everything was pawed through. It was creepy."

Ella had a plastic iced tea bottle in one hand and a wadded-up piece of aluminum foil in the other. When she stopped what she was doing long enough to see that I was doing absolutely nothing, I knew what she wanted. She might be concerned—about me, my safety, and my possessions—but that didn't excuse me from not doing my part.

There was a different trash can in front of me, and just to make it look like I was a team player, I bent over it and, with two fingers, plucked out a paper coffee cup. "Jim's kidding about this recycling stuff, isn't he?"

She sorted her found objects into neat piles. "We need to do all we can to help. If we're diligent about going through what people throw away, we can get money for some of it."

"And get cooties from the rest." I peered into the trash can and made a face when I saw a half-eaten sandwich and an empty bag of potato chips staring back at me. Knee-jerk reaction. I backed away, scraping my hands against the legs of my pants, just in case any of those cooties decided to hitch a ride. "Can't do it," I said.

"You've got to. We all have to pitch in and—"

"Get E. coli?"

I should have known Ella wouldn't let something like a deadly disease stand in her way. Not when she was on a mission. We were in a back room of the administration building, and when she continued to stare at me, and tap her foot, too, I folded like a flip phone. I grabbed a pen from a nearby desk and poked it through the garbage, careful not to get too close. Or too much of a whiff of what smelled like rotten fruit. There was a discarded Coke can in there somewhere—I saw the flash of red—and hoping that a show of good sportsmanship and this one piece of garbage Jim could turn into cash would change Ella's mind about this ridiculous quest, I snared the can with the tip of the pen.

"I'll bring gloves for you tomorrow," Ella said.

When I dropped the soda can, it landed right back where it came from. "We're going to do this again tomorrow?"

"Now, Pepper . . ." I hate when Ella starts a sentence like that. Any sentence. "It doesn't hurt to help," she said. "And we won't have to worry about these sorts of cost-cutting measures forever. Besides, keeping busy will take your mind off that burglary at your apartment."

"I don't think it's a burglary if nothing is taken," I said, repeating back what the uniformed cop who finally showed up at my place told me. In my mind, I watched a replay of the scene: the cop walking me through my place, room by room, asking me what was touched, what might be missing.

My bedroom was almost exactly the way I had left it, but believe me, when it comes to my wardrobe, I know what's what. The skirts hanging from the lowest rod in the closet had been shoved to one side, and the shoes on my closet floor were jumbled.

As if someone had been looking for something in there. I thought about this, realized I was tapping my hand against the side of the trash can as I did, and jumped back. Where was a bottle of hand sanitizer when I needed it?

"It was all there," I said, thinking out loud because it beat doing what I was supposed to be doing. "My jewelry. And my TV. And my MP3 player. And—"

I froze.

"What?" Ella darted forward. "You look like you've just seen a ghost."

If she only knew!

I shook off the thought. "My leather portfolio was on the kitchen table when I left the apartment to go to dinner," I told her. "And it wasn't there when I got back."

"Somebody broke into your apartment to take your leather portfolio?"

Yeah, it did sound weird, so I didn't blame her for using that tone of voice.

"I know it was there," I said, but of course, I didn't. I mean, I have a busy life, and it's pretty hard to keep track of stuff that isn't very important in the first place. Like the leather portfolio no self-respecting burglar would want. "I had it when I went to Patrick Monroe's poetry reading. And I had it when I went to see Will, and Janice, and Darren. But it's not there anymore."

Ella's eyes shone. "What does it mean? Do you think it has anything to do with Lucy?"

This, I couldn't say. But, oh, I intended to find out!

W orking in the cemetery biz like I do, I'm pretty used to funerals. They are not often—thankfully—the funerals of women whose bodies I find hanging in their offices. When I cut out of my own office the next afternoon so that Ella didn't have to go to Janice's funeral alone, I told myself I was not allowed to think about the whole body-swinging-from-the-fan thing. I was there to support Ella. Pure and simple.

And if I could do a little investigating while I was at it, that would be a real plus.

As luck would have it, the Sherwin family had a plot right at Garden View. Ella and I didn't have to drive far in her car, and that, too, was a lucky thing. That day, Ella was quiet, and when she wasn't quiet, she was weepy, and when she wasn't weepy, she sat staring off into space. I guess I couldn't blame her. The morning's paper had reported that the county coroner had announced that Janice's death was a homicide. Don't ask me how they figure out these things, but they know, and personally, I wasn't all that surprised by the ruling. Ella, predictably, was more shaken than ever. I knew she wouldn't begin to put any of it behind her and get back to her ol' Ella self until the funeral was over.

Then again, with all those memories about Lucy at the surface and no closure in regards to her disappearance or her body, I wondered if anything would ever be the same for Ella.

When we neared the line of cars parked along a shady, curved lane, I automatically looked for the turquoise Mustang. Ella hadn't spoken a word all the way from the administration building and the silence was starting to get to me. I said out loud, "Darren Andrews isn't here." The sigh that escaped her brought her back from wherever her thoughts had wandered.

"He's a busy man. And for all we know, he and Janice haven't seen each other in years. There's no reason he should be here."

No reason, except that if he was, I would have had the chance to corner him and ask a few more questions.

We parked and picked our way across the lumpy ground to a place where a couple dozen somber-faced people were gathered around a fancy-schmancy copper coffin. Good for Janice for being successful. Too bad she didn't have more of a chance to enjoy it.

"We're gathered here today . . ." The minister started into the service. He looked too young to be out of college.

I tuned out.

At least to the prayers and the thoughts and reflections of the people who stepped forward to say a few words about Janice.

But then, I was too busy glancing around, wondering how much any of these people knew about the woman they were there to honor, and if anything they knew might shed some light on Janice and Bobby's deaths, Will's disappearance, and Lucy's missing body.

When I realized I wasn't the only one eyeballing the crowd, I guess I must have flinched, because Ella mouthed the words, "What is it? What's wrong?"

I backed away from the service, holding up a finger to signal that I'd return in a moment. It seemed simpler than telling her that her youngest daughter—who most definitely should have been at school at that time of the afternoon—wasn't as unobtrusive as I bet she thought she was. But then, she was standing on the roof of a mausoleum about fifty yards away and watching the proceedings through a pair of binoculars.

I skirted the cluster of mourners, circled around to the other side of the grave, ducked behind a couple head-tall tombstones, and sidled between a gray granite monument with an angel at the top of it and a pink marble bench.

Here's the thing about sneaking up on someone using binoculars—they're so busy looking into the distance, they don't know what's going on right in from of them. When I cleared my throat, I thought Ariel was going to tumble off that roof.

"The cemetery's insurance company would have a fit if they knew you were up there," I told her while she was still trying to catch her breath. "And your mother would have a coronary. And not just because she'd be worried about you. That mausoleum is over a hundred years old. I bet it's a national treasure or something. Come on down." I held out one hand to help. "And do it carefully. If you fall and break something, your mom will kill me."

"Only if you tell her."

"What, that you fell and broke something?" I watched Ariel crab-step to the edge of the mausoleum roof and skitter down the side, just waiting for her to fall and break that unnamed something. When she landed on her feet, none the worse for wear, I let go the breath I was holding. "What the hell—"

"Is that any way to talk at a funeral?" Ariel grinned. She was dressed in jeans and a dark T-shirt. Her red locks were wound into a braid, and those binoculars hung around her neck. She'd stashed a canvas bag near the mausoleum door and she went and got it, pulled out a legal pad, and scribbled some notes.

"What are you doing?" I had to fight to keep my voice down. Sounds carry in a quiet cemetery, and I didn't want to interrupt the funeral. "And why aren't you in school? And what are you doing here?"

She finished what she was writing. "I'm investigating, of course. You heard Janice was murdered, right?"

I nodded.

"And I can't believe you don't think that has something to do with our other case."

"*We* don't have another case."

She was not one for subtleties. "That's why you're here, isn't it?" she asked. "To investigate?"

"I'm here because your mother shouldn't be at the funeral of a friend all by herself. And now she is all by herself, because I didn't want to be standing over there"—I pointed—"and watch you over here"—I swung my outstretched arm in the other direction—"taking a tumble off that mausoleum and breaking your neck. And what do you mean, anyway? What do you mean you're investigating?"

"I'm starting my own private investigation firm. You know, like the one you have."

"Except I don't have a private investigation firm."

"But you investigate. Privately."

"Sometimes, yes. But not because I want to."

She folded her arms over her chest. It was the first time I noticed that she must have made a trip to Victoria's Secret for one of those push-up bras with the gel cup inserts. Ariel had curves! "You want to keep all the business for yourself."

"I don't. I don't even want the business I have. Not most of the time, anyway. But this time I do, because this time is different. I want to help your mom find out what happened to her friends. But investigating . . ." I glanced back toward the gravesite. While I'd been busy keeping Ariel from doing a header off the mausoleum, the funeral service had already broken up. Some of the mourners were standing in knots and talking softly. Others were headed to their cars. "Investigating is exactly what I'm not doing."

"Then what are you waiting for, girlfriend?" So much for the power of a lecture from me. Laughing, Ariel took off toward Janice's gravesite. "I'll bet one of those people over there is the murderer, but we're not going to know until we grill every one of them."

She could move pretty quick. But then, she was a dozen years younger than me and she was wearing sneakers. By the time I got back over to the funeral, Ariel had managed to buttonhole a white-haired granny.

Not the murderer type, I was sure of it. But Ariel didn't need to know that. While she was busy chasing red herrings, I might actually be able to get down to business.

Ella was speaking to the minister, and I fully intended to join them and see what he could tell me about the people in attendance when I saw a familiar face watching the goings-on from behind a shaggy rhododendron.

As funerals went, this looked like the one the uninvited wanted to crash.

This time, there was no mausoleum roof involved so at least I didn't have to worry about broken bones. I did have to worry that Will Margolis would catch sight of me closing in on him and take off running before I had a chance to corner him. I quickened my pace, coming around at him from the side and stopping by a headstone taller than me when I got within five feet of him. Before he noticed me, I took a moment to gather my thoughts, and watched him watch the crowd.

For a moment, Will's gaze rested on where the casket glinted in the afternoon sun. Then it traveled over to the left, to the spot where I'd seen Ella and the minister only a minute before. The minister was walking back to his car, and Ella stood there all alone. She bowed her head, took a pink rose from the spray of flowers that had been left next to the grave, and set the flower on Janice's casket. When she stepped back, the sun glistened against the tears on her cheeks.

Rather than deal with the sudden lump in my throat, I looked back at Will. Since the last time I saw him, the left sleeve of his black cardigan had been ripped, and there was a smear of something muddy looking—like dried blood—across the front of it. The color matched the scrape on his right cheek and accented the dark circles under his eyes. The hair that hung out from the back of his stocking cap was limp and greasy. My guess? It hadn't seen a drop of shampoo since that day I'd gone to see him at the rehab center.

Ready to run after him if he bolted, I stepped closer. "You look like hell, Will," I said.

"Feel like hell, too," he said. He didn't look surprised to see me. In fact, he didn't look anything but lost and miserable. He swiped the cuff of his sweater under his nose before he turned to face me.

"I went over to the center to look for you. Where have you been?"

There was a couple days' growth of beard on his face and he scraped a hand over it. "Thought I was really going to make it this time."

"That doesn't mean you can't try again."

"I dunno." He shifted from foot to foot. "Can't remember where I've been. Or what I've been doing. Can't remember much of anything. I woke up this morning behind some downtown bank and my face hurt like the devil." He touched a finger to the raw, swollen skin of his right cheek. "Don't even remember who I was fighting with, but I guess I lost, huh? And then I walked by one of those buildings with the newsstand on the first floor. And I saw this morning's paper. And the picture of Janice." His cheeks went ashen, and I knew I had to keep him focused or I'd lose him.

I dared to step closer. "Do you remember when you left the rehab center on Saturday? Where did you go, Will? And why did you leave?"

His shoulders trembled. He shook his head.

"I'll bet if you try hard, you can remember. Maybe someone came and got you? Asked you to do something?"

Will twitched. "You mean something like kill Janice?"

I guess Will and I had something in common after all. He wasn't one to beat around the bush, either. "It wouldn't be your fault," I said, and hoped what I was trying to make sound like quiet reassurance would work its magic. "Not if that person made you do it. Not if he took advantage of you."

His head moved faster, back and forth. "I didn't kill her. No. Not me. Not this time."

My breath caught behind the ball of anticipation that made it hard to breathe. I forced out the words, nice and slow. "Are you telling me—"

"Not telling you anything." Will's face twisted. His cheeks flushed as muddy red as that wound on his face. He paced over to a marble headstone with a lamb carved on top of it, and his voice was choked and angry. I swear, he wasn't talking to me. I don't think he even remembered I was there. Will was talking to himself. To his demons. And his voice rose and echoed against the gravestones all around us.

"I'm not telling anybody anything," he yelled. "I never have. I never have, that's what I said. And still, Janice is dead. And Bobby's dead. And Lucy . . ." His eyes cleared and he froze, and aimed a laser look in my direction. "You know Lucy's dead, too, don't you?"

"I do know that." I took another step in his direction, but as soon as I did, he started up again. He stomped out the distance between the lamb gravestone and the bush he'd been hiding behind to watch the funeral service, and I scrambled for a way to calm him down and keep him talking. No easy thing considering he was sobbing now. He swallowed gulps of air and moaned.

"How do you know Lucy is dead, Will?" I asked him. "Did someone tell you? Or did you—"

He stopped, as still as the statue that watched us from a nearby monument. He didn't look my way. Will looked down at the grass at his feet, then up to the dome of blue sky over our heads. He balled his hands into fists and flexed his fingers, and balled them up again, and he pounded them against his own chest. "I know, I know, I know," he wailed. "But I'm not telling. I'm not going to tell. I'm not ever going to tell."

I was so busy wondering what on earth I could do to calm him down, I didn't realize we weren't alone until Ella stepped up beside me.

"Hello, Will," she said.

With the cuff of his sweater, Will wiped away the tears on his cheeks. He gasped for breath, choked, coughed.

Ella's expression didn't give away a thing, and even as I watched her take a step closer to him, I wondered. Was she disappointed to see what the years had done to Will? Repulsed by him? Had she already called cemetery security and asked them to hightail it over there and toss the guy out onto the street?

"I'm glad you came," she said, and since *glad* was something I hadn't even considered, I could only watch and go on wondering. "Janice would have liked that."

"She's dead." His voice, so blistering just moments before, was no more than a whisper. His shoulders were stooped. He hung his head. "She doesn't know nothing. Janice is dead."

"I like to think that the dead still watch us."

That sure wasn't me who spoke. I knew the dead *did* watch us, and thinking about it was enough to give me a major case of the willies.

"Do you believe that, Will?" Ella tipped her head, watching him, and when he didn't move and he didn't say a thing, she smiled. "We've got a lot of catching up to do, don't we? It's late." It wasn't, and since she looked at her watch, she should have known this. "I've got work to do at home this evening and I know I won't have time to make dinner. I was just going to head over to the Academy Tavern for a burger. You want to come along?"

He didn't say yes, but he didn't say no, either, not even when Ella wrapped her arm through Will's. Side by side, they walked over to where her car was parked.

"Where's my mom going with that weird guy?" I glanced to my left to see that Ariel had been watching, too. She made a face. "You're not going to let her get into the car with him, are you? Are you nuts, Pepper? He's dirty and crummy. He's disgusting." She darted forward, eager to follow Ella and stop her.

I clamped a hand on her shoulder to keep her in place. "He's not disgusting," I said. "He's an old friend."

14

Remind me next time one of the not-so-dearly departed needs my help . . . it's not a good idea to get involved with a ghost stuck in a place that requires an admission charge.

With Ella gone, I knew nobody would miss me, so I dug the last of my dollar bills out of my purse, cut out of work early, and hopped on the rapid.

The Indians had an evening game scheduled, the rapid was heading downtown, and I found one of the last empty seats, but lucky for me, the guy sitting next to me got off at the next stop. Just as soon as he did, Lucy materialized in the seat next to me out of the nowhere ghosts go when they aren't hanging around complicating my life.

"We've got a lot to talk about." Yes, I had my cell out and up to my ear. Better that than having people stare at me the way the mourners leaving the funeral gaped at Ella and Will when they walked to her car together. "I had a talk with Darren."

She didn't look surprised. But then, I imagine once you've been kidnapped and murdered, everything else is pretty small potatoes in the taken-by-surprise department.

"Does he miss me?" Lucy asked.

I was not in the mood for teenaged drama. "Why did you break up with him?"

Lucy pressed her golden lips together.

"Fine." I slapped my hand down on my lap. "If that's the way you want to be, let's see how successful you are at finding your own body. Especially since you're stuck on this train."

When the woman in the seat in front of me looked over her shoulder, her eyes wide and her mouth open, I realized the hand I'd slapped onto my lap was the one holding the phone. I quickly lifted it back up to my ear.

"Yeah, that's what I said," I growled into the phone. "Find your own body of evidence. Let's see you do that when you're stuck here on the train in rush hour."

Apparently, this satisfied her, because the woman spun back around. I lowered my voice and turned in my seat so I was facing Lucy.

"Why did you break up with him?" I asked her again, this time right into the phone, and in barely more than a whisper.

She tossed her head. "What difference does that make? It can't possibly have anything to do with my death. I was—"

"Murdered. Yeah. I know." I beat her to the drama punch and Lucy didn't like it. No one pouts as well as a teenaged girl. "He's sleazy."

I expected an eye roll. What I got instead was a sidelong

look that told me Lucy wasn't all that surprised to hear this news.

"What?" I inched closer. We weren't touching, but I could feel the icy aura that enveloped her. The chill hit me in little waves that sent goose bumps up my arms. "You're not surprised to hear me say that Darren is a scumbag. Is that what you're telling me? Does that mean him being sleazy, does that have something to do with why you broke up with him?"

She clicked her tongue. "What difference does it make? Darren didn't kill me."

"How do you know?"

"He got off the rapid before me with the rest of them."

"But he was mad at you. Because you broke up with him."

She shook her head. "Darren? He wasn't mad. In fact, I think he was relieved. See, I was the one who was mad. Darren . . . Well . . ." She drew in a breath. Or at least she would have if she were alive and breathing. "Darren was stealing tests," she said. "Don't ask me for details, I never did figure out how he was doing it or how he got away with it for so long. But he did. See, Darren wanted a bigger allowance, and Mr. Andrews wouldn't give it to him. He said Darren had to learn the value of hard work, that he had to realize that most people didn't get everything just handed to them. So Darren got ahold of those tests and started his own little business. History tests. Math tests. English tests. He'd sell the questions, he'd sell the answers. It was how he got enough money to buy that fancy car of his."

I remembered the Mustang. "And so . . ."

"So . . . that's it. That's all there is to it."

I didn't think so. There had to be more to any answer that came out that fast—and that definitive. "That still doesn't explain why you broke up with him."

Lucy's big blue eyes filled with tears. Her lower lip trembled. When she looked me over, she said, "You just don't get it, do you? I guess a girl who looks like you never would. In your whole life, you've probably never had trouble getting a boyfriend."

Getting them? No. It was keeping them that seemed to be my problem.

Rather than explain and risk getting into the whole thing—Joel, my ex-fiancé, and Dan, the paranormal researcher who'd left the country after we worked together to solve a case, and Quinn, of course—I glommed on to what I saw as the subtext of her comment. I studied Lucy's gorgeous, golden hair, those long, shapely legs shown to perfection by her miniskirt, that cute figure. "You had trouble getting boyfriends? No way!"

"Looks aren't everything. But then, you probably know that, too. I might have been cute, but I never knew when to keep my mouth shut. I had opinions. And I didn't keep them to myself. Back when I was growing up . . . well, that wasn't the way a girl was supposed to act, and when guys realized there was more to me than just my looks . . ." She shrugged like it was no big deal, but I knew it was.

I have a hard-and-fast rule about dealing with the dead: I never let them know what I'm thinking. At least when it comes to my love life. It keeps things simpler and it keeps them from butting their ectoplasmic noses in places they don't belong. I violated the rule and lowered my guard—just this one time. But then, I figured I owed it to the girl who'd never had a chance to get as old—or as wise—as me. "I had a guy walk out on me," I confessed. "Because I told him I talk to the dead."

"And he didn't believe you." Lucy shook her head in disgust. "I get it. I mean, I don't get how he could be so horrible, but I've seen it a thousand times. A girl speaks her mind, a boy can't handle it. Gosh, that's too bad, Pepper. I mean it." She sighed a sigh that didn't ripple the air between us. "I thought things would be different by now. I thought that's what the sixties were all about—all of us, men and women, young and old—finding our ways and our own true voices. That summer I died, I could feel the first quiverings of it in the air. Free love. Free speech. Free thought. Finally, I felt like I was going to fit in. Like I could speak up and guys wouldn't look at me like I had two heads. But I never had the chance to enjoy the freedom. I wasn't alive to be part of it. That's what the poem was all about, you know? Girl, crimson and golden, awake to the dawn. Alive to the pulse. The vibration. The beat."

Maybe that's what Lucy believed. Personally, I think Patrick Monroe was thinking of a whole different pulse and vibration when he wrote those words.

But I was getting philosophical. And toeing the edge of more than mildly disturbing when I thought of what Patrick Monroe must have been thinking of when he penned that poem.

"So what does you having trouble keeping a boyfriend have to do with Darren?" I asked her. "Unless you spoke your mind about something and he dumped you for it?" I knew that couldn't be possible since Lucy was the one who broke up with him. Besides, that was too much like what had happened to me and Quinn. I shivered at the thought.

Lucy's cheeks flushed. "Just the opposite," she admitted. "I found out he was selling test answers and I . . ." She glanced away. She folded her fingers together and clutched them in her lap. "We were just friends back when I first found out. We hung around in a group. Me and Darren and Bobby and Janice and Will. We'd go for Cokes after school, hang out at dances. You know, that kind of thing. But I'd had a secret crush on Darren since back in middle school. He liked me. As a friend. But I really wasn't Darren's type. He liked . . ." She gave me a sidelong look. "You know . . ." I had to lean closer to hear her when she whispered, "The bad girls. The loose girls. You know, like Janice."

This was news, though I can't say I was surprised. There was something about the bleached hair and the beehive that practically screamed, *Come and get it!*

Lucy was probably thinking the same thing. She lifted one shoulder to brush off the thought and got back on track. "I told Darren . . . well, you're going to think less of me."

She waited for me to deny this, and when all I did was wait for her to explain why she was suddenly chewing on her lower lip, she blurted it out. "I told Darren I was going to report him to the principal if he didn't go out with me."

"You blackmailed him into dating you?" All right, I'd never been that desperate. I'd never even been desperate enough to think of being that desperate. This did not seem the time to mention it, so I bit back a lecture that was all about self-respect and just said, "So why break up with him?"

"Because when I told him I was going to report him, Darren swore he was going to change his ways. He said I'd shown him the light, that what he was doing was stupid and that he was grateful to me for giving him another chance. He said he'd never do it again. We dated all that spring before I died, and we dated into the summer. And all that time, I thought he was being true to his word. And then . . . well, there was the whole Janice thing. You know . . ." She stared down at her lap. "I think he was dating her, too. Behind my back."

"And you put up with that?" It came out too judgmental, but then, I had trouble not speaking my mind, too.

Lucky for me—and my investigation—Lucy didn't hold it against me.

"Then I found out that Darren had been lying to me. I caught him selling test answers to one of the football players who was in summer school. That's when I had it out with him. I told him I didn't want to see him anymore."

I remembered what Ella had said about seeing Janice and Darren together at the Beatles concert, and about how Janice had looked pushy and insistent. "And Janice cornered Darren at the Beatles concert because once you were out of the way, she wanted him all to herself."

Lucy shrugged. "I can't say. I only know that once I found out he lied to me, I didn't care if I ever had another date ever again in my whole life." She gulped. "I guess that's pretty much what happened, isn't it? I told Darren I'd had it with him. That I never wanted to see him again."

"And if he thought that meeting you had scheduled with the principal was about him . . ." For the first time since I'd gotten involved in this quagmire of an investigation, I felt my hopes rise. "He might have wanted to shut you up."

"Yeah, sure he might have. But he didn't. He couldn't have. He was with Bobby and Janice and Will. They were all going to his house to listen to albums. If Darren left and was gone long enough to kill me, somebody would have noticed, don't you think?"

Yeah, there was that.

How I hate it when ghosts are right!

I was sitting at Ella's kitchen table, sorting through the stacks of old Garden View employee newsletters she'd brought home from the office to shred (and yes, recycle). Bad enough that I was bored out of my mind. Worse, because something was up. And I hated not knowing what it was.

I glanced over to where Ella was busy removing staples and tapping old newsletters into too-neat piles. Her head was down, her eyes were focused on her work, the saggy skin under her chin shimmied as she went through the motions: Grab a newsletter. Pull the staple. Set the pages aside.

I looked the other way at Ariel, who was sitting on the other side of me, doing the same thing. Her head was down, too. Her eyes were focused on her work. The muscles in her jaw were pulled so tight, I swear before the night was over, I was going to hear the *ping* when they snapped.

The two of them hadn't spoken two words to each other since I'd gotten to Ella's thirty minutes earlier. They'd barely spoken to me.

Maybe I was curious. Or just plain uncomfortable. Either way, I couldn't stand it anymore.

"So . . ." I looked from one of them to the other. "What's up?"

"Nothing." They answered in unison and glared across the table at each other, then silently fell back into the grabbing, pulling, setting aside routine.

This reminded me of the Ella-Ariel relationship of old. And that was not a good thing.

I found myself in the uncomfortable position of peacemaker. It might have been a whole lot easier if I knew what was going on.

Determined to get them talking so I could find out, I settled for the most obvious subject. It was Friday night, the school week was over. "Any plans for this weekend?" I asked Ariel.

Innocent question, yes?

Which says something about how surprised I was when

she punched the nearest pile of newsletters, hopped to her feet, and stomped to the kitchen sink. She poured a glass of water, drank one sip of it, then tossed the rest away with so much oomph most of the water ended up not down the drain, but on the floor. She didn't bother to clean it up. Instead, she stomped back the other way.

"*Some* people have things planned for this weekend," she said, completely ignoring me and focusing on her mother. "But then, *some* people don't live in a dictatorship."

"Now, honey." This comment came from Ella, of course. She clasped her hands together on a stack of newsletters and tried for a smile, but since it wobbled around the edges, I knew this wasn't the first time they'd had this discussion. "Some people," she said, so much more sweetly than Ariel had, "have to learn to live by the rules."

Ariel dropped back in her chair. She shoved the nearest pile of newsletters aside. "This recycling stuff is stupid," she grumbled.

"I'll second that." I was going for funny, but neither of them laughed. It was exactly the opening I needed.

"You two . . ." I looked from one of them to the other, suddenly sounding so much like Ella when she's trying to be sensible, it made me a little queasy. "You two are obviously not getting along. And I need to know why."

"She doesn't trust me," Ariel blurted out.

"She'll thank me for it later when she calms down and realizes it's for her own good." Ella's words washed over her daughter's.

And I was left just as confused as ever. I tried a no-nonsense look again, and when that got me nowhere, I knew it was time to change the subject. A little end run, and with any luck, I'd get them back to where we started before they ever realized it—and I'd get some answers, too. As I'd seen in the past weeks, nothing could get these two going like talking about my investigation.

"I've spent a lot of time working through the whole Lucy thing," I said as if it were the only thing on my mind. "I'm pretty sure Darren did it."

Ariel grunted and rolled her eyes.

Ella shook her head. "Absolutely not!" She pressed her lips together. "Lucy and Darren were friends."

"And she had something on him." I told them about how Darren had been stealing tests and answers. Since they were both in such foul moods, they didn't ask how I'd discovered this. Even after hearing this news, Ella dismissed my theory out of hand. "And you said Darren and Lucy had been dating, though I'm really not so sure about that, either. If they were, though . . ." The way she wrapped her tongue around that *if* pretty much said that my information about them dating wasn't only wrong, it was impossible. "That would indicate that they had feelings for each other."

Or not.

I didn't elaborate because really, there was no way I could tell them about how Lucy blackmailed Darren into being her boyfriend. Not without confessing about this Gift of mine. And not without betraying Lucy's confidence. I told myself I was doing it for the first reason. I knew it was really for the second. I couldn't see the point of adding major embarrassment to everything else Lucy had already suffered.

"All the more reason he would have been pissed if she was going to turn him in," I told Ella. I'd like to think I was telling Ariel, too, but she was so busy shaking her head like I was an idiot, I decided it was better to ignore her. "Lucy had that appointment with the principal. You told me about that. And yes, she might have made it to discuss that grade she got in her summer school class, but Darren didn't know that. If he thought she was going to rat on him—"

"That's just bullshit."

At the comment from Ariel, Ella gasped, and her shoulders shot back. She held her temper. But just barely. I have a feeling the only way she was able to do it was to pretend Ariel didn't exist. "You're forgetting," she said to me through gritted teeth, "that Darren was with the other kids that night."

I hadn't forgotten this; I'd just chosen to ignore it because then I could pin the crime on Darren. After only one meeting with him, I knew I didn't like him so I'd be thrilled if he was guilty. Leave it to Ella to introduce the logic that shot my case to hell. Even when she was deep in the drama zone with Ariel.

I sighed and fed a pile of papers into the shredder near my chair.

Ella tapped and organized. "I think it was Chuck Zuggart, the guy from the biker bar."

"Because you saw him talking to Lucy once about a thousand years ago?" Ariel barked out a laugh. "If you were a real detective like me, Mom . . . If you were paying attention and keeping notes like I do . . ." She reached over to what I thought was the empty chair beside her, and came up with her cell and a legal pad. She set her phone on the table and brandished the pad. "There's absolutely no other connection between Lucy and Chuck Zuggart. And there's never going to be. Not that either of you are going to find, anyway. That's because Patrick Monroe did it."

I wasn't sure she was right, but I didn't know she was wrong, either, so as much as I would have liked to meet Ariel's show of attitude with a little of my own, I didn't.

Besides, she sounded awfully sure of herself, and I wondered if her version of an investigation had turned up something mine had not. I plucked the legal pad out of her hands.

"I'm organized and efficient, see." Ariel leaned over and
tapped the pad with one finger, and I saw she was right.
She'd made columns that listed suspects, motives, alibis.
There was nothing new or surprising on her list, but it was
pretty darned impressive, anyway. "I've even done a spreadsheet on the computer," she added as if she knew what I was
thinking and had to get in this one last dig. "You know, who
was where when and what they know and say they know.
And I've even been through Mom's old scrapbook over and
over again. You know, the one about Lucy."

This was news, and I looked Ella's way. "You have a
scrapbook about Lucy?"

She brushed off the information. "There's nothing important in it. Just the old articles from the newspaper, and
the one that appeared on the twenty-fifth anniversary of her
disappearance. There's nothing in any of those articles that
we don't already know, right, honey?"

Her attempt at smoothing things over with Ariel was met
with icy teenaged contempt.

"Your theory about Darren Andrews . . ." When she
looked at me, Ariel dispensed with the contempt. But she
wasn't above a little one-upmanship. "Pepper, you're way
off base. It was Patrick Monroe. It had to be. He's still in
town, you know. He's working on a video of 'Girl at Dawn,'
and they're filming it here since this is where he wrote the
poem. If I could just get him alone, I know I could make
him talk."

"That"—I emphasized my point by slapping her legal
pad back down on the table—"is a really bad idea."

I had meant it more as advice than as a pronouncement,

but I'd forgotten that when a fifteen-year-old girl is feeling touchy, even the most well-intentioned comment sounds like a decree.

"Oh, you're going to gang up on me, too?" Ariel pushed back her chair and stomped to the door and back again. "What, you guys are tag teaming me? Is that why you asked Pepper to come over tonight, Mom? So the two of you could—"

"Now, honey . . ." Ella pulled herself to her feet so she could face her daughter.

I got up, too, the better to look my imposing tallest and to send the message that I was past putting up with their sniping. "All right, you two," I said, swinging a look from one of them to the other. "Somebody better explain what's going on. And don't tell me you live in a dictatorship," I warned Ariel. "I'm not buying it, and it doesn't explain anything, anyway."

Ella folded her arms over her chest.

Ariel balled her hands into fists and held them close to her sides.

There couldn't have been a worse time for the oven timer to ring.

Ella had put a frozen pizza in when I arrived, and ever the mom, she went to get it out. She set it aside to cool, put napkins and silverware at the places where none of us were sitting anymore, and cut the pizza into slices. She slid pizza onto plates, handed them around, and sat down with hers. It wasn't until she'd cut it into neat pieces that she set her shoulders, lifted her chin, and said, "Ariel wanted to go out with Gonzalo tonight."

This was a surprise! I turned to Ariel. "So he's back, huh?"

Ariel might be plenty pissed at her mother, but she was

a teenager, after all. She'd attacked the pizza with gusto, and her mouth was full. "He's forsaken his plebeian ways," she said.

"And Tiffany Slater? Has he forsaken her, too?"

Ariel chomped, her mouth clamped shut.

"I told her that I don't have a problem with her seeing Gonzalo again but—"

"That's not what you said, Mom." Ariel swallowed around the protest. "You said he wasn't good enough—"

"I never did." There were spots of color in Ella's cheeks when she looked my way. "You know I'd never say that, Pepper. Not about anyone. I simply pointed out that after Ariel's irresponsible behavior a couple weeks ago—"

"Oh, am I going to be made to suffer forever just because of one little mistake?" Ariel flopped back in her chair and groaned.

"I explained . . ." Ella was always reasonable, even when the situation wasn't. "I *tried* to explain," she said, "that I don't have a problem with Ariel seeing Gonzalo again. Once she proves she's trustworthy."

"I'm going to have to join a convent before I can prove that to you," Ariel wailed. "Are there Jewish convents? I'll have to found the first order of Jewish nuns."

I didn't wipe the smile off my face fast enough. Ariel saw it, and her irritation knew no bounds. "You're just as bad as Mom." She pointed at me, her voice sharp. "I thought we were colleagues, fellow detectives. But she's pushing me around and you . . . you're laughing at me."

It wasn't all that long since I'd been a touchy fifteen-year-old whose irritation knew no bounds myself, and I never have been one to put up with this kind of crap.

"You're just a kid," I said. "You don't—"

"See, that proves it." She stomped one sneaker-clad foot.

"You and Mom, you both think alike. 'Don't do this, Ariel.' 'Don't do that.' But the two of you, you do whatever you want. You investigate, Pepper, and nobody ever said you were a real detective. But you don't let that stop you. And Mom goes right ahead and does whatever she wants to do, too. Even with that creepy homeless guy who was at the cemetery the other day."

The color drained from Ella's face, and her mouth fell open. "Ariel, honey, if this is about Will—"

"You can see that grubby guy and I can't see Gonzalo?" A single tear splashed down Ariel's cheek. "That not fair, Mom, and you know it."

"It's not fair. It's not anything. Because I'm not *seeing* him." Ella wrung her hands. Her breaths came in sharp gasps. "Honey, if you're having issues because of Will—"

Ariel threw her hands in the air. "I am not having issues. I'm having a life crisis. And if the two of you weren't so old and out of touch, you'd realize it."

So much for me acting the peacemaker. Since I'd tried to make things better, they'd only gone from bad to worse. I scrambled for a way to save the situation, and keep these two from going at each other's throats.

"Ariel . . ." I pivoted her way and kept my expression neutral, so I couldn't be accused of anything. "I'd love to see that scrapbook of your mom's."

"Why, so you can look through it and tell me I don't know what I'm talking about? I do. I'm a good detective. I'm a better detective than you are, Pepper. I could prove it if I could just get Patrick Monroe alone."

The tips of Ella's ears were pink. "Even back in high school, the girls talked about how Mr. Monroe paid too much attention to them, honey. It wouldn't be a good idea for you to talk to him."

"You think I can't take care of myself?" Ariel snapped.

I hadn't signed up for family drama night; I groaned. "Nobody said that."

"But it's what you were thinking."

"I wasn't. OK, I was," I admitted. "And I'm also thinking that I've about had it with you, Ariel. Your mom says you can see Gonzalo again when you prove she can trust you, so start acting like a grown-up. That's the only way you can convince her."

"Yeah, I'll act like a grown-up, all right." She grabbed her legal pad and stormed past me and out the door that led into the front part of the house. "This grown-up is spending the rest of the night in her room."

The last we heard from her was her footsteps stomping through the upstairs hallway.

"Well . . ." Wiped out, Ella collapsed back into her chair. "I'm sorry about that, Pepper. You shouldn't have had to put up with it. Ariel's made such great strides these last few weeks, I thought she'd understand when I said I wasn't ready to let her go out again without supervision. I told her she could talk to Gonzalo on the phone. I never thought she'd react like that when I said she couldn't see him yet."

"Except I don't think that's what she was reacting to, do you?"

Ella reached for the pizza that was getting cold on her plate. She took a bite and chewed.

I knew a dodge when I saw one.

"You're not really dating Will, are you?"

Luckily, she had a glass of Diet Dr Pepper close at hand. Otherwise, she might have choked on her pizza. "Dating?" Ella coughed and pounded on her chest. "Of course not! Ariel can't possibly think that's true."

"Who knows what a teenaged girl thinks."

She acknowledged this with a tiny nod.

And I saw an opening. I'd been meaning to talk to Ella about Will since the day of Janice's funeral, and there just never seemed to be time. "What about him?" I asked her. "You haven't said a word about that dinner you had with Will at the Academy Tavern. What was he talking about, Ella, when he said that thing about how he hadn't murdered anyone, *not this time*?"

She set aside her pizza and got busy with the newsletters again. "It wasn't exactly something I could bring up in casual conversation," she said and added quickly, "I know, you would have done it. But the way you investigate and the way I investigate—"

"You're not investigating." I don't know why I bothered to even mention it.

"Will is just too fragile. I didn't have the heart to put him on the spot. I tried to keep things light. I asked about his mom. I asked if he'd seen anyone else from school."

I fed a stack of papers into the shredder. "You didn't happen to ask why he disappeared from the rehab center and where he was the day Janice died, did you?"

Even when Ella scowled, she looked like a huggable gnome. "Like I said—"

"Fragile. Yeah."

The shredder groaned, and I turned it off and took a moment to pull out the strip of paper that had jammed it, then sat back and stared across the table at Ella.

She's the sensitive type. It didn't take long to get her attention.

"What?" she asked.

"I was just wondering. About Will. About what Ariel said. What she was thinking. Do you still have feelings for Will?"

"Don't be silly." Ella got back to work. "Will was a great kid back in high school and yes . . ." She thought if she concentrated on the newsletters, I wouldn't see that her cheeks were flushed, and this time, it had nothing to do with trying to reason with Ariel. "Back then, I did have a crush on him. But as you no doubt noticed, life hasn't been easy for Will. He's a kind, sensitive soul. And if things were different, yes, we might still be friends. But really, Pepper, I hope you realize that's all he could ever be. I've got the kids to worry about. And my job. And yes, you, too, since I think of you as one of my girls. I don't need to complicate my life with a man who has serious problems."

"And one of those problems could be that he killed Lucy."

"He feels guilty about Lucy's death, that's for sure," she said. "I'm no psychologist, but I think that's why he turned to alcohol and drugs in the first place. I think he just couldn't handle Lucy's disappearance any other way."

"Which might explain why Bobby felt so guilty, too."

In agreement with me, Ella nodded.

"But it doesn't explain why someone would murder Janice," I said, only since I had a mouth full of pepperoni and mushroom pizza, it didn't sound as authoritative as I'd hoped. I swallowed and wiped a string of mozzarella off my chin. "Janice must have known something about Lucy's murder—"

"Disappearance," Ella corrected me.

I took another bite of pizza, the better to keep myself from telling her how wrong she was.

Ella took a sip of her soda. "Maybe Janice's murder has nothing to do with Lucy," she said, and yes, I'd thought of this myself; I just wasn't willing to believe it. "Maybe Janice sold somebody a bad house, or made a neighbor angry, or had an ex-boyfriend with an ax to grind."

"Maybe. Or maybe I'm right, and Darren's the one who really did it. Or Ariel's right, and it was Patrick Monroe. Or—"

It was just as well that Ariel's phone rang; I was fresh out of theories.

Ella jumped up and grabbed it. "It's Molly," she said. "Ariel's best friend. Why don't you run the phone up to her, Pepper? You know, as a little peace offering. Talking to Molly will cheer her up."

I doubted I could run fast enough for her to take the call, but I made the effort.

I got to Ariel's bedroom door just as the phone stopped ringing and made the little twinkling sound that indicated there was a voice mail message.

"Hey, Ariel!" I tapped on her door. "You left your cell downstairs. Molly called."

The kid didn't answer.

And I knew what I was going to find even before I pushed the door open. But then again, like I said, it wasn't that long ago that I was a dramatic fifteen-year-old.

The room was empty.

Ariel was gone.

I t didn't take a rocket scientist to figure out what Ariel of
the Nasty Mood had in mind.

She wanted to prove she was a better detective than me,
of course. Poor thing was too young to realize that was
never going to happen!

No matter, I would have bet my next manicure that she
was headed out to find Patrick Monroe.

Fortunately—for me, anyway, since I couldn't take much
more of Ella wringing her hands and moaning about what a
bad mother she was one moment, and the next about what
an ungrateful child Ariel had turned out to be—it didn't take
me long to locate Monroe. The guy had an ego the size of
Arizona, remember, and thanks to the wonders of the Internet, a blog to celebrate it. One of the things he talked about
on that blog was how poetry lovers in northeast Ohio were
in luck—he was doing a reading that evening at a tavern

called the Barking Spider, a funky little place near the campus of Case Western Reserve University.

Notice my use of the word *funky*. That's a kind way of me saying it is not the sort of place I hang out. Ever. The Spider is located in what looks like an old garage. It features folk and jazz entertainers, serves about a million different kinds of beers, and doesn't pay as much attention to its decorating scheme as it does to what's charitably called *ambience*. Hello, picnic tables outside the back door do not qualify as atmosphere. But that, as they say, is a discussion for another day.

For now, I had one teenaged fugitive to worry about.

Keeping that thought in mind, I talked Ella into staying home on the pretext that if Ariel did happen to show up before I got back, it wouldn't look like Ella had run out looking for her because she didn't trust her. Alone and grateful for it, I paused just inside the door of the Spider, and since it was dark, I had perfect cover and the chance to look around. I was just in time to see Patrick Monroe finish one of his so-called poems, take a bow, and down the amber liquid in the rocks glass someone handed him. It was apparently intermission. The fifty or so literary types gathered around clapped like crazy.

Go figure.

I was not fast enough to stop Ariel when I saw her dash out of the crowd and approach the stage.

I elbowed my way through the people streaming toward the bar and the restrooms, lost sight of Ariel, then picked up her trail again. I watched her wait for Monroe to sign a few autographs, then step forward and introduce herself. Monroe leaned back against the bar stool near the microphone. He smiled down at the kid.

Yeah, like the big bag wolf licking his chops at the sight of one of those delicious little piggies.

By the time I made it over to where they were chatting it up like long-lost friends, the last thing I cared about was civility.

"Where's Gonzalo?" I asked Ariel, because let's face it, she must have had an accomplice to make her getaway, and it was no leap of faith to figure that the Clyde to her Bonnie was good ol' Gonzalo. I wouldn't have been surprised to find out he had been outside Ella's place all night waiting for the perfect opportunity to swoop down and scoop up his ladylove.

I did another quick scan of the bar. No emaciated under-agers. Except for Ariel, of course. I swung back her way. "Where did you leave him?"

"He's . . ." Ariel's face was the color of the nearby crimson neon sign that advertised some brand of beer I'd never heard of. She spun around so that Monroe couldn't hear her. "He's back at the car," she said out of one side of her mouth, and in a stage whisper, "You know, so that it's easier for me to question the perp. Which I can't do with you here." Just in case I didn't get the message, she added a sneer like the one I'd seen from her back home. "What kind of detective has a babysitter hanging around, anyway?"

My question exactly, and we'd discuss it when we were home and I had a chance to lecture Ariel in private. For now, I was more concerned about the fact that Gonzalo actually let her come into the bar alone. It looked like Ariel's mother wasn't the only one in the family who knew how to pick a loser.

Since it was not the time to talk about Ariel's father, either, I gritted my teeth and greeted Monroe. He remembered me. But then, I'm pretty hard to forget. The skinny jeans, the emerald scoop-neck tee, and the open-toed sandals helped. Until I realized that when Ariel had disappeared into her room, she'd put on almost the exact same outfit.

That was just downright embarrassing.

"How nice to see you again." When Monroe stuck out his hand, I shook it. Maybe if he was busy looking at me, he wouldn't notice Ariel was my clone. "How's that thesis of yours coming along?"

"Oh, I'm working as hard as ever," I said, even though it wasn't true. "This reading tonight, this is really wonderful."

"And how nice that you brought your little friend." He patted Ariel's shoulder.

She didn't like that one bit, and I couldn't say I was crazy about the touchy-feely familiarity, either. I clamped a hand on her shoulder and dragged her over to stand beside me and out of Monroe's reach.

He took the not-so-subtle message in stride, yanked a pack of cigarettes out of his shirt pocket, and moved toward the back door. Even though he didn't ask me to, I walked along with him, and since I wasn't about to let Ariel out of my sight in a place she shouldn't have been in to begin with, I tightened my grip on her shoulder and hauled her with me.

Outside at one of those unatmospheric picnic tables, Monroe sat down, stretched his legs out in front of him, and lit up. "Still looking into every little nook and cranny of my past?" he asked on the end of a trail of smoke. "Find out anything interesting?"

I have a rule about picnic tables in public places. I broke it this one time, dropping down onto the seat next to Monroe. While I was at it, I tugged Ariel into the empty seat on the other side of me. "I found out you don't have an alibi for the night Lucy disappeared."

Monroe smoked in silence.

I didn't have much time. Intermission wouldn't last forever. Though I would rather play it cool and pretend I didn't care, I couldn't afford not to push. Just a little. "I guess that doesn't worry you," I said.

"Why should it? I didn't do anything to Lucy. Before or after she disappeared." He slid me a look. "But you already know that, don't you?"

Before I had a chance to tell him I wouldn't be sitting at a picnic table with a smoker if I was as sure of myself as he seemed to think I was, a middle-aged woman approached. She had a copy of Monroe's *Collected Works* in one hand, and a pen in the other. "Please!" She handed him the pen and opened the book to the page she wanted signed. "You changed my life, Mr. Monroe . . . er . . . Patrick." The woman grinned like a homecoming queen. "Your work is so profound. So intense."

"Yes," he said, "it is." He scribbled his name and offered the book back along with a smile that was so world-weary there was no doubt that the life of an artist was not an easy one.

I found myself hoping the woman wasn't there alone, because the way she hyperventilated, I was pretty sure she was going to faint, and she'd need somebody to drive her home. "'Girl at Dawn' . . ." She whispered the words like a prayer. "That poem changed my life. I was a senior in high school that fall when it was published, 1967. My friends and I, we read it every single day after school. We talked about what it meant. And what it meant to us." She clutched the book to her ample bosom. "Thank you." Tears filled her eyes. "Thank you for helping me grow up."

Monroe stood and gave her a peck on the cheek.

And it was a good thing that I had to sit there and put up

with all the gushing and blubbering the woman did after that.

It gave me time to think. And what I thought knocked my socks off. Maybe I was way off base, but what the hell. If I was wrong, it wouldn't be the first time I'd embarrassed myself in the name of an investigation. If I was right . . .

I waited until the woman walked away. When the great poetry guru sat down again, I was ready for him.

"Remember what I asked you about last time we talked?" I didn't wait for him to answer, because of course he didn't remember. Patrick Monroe's brain was so full of himself, there was no room in his memory banks for anything or anyone else. "I asked if you'd written 'Girl at Dawn' for Lucy. You said you hadn't. One of the things I've learned recently is that you were telling the truth about that."

"Of course I was." I think he would have patted me on the head if he thought he could get away with it.

I waited for the right moment, poking Ariel as I did. Just so she didn't miss the master at work.

"It wasn't *for* Lucy. But it was *about* Lucy, wasn't it? The girl at dawn *was* Lucy and nobody knew better how she thought and felt and what growing up was all about to her. That's because Lucy wrote that poem."

I don't think people are supposed to be the color of gray Monroe turned. He hopped off the bench. "You can't possibly know that. Your notes—"

Too late, he'd given himself away, and realizing it, I jumped to my feet, too, as fighting mad as I was that day I realized someone had kicked in the door to my apartment. "You're the one who trashed my apartment. You son of a—" It wasn't like I thought Ariel had never heard the words before, but I bit my tongue, anyway. There were lots of people around, and if I pissed off Monroe too much, he'd walk away. I wasn't going to let that happen. Not until I had all the facts, anyway.

I controlled my voice and my temper. "I had my portfolio with me when I went to your poetry reading so, of course, you figured I kept my notes in it. It was the only thing missing from my apartment because that was the only thing you cared about. Oh, you looked through the rest of the place, but you didn't find any notes stashed anywhere else. How surprised were you when you saw there weren't any in that portfolio, either? You were hoping for a clue, right? You were thinking that when I asked about Lucy and the poem, I must have discovered something that proved that she wrote it. That's what you were trying to get your hands on. The proof. So you could destroy it."

"I . . . I . . ." Monroe stuttered into an explanation I knew was going to be lame. That's why I didn't give him a chance to even get started.

"I've got news for you," I told him. "You wasted your time with the whole breaking and entering thing, because I didn't know about Lucy and the poem then. I just figured it out. Right here. Right now. Right when that lady reminded me that 'Girl at Dawn' was published in 1967. Lucy died in '66, see, and she knew enough of the poem to recite some of the lines. She shouldn't have because when she died, it hadn't been published yet. There's no way she could have read it. Except if she was the one who wrote it, of course."

"She could have . . . she might have . . . she couldn't . . ." It was kind of fun to watch him sputter. Too bad he finally shook his head and scratched a hand through his shaggy hair, settling his thoughts. A muscle twitched at the corner of his mouth. "You said Lucy knew the words. Are you telling me she . . ." He swallowed hard. "Had she kept a copy? A dated copy? You found it?"

It would have been far more fun to tell him I'd heard the poem from the horse's mouth, but I thought Monroe had had enough surprises for one night, and besides, a guy as scummy as him doesn't deserve the truth. I went along with the lie he'd put into my head.

"Found it? You bet. And the paper and ink she used is being authenticated even as we speak. You know, so the experts can tell that it really is forty-five years old. They'll find out it's not a copy, it's the original. And you're going to have to explain how you ended up getting your hands on it. And—"

I would have slapped my forehead if it wouldn't have made me look very un-detective-like. "That's why you gave her an F in that summer school class and said she didn't turn in her assignment. Her assignment was 'Girl at Dawn,' and she handed it in, all right, and you read it and you knew it was good. Your own poetry is crap." As far as I was concerned, I didn't need any corroboration. All anybody had to do was look at the body of Monroe's work since "Girl." All they had to do was listen to the flat, flavorless verses everyone assumed were high art just because "Girl" was so good. "You decided to keep the poem and claim it as your own. By the time you found out Lucy was going to see the principal about her grade, I'll bet you'd already submitted that poem to one of those weird literary magazines. Maybe they'd even already accepted it and paid you for it, too. And they were singing your praises, right? They were already calling you the next best thing. And you were all too willing to believe it. No wonder you thought you had to get rid of Lucy."

The ashen color of Monroe's face was relieved by the two spots of color that popped in his cheeks. "No! I . . . I didn't!"

"You swiped her poem and you built your career on it.

It's the perfect motive for murder." It was, too, and I was so proud of myself for figuring it out, I could have burst.

"It wasn't me." Monroe's jaw looked as if it was about to snap. "The cops never found anything to prove it was. If they did, they would have arrested me. Besides, I have an alibi for that night."

Ariel stood up beside me. It was a good thing she had that spreadsheet of hers memorized. She also had her legal pad with her, and she waved it in under Monroe's nose as if that would somehow prove she knew what she was talking about. "You told the cops you were home alone the night Lucy disappeared," she said. "You're quoted as saying that in the *Plain Dealer* the morning of August eighteenth, and in the *Press* on the nineteenth and again on the twenty-first and—"

"I did tell the cops that. But it wasn't true. I was . . . well, I can't imagine it would make any difference anymore . . ." He pulled in a breath and let it out in a huff that smelled like nicotine. "I spent that night with Violet Beck."

"The vice principal?" Again, Ariel was information girl, and I was grateful.

Monroe nodded, confirming what she'd said. "Violet was married, and if the school board had found out we were involved, we both would have been fired. I couldn't tell anyone I was with her. She would have . . . she would have come forward, she told me as much. She would have come forward if the police had ever thought of me as a serious suspect."

"And when they didn't?"

In answer to my question, he looked my way. "When they didn't, there was no reason for Violet to say anything. I left the school soon after, and she went on with her career. There was never any reason to mention it to anyone."

I glanced at Ariel. "Is this vice principal still around?" I asked her.

She consulted her notes. "She was in Punta Cana last time I tried to call her."

"Call her again. Right now." I handed Ariel my cell and she took it and walked away to where it was quieter. "If Violet Beck confirms what you told us before you have a chance to coach her—"

Monroe barked a laugh. "What, you think I'm going to run to the phone and tell her what to say? I wouldn't coach Vi. I haven't even talked to her in forty-five years."

"Love 'em and leave 'em, eh?" It didn't make me think any less of him. That was impossible.

Then again, his groveling didn't do much to improve my opinion of him, either. "Look, if word of this gets out . . . my career . . . my reputation . . ."

"Personally, I don't care much about either. I do care if you threw Lucy in the trunk of a car, then smothered her."

I was hoping for another appearance of that murky gray expression that had guilt written all over it. Too bad for me. Monroe simply blinked.

"She says she remembers being with him that night, all right." Ariel came back over and delivered the news along with a glare she aimed in Monroe's direction. "She says she remembers because the next day, all anybody could talk about was how Lucy had vanished. She says . . ." Three cheers for the kid, she raised that stubborn little chin of hers and looked Monroe in the eye. "She says that's why she remembers, not because he was anything special in bed."

"There you have it." Monroe backed away from us, his smile so sickly sweet, it turned my stomach. "Now that you know I'm not a killer, perhaps you won't be so eager to trash my reputation. We can work something out. We can make some arrangement. If you don't tell anyone—"

"In your dreams, buddy!" Ariel flipped him off.

And at that moment, I had to admit, there were times I actually liked the kid.

Since he was a heartless creep who didn't deserve any better, we left Gonzalo in his car and didn't tell him we were heading home. We were back in my car, and Ariel was deep in thought.

"We can't actually prove it, right? I mean, you're sure Lucy wrote that poem, but there's no way we can tell anyone because there's no way we can prove it."

We were stopped at a red light, and I slid her a look along with a smile. "Monroe doesn't have to know that."

She didn't laugh like I expected her to. Instead, her brow furrowed and her eyebrows dropped low over her eyes. "I was wrong. Patrick Monroe didn't kill Lucy. But if he didn't—"

We'd just pulled into Ella's driveway, and we got out of the car. Ariel trudged to the back door. My steps were more confident.

I pushed open the door and stepped into the kitchen.

"Think of it this way," I told her. "When a detective finds out somebody didn't do it, it puts that detective one step closer to finding out who did."

"Are we one step closer?" Ariel grabbed a can of Mountain Dew out of the fridge and cracked the top. "It doesn't feel like it. It feels like we're at a dead end."

"Not so!" It was far too late to be sucking down caffeine, but I didn't think I'd sleep that night, anyway. My head was spinning with too many possibilities. I grabbed a Mountain Dew, too. "We know Monroe didn't kill Lucy, and like I told your mom earlier this evening, I don't think it was Chuck Zuggart, either. He never really was much of a suspect."

"That leaves only one person." Ariel's eyes lit. "So we do know something. We know who did it."

I slapped Ariel a high five. "You got that right. We know our murderer is none other than Darren Andrews."

"That's not exactly right."

The words came from the darkened hallway that led into the dining room and the living room beyond, and both Ariel and I squealed our surprise and spun around just in time to see Ella walk in the room. Will Margolis was with her.

Ella's eyes were red. Her cheeks were stained with tears. "Will has something to tell you," she said. "He thought . . ." She patted his arm. "He was considerate enough to think you'd want to hear it before he went to the police and told his story."

I looked to Will to start explaining.

"It's like this," he said. He plucked at the sleeve of his black sweater with twitchy fingers. "Darren didn't kill Lucy. Not all by himself, anyway. We all . . ." He swallowed hard and lifted his chin. "Darren and Janice and Bobby and . . . and me. We all killed Lucy."

16

In the light of the chandelier that hung over the dining room table, Will's eyes were shadowy pits. There was a cup of coffee on the table in front of him, and he wrapped his left hand around it. Against the cobalt blue cup, his knuckles were the color of skeleton bones, and when we were all settled and he finally started talking, his voice was husky. "That night after the Beatles concert, Lucy was bragging about how brave she was. You remember, Ella." He glanced to where she was sitting to his right, but he never met her eyes. "You remember how she was showing off."

Ella rested a hand against the sleeve of Will's black sweater. "Lucy was excited because she was one of the kids who ran out onto the field," she reminded me and Ariel. "She made it all the way to the stage, and she jumped up there and kissed Paul McCartney." Her smile was bittersweet. "I was terrified that she'd get hurt, but Lucy . . . Lucy was so brave and so daring. She was so . . ." She hiccupped out a sob. "She was so proud of herself."

Will nodded. "And all the way home . . . you remember that, too, right, Ella? All the way home on that rapid, she was telling us—"

"That she was the bravest girl in the world, yes." Ella's expression settled, as serious as Will's. But then, he'd already told her the story so she knew what was coming.

I knew the ending, too. It was the in-between part that had me baffled.

I couldn't catch Will's eye so I didn't even try. I just raised my voice a little and acted as calm as I wasn't feeling. "So Lucy was bragging. And you and Darren and Janice and Bobby . . ."

"We got off the rapid and Darren, he said we should teach Lucy a lesson. You know, as a joke. He said we needed to show her she wasn't as brave as she thought she was." He took a cigarette out of his pocket but he didn't light up. Maybe he knew about Ella's no smoking rule. Or maybe he was just a polite guy. He tap, tap, tapped one end of the cigarette against the cherry table. "We ran over to his house, and we got in his car and—"

"So you weren't upstairs all night playing records?" It wasn't what I'd heard or read in the old newspapers articles, and I wasn't going to let it pass. "Darren's mother said you were home. She said she heard music. That's what she told the cops."

"She did hear the music. Because when we got there . . . I mean, before we got in Darren's car . . ." Will's green stocking cap was on the table beside him. He scratched a finger behind his right ear. I guess I couldn't blame him for being confused. Forty-five years of pickling his brain, and the results weren't pretty. He scraped a hand over his nubby chin. "When we got to Darren's house, we already knew what we were going to do. I mean, about playing that joke on Lucy. And we knew Mrs. Andrews would have had a fit if we were out late, so we ran upstairs as fast as we could, and we put a stack of albums on Darren's stereo." It was the first time since we sat down that Will dared to raise his head. "You two . . ." He looked from me to Ariel, who was sitting beside me. Yeah, the subject of murder—especially among friends—wasn't exactly PG-rated, but I figured we owed Ariel this much. Right or wrong, she thought of herself as part of the investigation, and she deserved to hear the truth.

"You two wouldn't understand because of all these CDs and DVDs and iPods and such that you have these days. But back when we were young, you put a record on a turntable and that's how you played it. And on some turntables, you could stack the records up on the spindle that went through the hole at the center of the record. Five or six or seven records, one on top of the other. And when one finished playing, the next one would drop down, and then that one would play, too. That's what Darren did when we got back to his place. He grabbed his Beatles albums and his Stones albums, and he stacked them on his stereo and he turned it on. He said it would make his mother think we were there, and that way she wouldn't know what we were up to."

Ariel scribbled this bit of info onto her legal pad.

"We got back downstairs fast, and we got in Darren's car and raced over to the rapid station. You know, Lucy's stop." Will's Adam's apple jumped. "We got there just a little bit before the train pulled in and Lucy got off."

One hand still beating out a rhythm with his cigarette, his other rapped the side of his coffee mug. A muscle twitched at the corner of his eye. Will stared over my head, his eyes unfocused. I was afraid we were going to lose him, and I couldn't afford to let that happen. If I waited any longer to hear what had really happened that night, I was going to have a coronary. There was no use waiting for Ella to jump in and help out. Tears streamed down her cheeks and she stared into her teacup.

I scooted my chair a titch closer to the table and leaned forward. "You were only trying to scare Lucy. That's what you said, Will. You said you were only trying to teach her a lesson."

"Y . . . yes." Once he started nodding, he didn't stop. "Darren, he said we should pretend we were kidnappers. That we should sneak up on her and grab her, and that way, Lucy would get real scared and that would prove she wasn't so brave after all." He scrubbed his knuckles across his eyes, and when he spoke, his voice was no louder than a whisper. "We all thought it would be pretty funny." His focus faded away along with his voice.

"So you attacked her when she got off the rapid and killed her?"

I elbowed Ariel in the ribs to shut her up and went for a smoother approach. "Whose idea was the blindfold?"

Will was too lost in his memories to ask how I even knew this detail, Ella probably couldn't hear much of anything above the sounds of her own soft weeping, and Ariel was busy taking notes.

They took my question at face value. "The blindfold . . ." Will thought about it. "I don't remember. Darren's maybe. Yeah, it was. He said if Lucy saw us . . . well, then our joke wouldn't work, would it? She wouldn't be scared if she knew it was us. And gagging her . . . well, we had to do that or she'd scream and somebody would hear her."

"And tying her hands?"

He lifted his coffee cup, but he didn't drink. When he set it back down, the cup clattered against the saucer. "We had to do that so she wouldn't fight back. So she wouldn't make a scene and so she couldn't take off the blindfold."

It was clear—at least to me—that Will had been over this part of the story in his head a million times in the past forty-five years. I could hear the familiar ring of logic in his voice, as if going over the details and justifying every little thing would finally show him the flaws in the plan that had resulted in Lucy's death. A million and one times, and he was no closer now to figuring out what had gone wrong than he had been then.

"It made sense," he mumbled. "We were kids and we were stupid, and it all made so much sense to us."

I couldn't let the desperation that tinged his voice get a foothold.

I sat back, and as casually as if we were talking about the weather, I filled in the blanks. "So you waited for Lucy to get off the rapid, and when she did, you were ready for her. You came up behind her, right? I mean, it was the only way she wouldn't have seen you. And since you were all working together, it would have been easy to grab her and blindfold her and gag her and tie her hands."

Ella choked out a sob.

Will dropped his head into his hands. His shoulders trembled. He sat that way for a long time, and I counted out every painful second, eager for him to continue. But then, I didn't exactly have the right to hurry him along. It had taken him forty-five years to get this far.

When he finally looked up, there were tears on his cheeks. "It was supposed to be funny," he said. "We put her in the trunk of Darren's car, and it was supposed to be funny and we . . . we drove to the park, and we pulled over and we were trying so hard not to laugh because we were going to go get her out of the trunk, and when we did, we couldn't wait to see the look on Lucy's face when she realized it was us. And we were going to ask her . . . then we were going to ask her how brave she was feeling. Only . . ."

Ella sniffled. "Will's never told anyone any of this," she said. She dabbed her nose with a paper napkin. "Not until tonight when he showed up here to talk to me. He's spent a lot of years . . ." The words caught in her throat and she coughed them away. "Will has spent a long time thinking about what happened that night and wondering what he could have done differently."

I thought back to Lucy's side of the story and a rush of anger pounded through me like a jackhammer. I clutched the table. What they could have done differently was not held that blanket over Lucy's face and suffocated her.

But I was getting ahead of myself.

I forced a calming breath that hit my lungs and burned like the devil. Pain was good. It made me focus.

"Was Lucy surprised when you opened the trunk and she saw it was you?" I asked.

Will tugged on his earlobe. "Like I said, we were going to surprise her. Oh man, we thought we were going to laugh so hard. And we parked the car, and Darren, that's when he said he'd go get Lucy out of the trunk."

I sat up like a shot. "He opened the trunk? Alone? By himself?"

If Will thought my questions were a little anxious, he didn't let on. "That's right. Darren said he'd get Lucy out and we could all be sitting in the car, and when she walked around to the front of the car, we'd pop out and surprise her. But then . . ." His mouth twisted. He closed his eyes, and his chest rose and fell. "He came back to the car . . . and . . . and Darren . . . he said . . ." Will jumped out of his chair and shot to the other side of the room.

"I can't do it," he wailed. "Ella, I can't do it. I can't say it. I told you, and I can't say it again."

She went to stand beside him and soothed him, one hand on his back.

"You don't have to tell us," I said, because let's face it, I knew exactly what had happened. "I'll tell you what I think, Will, and you tell me if I'm right."

He nodded.

"I think Darren came back to the car and told you there was a problem."

"That's right. Yes, yes. That's what happened." Will came back and sat down. He balled one hand and rapped the table with his fist. "He said we did something wrong. Maybe . . . maybe we put the gag on too tight. Or maybe . . . maybe there was a leak in the exhaust system and the carbon monoxide built up in the trunk. By the time Darren went to let her out—"

"Lucy was already dead." I felt a breath of relief whoosh out of me. Finally, we'd gotten to the truth. Or at least to part of it.

Because I was the only one who knew the rest of the story.

I thought it over, watching Will's face to gauge his reaction when I asked, "And you came up with the story about how you were all at Darren's when Lucy disappeared, and Mrs. Andrews confirmed it."

"We were scared." He gulped. "We thought if we told anybody what happened, we'd all get into real big trouble. And Darren, he was the one who said we should all just stick together. That if we kept our mouths shut, everything would be OK."

"But it wasn't OK, was it?" Understatement of the year! "Ella has spent all these years thinking about Lucy and worrying. And you, Will, you decided it was better to drown yourself in a bottle than face the truth. And Bobby—"

"He wanted to die." Will rasped out the words. "That's what we heard later from his buddies. Bobby just walked into the middle of that battle and never tried to stop or hide or defend himself. He let them kill him. I wish . . . I've spent all these years wishing I had the nerve to do something like that."

"Do you think Janice felt the same way?"

Will knew better. He read the newspaper, the same as the rest of us. "The cops said Janice didn't kill herself. Somebody tried to make it look like a suicide."

"Do you know who?"

He scraped his hands together, but he didn't answer.

I tried again. "Do you know why?"

"I don't think it's my fault. I mean, it couldn't be, could it? Not a second time." Will was trying so hard to convince himself by convincing us, it hurt. Ella sat back down beside him. By this time, Ariel was so caught up in the story, she wasn't even writing anything down. Her nose was red, and I reached for the pile of paper napkins on the table and slid one her way.

"I called them," Will said. "Janice and Darren. I called them after you came to see me at the rehab center, and I told them somebody was asking questions about Lucy. Darren . . . he said he wanted to talk to me about it."

"So that's why you left rehab."

Will nodded. "Darren came to talk to me. He told me not to worry, that nobody could ever really find out what we did to Lucy. It was too long ago. And there was no proof. He brought me—"

"Let me guess, a week's supply of Seagram's VO."

"A week's supply, yeah, and it lasted me exactly three days." He hung his head.

"And Janice?"

Will was so lost in thought, he flinched. "Janice, she told me to go away and never call her again and not to bother her. She said she didn't remember anyone named Lucy and she didn't know what I was talking about."

"Doesn't that just figure." Ella sat back and crossed her arms over her chest. "They were supposed to be best friends."

"And they might have been if they weren't fighting over Darren," I said. "These days, I'll bet Janice thought everybody had forgotten all about Lucy. You were a threat, Will."

"But nobody killed me. Not like . . . not like Janice."

"Yeah, well . . ." I weighed the wisdom of scaring him then decided he needed to hear the truth. "Darren was probably hoping you'd drink yourself to death."

Will shook his head. "No. Darren has always been my friend. He knew I was thinking about the past. He knew I was feeling bad. He was just trying to make me feel better."

"The way he made Janice feel better?"

Ella's face went ashen. "You mean, you think . . . You think Darren . . . ?"

"Who else could it have been?" I stared at her long enough for this to sink in.

"But Darren . . ." Ella's expression was sour.

"Darren was in on it just like the rest of them were," I said. Only it wasn't what I was thinking. Because what I was thinking was that he was really in on it more. Because somebody held that squishy blanket over Lucy's face, and that somebody could only have been the person who went to get her out of the trunk. Of course, I couldn't tell Will that yet. I couldn't tell anyone. Not without proof. "Darren had as much to lose as anyone else."

"The police will talk to him, right?" Will asked me. "I'm going to . . ." He scraped back his chair and stood. "I'm going to go turn myself in. I'm going to tell them everything. Now. Tonight. Ella . . ." He looked her way. "Ella said she'd come with me."

"And I think that's the best thing you could do," I said. "But not tonight."

They all looked at me in wonder.

"You not letting Will go to the police, that's obstruction of justice," Ariel reminded me, and maybe she was just full of too much prime-time TV, or maybe she was right.

Either way, I wasn't about to let that stop me.

"You can turn yourself in tomorrow," I told Will. "And Ella will go with you, and I will, too, if you'll let me. But not until after you do me one favor. Will, you have to show me what you did with Lucy's body."

I suppose I should have paid more attention that night when I told Will what I wanted him to do for me and he clammed up like a . . . well, like a clam. My only excuse (and I'm not saying it's a good one) was that I felt sorry for the guy. All those years, he'd been keeping a secret, and it was literally eating him up from the inside out.

If I'd been less compassionate and more hard-nosed, the way a detective is supposed to be, it would have saved me the disappointment the next day when I parked the car in a shaded picnic area in one of the Metroparks that ring the city, and Ella, Will, and I got out and trudged to a spot where a winding creek snaked around the contour of a hill packed with just-about-to-burst-into-green trees.

"It was a long time ago," Will said, glancing around. "Things change. I haven't been back here, except that one time. The next day."

I perked up. "You didn't tell me you'd come back the next day."

Will stayed at Ella's the night before (I had it on Ariel's authority that he slept on the couch in the family room) and he'd taken a shower that morning. I'm not sure where Ella got it, but she'd managed to come up with a clean long-sleeved T-shirt that fit him. His jeans still looked like they'd seen too much wearing and too little laundry detergent, but the rest of him was clean and presentable.

He kicked one sneaker-clad foot through the dirt. "When we found out that Lucy was . . . When Darren said she was dead, we didn't know what to do. We panicked. You know."

I didn't. I never wanted to. But I could imagine.

"We . . . we took her out of the car. I think we were parked over there somewhere." He pointed back near toward where we'd left our car. "And we carried her over here." He walked a little farther on toward the trees. "Me and Bobby carried her. Janice, she was crying too hard. She kept saying how her life was ruined and it was all our fault."

"And Darren?"

Will glanced my way. He shrugged. "I remember him standing back over by the car for a while, smoking a cigarette. I think it was his way to deal, you know?"

I had a feeling his way to deal was a lot different, but for now, that didn't matter nearly as much as finding Lucy's body. I followed Will farther into the woods. "Do you have any idea where her body might be?" I asked him.

"Well, that's just it." He paced the banks of the swirling

creek. "We carried her here and we laid her on the ground.
You know?" Demonstrating, he motioned toward the dirt.
"And that's when Darren, he finished his smoke, and he
came over and he said we shouldn't just leave Lucy here
like that, that we should cover her up with leaves and things.
We did. We collected leaves and branches and stuff, and we
covered her, that made sense at the time. But the next day,
me and Bobby talked, and we said that was no way to leave
Lucy. We came back. You know, to move her."

"And you took it where?"

"Well, that's just it." Will's chin quivered. "We came
back the next day and Lucy . . . She was gone."

My hopes of finally seeing Lucy at peace fell. "Are you
telling me—"

"We were terrified. You get that, don't you, Pepper?" He
swung the other way to where Ella was standing in the
shade of a giant oak, staring at the ground and looking
miserable. "Ella, you understand how we felt, don't you?
Somebody took Lucy's body, and that could only mean one
thing: somebody must have seen us take her out of the car
and leave her there. Oh, man!" He swiped his nose and
moaned. "I've never been so scared in my life. We were
all scared. Somebody saw us, and that meant somebody
knew what we'd done. We waited. Every day. We waited for
the cops to knock on our doors and tell us we were under
arrest."

"But they never did."

Will looked my way and nodded. "It was years before I
slept through the night. Every time I closed my eyes, I saw
Lucy looking like she had when we were at the Beatles concert, all pretty and happy. And then when I did fall asleep,
I'd dream there was someone knocking at the door, and it
was the cops, and they were coming to take me away."

I was afraid I knew the answer, but I asked, anyway. "So you don't know what happened to Lucy's body?"

Will shrugged. "I can't say. I only know that whoever took it and wherever it is, nobody ever found it."

True.

And I was right back where I'd started from.

17

I haven't mentioned Winston Churchill in a while, and really, it's no wonder why. For one thing, all that hoopla about the cops having a city neighborhood surrounded because the killer was hiding somewhere nearby? Well, that turned out to be a big ol' nothing. As usual, the local media was all over it, anyway, savoring the fact that the guy was still on the run and milking the story for all it was worth. An exclusive interview with the killer's kindergarten teacher? Please!

For another . . . well, obviously, thinking of the whole serial killer thing made me think of the guy who caught the serial killer in the first place, and thinking about the guy who caught the serial killer in the first place . . .

No good was going to come from that.

I also had a new and bigger worry, one I hadn't even imagined before Will took Ella and me out to the park where Lucy died and told us how he and Bobby had returned there the day after the Beatles concert. If Will didn't know where Lucy's body was even back before he fried his brain . . . if someone actually had moved it . . . then I really was up that famous proverbial creek without a paddle. And in a leaky canoe, too. Even though I knew what had happened to Lucy, I was farther from the truth than ever, and farther than ever, too, from finding her body so that Lucy could finally rest in peace and Ella could get some closure.

With all that whirling around inside my head, there was no room for Winston Churchill. I figured there was no room for any more worries, either, but oh, how wrong I was!

Try as I might, I couldn't stop thinking about how poor Will Margolis and his friends had spent forty-five years believing they'd been responsible for Lucy's death. In light of that info, it was no surprise that Bobby sacrificed his life in combat and Will had turned to the bottle for comfort. Imagine the kinds of demons that must have haunted them after that fateful night.

As for Janice?

Ah, that's where things got really dicey. See, I knew there was a flaw in Will's story. Because I knew what nobody else did—Lucy didn't die because those stupid kids pulled a stupid practical joke and it went all wrong. Or because Darren's Mustang had a faulty exhaust system. Somebody killed her.

It could only have been one person, and that one person could only have been Darren Andrews.

Which meant that Darren might also have had something to do with Janice's murder.

And I didn't have a clue how to prove any of it.

Was it any wonder that I was preoccupied? Not to mention moody, touchy, and with my brain working so much overtime, I was pretty sure my skull was going to split.

In an effort to forget my troubles when I got home from work the day Will took us to the park, I planted myself on the couch. By eight o'clock, I realized I was still there, and since staring into space had gotten me nowhere, I flicked on the TV.

There was a photo of Winston Churchill gazing back at me.

Before I even had time to surf my way to another channel, a local news guy with too-blue eyes and too-perfect hair informed me that the cops had Churchill cornered in an abandoned warehouse somewhere over on the west side of town. This time it was for real. There had even been an exchange of gunfire.

Ho-hum.

Like I said, I had other things to worry about.

I did that by devouring most of a pint of Häagen-Dazs Midnight Cookies and Cream and watching every DVR-ed episode of *Real Housewives* that I'd hoarded for just such an occasion.

It must have been ice cream overload.

I fell asleep on the couch.

And all that chocolate and fudge and those cookie wafers conspired against me—I dreamed about Quinn.

In my dream, he was standing next to the couch, looking down at me. He was dressed in one of those tailor-made suits of his, the kind that look like they come right off the cover of *GQ*. This one was charcoal gray—dark, but not nearly as inky as his hair. His white shirt was stylishly striped with winey purple and his tie was understated elegance itself, tone on tone, grape-colored paisley.

Leave it to Quinn to be tasteful and sexy all at the same time.

"Hey, Pepper, are you sleeping?"

Awake or asleep, I guess there's no way to keep the cynicism out of the voice of a woman who's been dumped for lousy reasons. Just in case Dream Quinn wouldn't notice, I gave an exaggerated yawn. "What does it look like I'm doing?"

He was all set to snarl right back at me, but he snapped his mouth shut instead and shifted from foot to foot.

It was a weird sign of hesitation from a man who was usually anything but. But then, those fudgy ribbons of deliciousness in the ice cream were doing strange things to my brain, too, so I didn't pay much attention.

I sat up. My couch is one that used to be in my parents' family room, and even in my dream, I knew it was a bad choice for sleeping. I fisted my right hand and kneaded the small of my back.

"What do you want, anyway?" I asked him. "Isn't it bad enough I think about you when I'm awake? It's not fair for you to show up in my dreams, too."

"You think about me? Really?" There was a momentary and all-too-familiar flash of green fire in his eyes. I held my breath, just waiting for him to jump on that little sign of weakness so that I could tell him it wasn't what I'd said at all and I made it a practice never to think about him, waking or sleeping. He didn't give me the chance. But then, he was looking around my living room as if he'd never seen it before.

"I'm in your apartment," he said.

I was going to say, *No duh!* But again, I wasn't quick enough.

"There's something I have to tell you," he said. He

dropped down on the other end of the couch, and truth be told, I was glad. Quinn and I had done some . . . er . . . interesting things there on that couch. I was grateful he didn't get any closer and spark any more memories. "It's about Winston Churchill."

I groaned. I mean, really, like anybody could blame me? After months of pining and being pissed and moaning and missing him, I was finally dreaming about Quinn. Thank you, subconscious! Anything could happen. In fact, I was counting on it. Now he was going to waste perfectly good dream time chatting about some killer who wasn't the killer I cared about in the first place?

A shot of anger propelled me off the couch. "You're kidding me, right? You show up out of nowhere and worm your way into my psyche or my unconscious or my . . . whatever . . . and you're going to squander a perfectly good opportunity for me to have a sexy encounter with you that I don't have to feel guilty about by talking about some scumbag I just saw on the news?"

One corner of his mouth lifted into that little smile that always sent tingles of electricity through me. "You think about it, too, huh?"

I knew he was talking about the sex. Sometimes I think it was the only thing Quinn and I ever did right.

I folded my arms over my chest. "Best sex I ever had," I admitted because, after all, it was a dream and there was no use lying to my own brain.

His smile bloomed full force. "Me, too. Except . . ." Leave it to Quinn to sigh without ever ruffling that perfectly starched shirt and that wicked fabulous tie. His expression grew serious in a way it hardly ever did except when he was thinking about some case he was trying to crack. "I thought there was more to us than that."

Like I said, there was no use lying to myself. "Yeah, me, too."

Stalemate.

Waking or sleeping, things were always the same between us.

Since there didn't seem to be anything else for us to talk about, I pointed at my TV. I remembered that just before I dozed, I'd turned it off. The screen was dark. "You're talking about Winston Churchill because I saw a picture of him before I fell asleep. That's how dreams work, right? Your brain processes things you saw that day. It makes perfect sense."

"Except you didn't see a picture of me, did you? But I'm still here."

There was that.

This was exposing a little too much of my psyche. Even to Dream Quinn.

Something told me he knew it, too. He stood up, and I braced myself. Now that I'd practically come right out and admitted that the sex was great, that I thought about him all the time, and that we'd both screwed up what might have been a good thing, I fully expected him to kiss me. Even asleep, the old, familiar tingle kicked into high gear.

Instead of coming closer, though, Quinn poked his hands into his pockets. "I can't stay long," he said. "And I've got important information that I've got to tell somebody. Only . . ." In silence, he studied me for a long time. Like he'd never seen me before.

Which was dumb. And made me uncomfortable. Not to mention antsy to get this dream over with.

"Only . . ?" I urged him to finish, and when he didn't, I stepped closer to him.

He took a step back. "Only I didn't think it was going to be you."

"Well, doesn't that make me feel all warm and fuzzy?" Was it possible for a smile to be so brittle it hurt? Even in a dream? I guess so, because for the sake of making an impression, I ignored the pain as well as the disappointment that flowed through me. Even in a dream, I couldn't catch a break. No sex. Just talk. And the same ol' go-round of fighting.

My voice was as sour as my mood. "Got anything else you want to say to boost my self-esteem before I send you packing back into whatever nightmare you stepped out of?"

That look of his—the one that had been so serious and careful only a moment before—softened into something more tender. "I guess I don't blame you for being mad, but really, you've got to see things from my perspective. When you told me you talked to the dead . . . Come on, Pepper, what did you expect me to do, jump up and down and tell you how cool it was? It sounds crazy. Even you have to admit that."

"Even me." He had a way of making those two little words sound like a condemnation. Honestly, I thought about marching over to the door, throwing it open, and telling him to get the hell out of there, but I figured that wasn't the way these things worked. If I couldn't get him out of my dream, maybe I could work things the other way around.

I commanded myself to wake up and squeezed my eyes shut, sure that when I opened them again, I'd be back on the couch. Alone.

It didn't work.

I swear my eyes were open. But there I was, still standing next to my couch, face-to-face with Quinn.

I propped my hands on my hips. "So it looks like the only way I'm going to get rid of you is to get this over with. Tell me what you want me to know. About Winston Churchill."

"Who?" Like he was the one pulling himself out of a dream of his own, Quinn shook his head. "Oh, Churchill. Yeah. That guy. I do need to tell you something about him only . . ." Frustrated, he grumbled and twirled around to pace as far as the kitchen door and back again. On his second time by, he stopped, just out of arm's reach.

"There's a whole lot more we need to talk about that's more important," he said.

"Maybe some other time. Like when I'm not trying to get my beauty sleep."

A smile glimmered over his lips. "You couldn't get any more beautiful."

"That's it!" I threw my hands in the air. It was my turn to pace, and I stomped for all I was worth. If I was actually awake, I would have felt sorry for the people who live downstairs. Once around wasn't enough to get rid of my anger, and I knew twice wouldn't help, either. I stopped right back where I'd started and pointed a finger at Quinn's nose. "You. Get out of my head. Right now."

"Can I come back?"

I growled and took a step closer. "You can come back when hell freezes over. And that would be when—"

He knew exactly when I realized what was really going on. But then, it was kind of hard to miss me turning into a block of ice in the middle of my living room.

That might have been from surprise.

Or because I was finally just close enough to feel the frosty aura that surrounded Quinn.

"Quinn?" I reached out a hand for him.

He stepped back. "You know you can't touch me."

I tried, anyway. "Quinn? This is some kind of crazy dream, right? You're not—"

"I need you to do something for me. I need you to tell the guys I work with that I went around to the back of the warehouse. There was a door back there that led into the basement. That's how Churchill got out. He jacked a car and took off. Dark-colored sedan. Ohio license plates AOY 6990. He headed toward the freeway, and that couldn't have been more than a couple minutes ago. If they're quick—"

"Quinn?"

Oh yeah, I sounded like a complete moron. I couldn't help myself. By this time, tears streaked down my face and my chest hurt so bad, I couldn't take another breath. I blinked and told myself my eyes were playing tricks on me because of the tears. Quinn couldn't really be fading right in front of me.

"You've got to get there and tell them," Quinn said. "Churchill is dangerous, and we can't let him get away. If he does, more innocent people are going to die. You've got to promise me you'll help, Pepper."

"But I can't—"

"Sure you can. You . . ." He swallowed hard and the green fire in his eyes tamped into a look far more smoldering. "I know the truth now. I know you're the only one who can."

It was the last thing he said before he faded away completely.

I'm not sure how long I stood there, staring at the spot where he'd been and wondering what had just happened. I only knew that the first thing I did was admit that I wasn't sleeping. No matter how much I wished I was.

The second thing I did was turn on the TV.

One of the local news channels was just cutting into a *Friends* rerun with breaking news.

Winston Churchill had escaped. But not before he'd had a gun battle with one of the cops who was after him. There was an officer down. They weren't releasing any names yet, but they didn't have to.

I knew Quinn was dead, and I'd just had a conversation with his ghost.

I may have ignored a couple dozen red lights on my way to the hospital where they said they'd taken the person they were calling "the wounded officer." I parked in a zone where it was clear I shouldn't have, and by the time I got off the elevator at the ICU, I wasn't just shaking, I was quivering like a bowl of Jell-O in an 8.2 magnitude earthquake.

"Police personnel only," the young uniformed cop just outside the elevator door told me.

"I'm . . . I'm not . . ." I was wearing what I'd changed into when I'd gotten home from the park visit with Ella and Will, the running shorts I never ran in and a T-shirt my mother had once brought home from a medical conference in New Orleans. I was just as surprised as the officer was to see I hadn't put on my shoes. "I just have to . . . I mean, I need to . . ."

It obviously wasn't my eloquence or even my tears that finally convinced her to step aside. It was the voice that came from behind her.

"It's OK, Barinski, I'll take over."

The man who stepped up was a middle-aged, balding

double for the Incredible Hulk. Big shoulders. Square chin. He even looked a little green, but I suppose considering the circumstances, I couldn't blame him. He was someone I'd met before at a Fraternal Order of Police picnic. Or a fund-raiser for the Police Museum. Or something. In better circumstances, I might have even remembered his name. He was wearing a suit and a badge on a chain around his neck. He took both my hands in his.

"Len Cranston," he wisely reminded me. "Pepper, how did you hear?"

"Quinn . . ." There was a flurry of activity outside one of the rooms down the hall, and I looked over his shoulder but once it was over and there was nothing to distract me, I had no choice but to talk to Len. And face the truth. "Quinn, he told me—"

"I know." Len patted my hands before he gave them back to me. "He told me you two were on the outs, too. This is a hell of a way to get back together."

"That's not . . ." I raked my trembling fingers through my hair. It was the first I remembered I hadn't bothered to comb it before I ran out of the apartment. "That's not why I'm here. I have to tell you . . ." I did my best to gulp down the ball of emotion that blocked my breathing and tried to sound calm even though it wasn't how I was feeling. Like cops everywhere, Cranston would be far more inclined to listen to a calm woman than he would to a shocky one who wasn't wearing shoes.

"I know how Churchill got out of that warehouse," I told Cranston. "He stole a car, too. He's in a dark-colored sedan and—"

"Quinn called you? He told you? Before that slime-bucket Churchill shot him?"

It seemed easier just to agree so that's what I did.
Right after I gave Len the license plate number Quinn had
given me.

He sat me down on a bench against the wall and went into
action instantly, making all the right calls, getting a bunch
more. It was five minutes or more before he remembered I
was there. It felt like five years.

"Sorry." He didn't need to say it, but really, it's the sort
of all-purpose word people use at times like this. "You want
to go in and see Quinn?"

I was tempted to tell him I already had, but even if I was
so inclined, I was sure the words wouldn't make it past the
lump in my throat.

"Come on." He made the decision for me, tugging me
to my feet at the same time he asked one of the nurses for
a pair of those funny, stretchy hospital slippers. "I'll take
you in."

I hung back. No easy thing to do considering the guy is
as big as a building. Still, I was determined. Talking to the
dead is one thing. Seeing a body . . . it wasn't like I hadn't
done it before. But before, it had never been Quinn, and my
heart had never been smashed and my legs paralyzed.

Cranston wasn't taking *no* for an answer. Before I knew
it, I had a pair of limey green slippers on my feet, and he was
half walking, half dragging me down a hallway. He stopped
just outside one of the rooms and stepped aside.

And me? I stood frozen to the spot, my chest aching like
somebody in thick boots had kicked the hell out of me, my
mind racing, grasping for any straw of logic in a situation
that was anything but.

I'd done what I came to the hospital to do. It was time to
run home and lose myself in the misery that made every
breath a chore. When I flinched and turned to hotfoot it to

the elevator, Cranston put his hands on my shoulders, spun me back the other way, and gave me a nudge inside.

The room was empty except for the body in the bed, a single light shining down on it.

It was quiet except for the swishing of some machine over on my left.

Rather than do what I had to do, and face the truth, I concentrated on details. Quinn's charcoal suit, his striped shirt, and that damned sexy tie of his were lying over a chair at the foot of the bed. There was an ugly maroon-colored stain on the shirt.

"Last time . . . I go anywhere . . . without . . . bulletproof vest."

I nearly fainted when I heard the raspy whisper from the bed.

"Quinn?" It wasn't a big room, but I closed the space between us in record time. "You're alive. Oh my gosh!" I grabbed his hand, which I probably shouldn't have considering there were IV tubes in it. His skin wasn't hot. I mean, not like the hot I was used to feeling when his skin met mine. But it wasn't ice, either. Not like the Quinn who'd been in my apartment. I hung on tight, even when I figured I was cutting off his circulation. Heck, we were in the ICU. They could fix things like that.

Quinn's eyelids fluttered. "Pepper . . . I think . . ." There was a smudge of blood in one corner of his mouth, and I found a cloth and wiped it. "I didn't think . . ."

He closed his eyes on a wave of pain, and I squeezed his hand tighter before I realized me hanging on like a limpet might have been what hurt so much. I loosened my hold, but I didn't let go.

I coughed around the tightness in my throat. "They said on the news that you were—"

For just a second, his eyes sparked with that old familiar flame. "Heard them talking . . . Nurses . . . Doctors . . . brought me back."

"But not before you told me where Churchill was."

The shake he gave his head was so weak, I wouldn't have noticed it at all if the tubes going in his mouth and nose hadn't moved. "Not possible."

"You know it is."

Another shake. "I was . . . just . . . dreaming."

"And you picked that particular moment to dream about me?" Like I hadn't smiled in a lifetime and didn't remember how to even begin, I tried for a bright expression. It hurt. "It wasn't the drugs, either, so don't try to tell me it was. You were there, Quinn. You were dead, and you were in my apartment. You remember, don't you?"

I thought he was drifting away, but actually he was looking me over. "Same T-shirt," he said. "Norleans. But . . . no. Can't be."

Recently dead and looking very much the worse for wear, and he could still make me mad enough to scream. I controlled the urge, but only because I didn't want to bring half the Cleveland Police Force running. "You were there. I talked to you. And you told me Winston Churchill escaped through the basement door of the warehouse. You said he got into a dark-colored sedan. You remember that happening?"

He did his best to nod.

"Then tell me how I knew about it if you didn't tell me."

"Not . . . possible."

If I could have ignored the tubes, the bandages, the machinery beeping around us, and the sickly smell of blood, I might have been able to remind myself to go easy on him.

Quinn had had a rough night, being dead and all. In my book, that wasn't much of an excuse.

I leaned in nice and close so that one of these days when he was up and around again and arguing with me about what a nutcase I was, he'd remember this moment.

"Ohio license plate," I said, slowly and carefully, "AOY 6990."

He shook his head.

And I guess we would have gone on just like that—me being the logical one for a change and him denying it for all he was worth—if Cranston hadn't poked his head into the room. "Highway Patrol just picked up Churchill outside the county line," he said. "He was driving that dark sedan, all right. That license number you gave us, Pepper, it was right on." He gave us the thumbs-up.

And I smiled down at Quinn in a very superior way. But then, I could afford to be self-righteous. I'd just helped capture a dangerous serial killer.

"Believe me now?" I asked him.

"Don't know . . . what to believe." He closed his eyes, and just at that moment, a nurse walked into the room.

"He needs to rest," she said.

And I knew a *get out of here* when I heard one. Even a polite one.

My knees were Silly Putty and my head was spinning, but I wasn't imagining it when I heard Quinn say my name just as I got to the door.

I turned in time to see the smallest of smiles lightly touch his lips. "I guess . . ." He pulled in a breath and a wave of pain crossed his face. "The dead do talk."

18

I spent the next couple days ping-ponging between relief that Quinn was alive and panic when I relived that awful time before I knew the truth, and yes—in my worst moments when the warm and fuzzies I'd felt at the hospital wore off and I was back to thinking about Quinn the way I had been thinking about him in the previous months— jealousy. That would be because I wasn't the lucky one who'd had the chance to take that potshot at him.

I cried a lot, too. Ella insisted that was just all the stress working its way out of my body.

It was more than enough to keep me busy, but not enough to turn off the thoughts constantly pounding through my head. No big surprise, they were all about Lucy and that empty spot at the park where her body had originally been dumped. While I was at it, I spent a lot of time obsessing over how I was never going to get at the truth.

And then there were Quinn's parting words to me, of course.

The dead do talk.

The phrase had become something of a mantra, and not because I wanted it to be. Every time I tried to work my way through the Lucy problem, my head was filled with memories of my visit to the hospital. There was Quinn, lying in that bed looking like nobody should ever look and scraping out those few words.

"The dead do talk."

"What's that?"

I hadn't realized I'd spoken out loud. In fact, I'd forgotten that Ella was sitting not six feet away. Like I said, I'd been preoccupied.

"Nothing." I shoved aside the new brochure about the cemetery's horticultural treasures that I was supposed to be checking for typos and looked across the desk at her. She was there in my office because she was—allegedly—convinced it was the best place for her to remove old paper clips from stacks of ancient interoffice memos. At least that's what she said. Since the conference room was just down the hall, no one was using it, and she could have spread her oldy moldy papers all over the table in there rather than keeping them balanced on her lap, I wasn't buying it. Ella was keeping an eye on me. I guess the least I could do in return is tell her what I was thinking.

"It's what Quinn said," I told her. Of course I'd already reported almost my entire conversation with Quinn to her. A couple dozen times. But I'd left out all the parts about how I thought I was dreaming about him when I wasn't, and about how he didn't believe me at first when I told him what he thought he dreamed was real. It took that license plate number to convince him. Yeah, it seemed best to gloss over that stuff.

"At the hospital. He told me the dead talk."

"He was delirious." Ella plucked off paper clip after paper clip and dropped them into an empty coffee filter box. "The poor guy. He must still be on some major medications, and I can only imagine it was worse the other night. You know, right after *it all happened*."

It was her way of sparing my feelings. Yeah, like substituting *it all happened* for *Quinn died* would make me forget that *it all happened*.

"I'm sure that was some of it," I said, even though I wasn't. "He was mumbling stuff about Churchill and all. But when I was leaving, that's when he said that stuff about the dead talking."

A shiver snaked over Ella's shoulders. "Well, I suppose he would know. You know what I mean, since he was *gone* for a little while. Has he said anything like it since?"

He hadn't. But that's because the couple times I stopped down at the hospital to see Quinn, he was always sleeping. Or maybe he was just pretending to be sleeping. On death's doorstep or not, I wouldn't put it past him. That way he wouldn't have to face me and the new reality that had dawned on him the night he died.

The dead do talk.

I drummed my fingers against my desktop, considering the words. It wasn't like it was some big revelation. I'd known that the dead could talk to me ever since that day I took a spill and clunked my head on a mausoleum.

So why wouldn't the thought leave me alone?

"What do you suppose he meant?" Ella asked.

I shrugged. It was a better strategy at this point than

mentioning he'd visited me while his spirit hung suspended between this world and the next. "It's just that every time I try to think about Lucy, I keep thinking about what Quinn said, and it's driving me crazy."

Apparently there wasn't much else Ella could say about it. She plucked in silence. I drummed my fingers and racked my brain and spun my wheels.

"You know . . ."

I don't know how long I'd been deep in thought. I only know that when Ella spoke, I jumped about a mile. She smiled an apology.

"You know," she said, "Will's just waiting for all the hoopla to die down. Before he turns himself in to the police."

It wasn't what we were talking about, but I was grateful for the change of subject. Maybe once my brain had a chance to disengage, it would settle down into thinking about what it was supposed to be thinking about. "You mean all the hoopla about—"

"About that terrible Winston Churchill fellow, and about Quinn being a hero. You've seen the newspaper, right?" She'd brought it into my office with her and set it on my desk, but I'd been so busy mulling and obsessing, I hadn't paid any attention to it. She tapped the front page with a rusty paper clip. "They're saying if it wasn't for Quinn, Churchill would have gotten away."

I craned my neck for a closer look. I was pretty sure those newspaper stories didn't mention me, and I guess I couldn't expect them to. It's not like Quinn could tell the press he'd provided me with the vital clue while he was dead.

I sighed.

"That's such a nice picture of your friend," Ella said with another tap at the photo of Quinn, the one right under the headline about how he was expected to make a full recovery and what a miracle it was. "He's so good-looking!"

Yeah, so good-looking, and so unwilling to believe it last summer when I told him the truth about how I talked to the dead, it took him dying to make him see I wasn't a liar.

Rather than look at Quinn's face looking back at me, I flipped the paper over.

"Hey!" I poked the newspaper, too, only not as delicately as Ella had. "You didn't tell me there was a story about Darren Andrews in here."

Antique interoffice memo in hand, she dismissed the comment with a lift of one shoulder. "It doesn't have anything to do with Lucy. Or with our case."

"We don't have a—"

"In fact, I'm surprised they bothered to put it on the front page at all. Must be a slow news day." I had no doubts the media thought so, too. Now that Churchill was behind bars where he belonged and Quinn's service record had been examined from one end to the other—both in print and on TV—there wasn't much else for them to talk about.

Ella brushed her hands together, picked up the box of paper clips, and headed for the door. "It's just about five," she said, and it struck me that this was probably the first time in the years I'd worked at Garden View that she'd ever had to remind me. "You going home? Are you sure you're OK to be alone?"

"I'm fine," I told her, because if I said anything else, she would hover.

"You can just throw those old memos into the recycling box on your way out," she said at the door. "And the newspaper, too, if you're done with it. Unless you're keeping a scrapbook for that handsome guy of yours!"

I'll bet she was twinkling when she said it. Since I didn't need verification, I didn't bother to look. Instead, I pulled the paper closer, ignored the story about Quinn completely, and scanned the article about Darren Andrews. It was all about that building of his down in the Flats, the one the city had scooped up through eminent domain. In spite of his feisty words about it at the news conference I'd crashed, it looked like Andrews had run up against a legal brick wall. Demolition had already started. Things like windows and copper plumbing—things that could be recycled—were already gone. What was left of the Andrews Building was set to come down the next day.

Ella was right. If that was front-page news, it was a slow day in Cleveland.

I tossed the newspaper aside, gathered my purse and the lunch I'd brought with me and hadn't touched, and turned out my office light.

I already had my hand on the door when that irritating mantra floated through my brain again.

And that's when it hit me.

That's what my subconscious had been trying to tell me!

If my hands weren't full, I would have given my forehead a slap.

The dead do talk.

All along, Lucy held the key to the mystery and all the proof I needed to put her—and this case—to rest.

And something told me Darren Andrews knew it, too.

It wasn't hard to find the Andrews Building. There was yellow construction tape printed with DO NOT CROSS warnings strung around the entire perimeter, and yes, just for the record, I crawled right under it like it wasn't there. It wasn't hard to get inside the building, either, but then, most of the windows on the second floor had already been removed, there was a conveniently placed Dumpster nearby, and—thank goodness—nobody was around to witness my less-than-graceful ascent.

It was practically an invitation to walk right in.

And walk right in I did.

Well, truth be told, I actually dropped from the window ledge. Fortunately, there was a small mountain of construction debris right under it, so I didn't have far to fall. I landed in a pile of splintered wallboard, wadded-up fast-food bags, and old floor tiles. Good thing, too, that I had dressed for the occasion in my oldest jeans and sneakers. If I'd risked a decent outfit, I'd be plenty pissed.

I scrambled down from the pile and took a moment to look around. In the gathering evening gloom, the hallway that stretched out in front of me was muffled in shadows. The good news was that since most of the windows were missing, I still had some daylight to guide me.

Some squeaky something scurried across the floor about a foot in front of me, and I gasped and jumped back. I waited until my breathing steadied, then flicking on my flashlight, I scanned what was left of the building. There was a stairway right in front of me, and a bank of elevators over on my left. What were the chances? Rather than try and just end up disappointed, I hoofed it up the steps, my sneakers silent against the green tile.

I stopped at the third-floor landing, listening, and when I didn't hear anything, I did a quick turn around the floor. The place was as creepy as hell, and except for the floors that creaked and moaned and the swoosh of the wind com-

ing off the lake and in through all those gaping window
holes, it was as quiet as everybody who doesn't know the
dead talk to me thinks it is over at Garden View.

There was no sign that Darren Andrews was anywhere in
the vicinity.

I legged it up to the fourth floor, and the fifth, and the
sixth.

By the time I'd scouted them all—and found them all
empty—I was discouraged. Not to mention winded.

I allowed myself a couple minutes to sit on the steps and
gather my thoughts.

So maybe I wasn't so good at putting together clues and
finding meaning in the words Quinn had mumbled when
he'd had one foot in the grave?

Or maybe I was.

My head came up when I heard a sound from the floor
above me, and I held my breath and listened for more. Sure,
it might have been another furry intruder, but if it was, it
was one with big feet, wearing hard shoes. My head tipped
so I could listen more closely, my steps careful and quiet, I
slunk up to the seventh and top floor.

The other floors I had examined each contained wide
hallways and rows of doors. This one was different. Just to
the left of the elevators, there was an archway that led back
into a suite of offices. Carved over it were the words AN-
DREWS INCORPORATED.

"Bingo!" I whispered to myself. It beat listening to
the sound of my heart knocking against my ribs. I stepped
through the doorway and paused to listen. This time, there
was no mistaking the sounds I heard. Pounding. Like somebody banging on a wall.

I followed the noise, and just outside an office at the end
of the hallway, I heard it change. No more pounding, this

was more like punching through. I heard the splat of plaster chips hitting the floor, and the grunt of labored breathing.

Silently, I stepped into the office. This was the corner suite, the one I had no doubt had once belonged to Darren's father. It was roomy, and once upon a time, I bet it had been elegant. Though most of it had been salvaged, there were still a few remnants of oak paneling on the walls and chunks of thick carpeting over in the corners where it had obviously been too difficult to rip up. Two of the walls had once contained windows and a killer view of Lake Erie beyond.

Darren Andrews stood opposite them, in the farthest corner of the room. He had a shovel in his hands, and he smacked the wall one more time. In the quickly fading evening light, I saw the last of the plaster fall away. And I saw the look of relief that swept Darren's expression.

But then, that's because he saw what I couldn't see. At least not until he stepped back and stepped aside.

An arm had flopped out of the wall.

Or I should say more precisely, what was left of an arm.

The bones were burnished the color of old brass, but there was no mistaking that the arm must have belonged to a woman. It was slim and delicate. The fingers were long and shapely. They clutched a gold chain, and I didn't have to get closer to know what was dangling from it—that Saint Andrew's medal Darren wasn't wearing in his senior picture.

"Son of a gun, Quinn was right. The dead do talk. I just wasn't listening. Lucy said she fought with you when you came around to the trunk and put that blanket over her face. She was so panicked, she didn't realize she'd ripped off that medal of yours. I bet you didn't, either. Not until it was too late. Bet you thought you lost it in the park. That's why you went back there the next day. You never knew it was clutched in her hand, did you? You were too scared to look too close."

Honest to gosh, I thought Darren was going to have a coronary, right then and there. His mouth open, his cheeks pale and pocked with plaster dust, he spun to face me. "What the hell are you talking about? You can't possibly know—"

"I know more than you think. Like about the tests you were stealing and selling. You thought that's what Lucy was going to see the principal about. News flash, it wasn't. You killed her for nothing."

Now that Andrews had a couple moments to compose himself, he pulled in a breath and threw back his shoulders. "Killed? What on earth are you talking about? You can't possibly think I know anything about this . . ." His top lip curled, he slid a look at the arm and I took a moment to peer farther into the cubbyhole it had fallen out of. Now that my eyes were more accustomed to the dim light, I saw the smooth contours of a skull, its empty eye sockets fixed on me.

I think it was that unwavering look from Lucy that kicked my adrenaline into high gear when Darren started with the excuses—just like I expected him to.

"I was here taking a last look at this magnificent building that was once home to my family business," he said. "I've made this terrible discovery. You're just in time. I was just about to call the police and let them know what I found."

Adrenaline, remember. And a healthy dose of chutzpah to go along with it. My chin high, I stepped closer to the skeleton. "You were going to call the police, huh? Was that before or after you were going to get rid of that medal of yours that Lucy's holding?"

His eyes snapped to mine. "That's ridiculous. There must have been a million medals like that made back then."

"Back then. You mean like back when Lucy Pasternak

was bragging about how brave she was at the Beatles concert, and you kids decided to teach her a lesson."

Oh, how I love to watch bad guys squirm!

He ran his tongue over his lips. "You're going to believe that stupid drunk? If that's what Will told you, then maybe he killed Lucy. Will and I, we used to hang around here sometimes after school. You know, watching the building being built. He could have known the last of the plastering was going to be done the day after the concert. He could have brought the body here and—"

"Except he didn't, because he thought the body was where you guys left it. You know, at the park. But Will and Bobby went back the next day, and Lucy's body was gone. That's because you . . ." I emphasized the word. "After you took the other kids home and swore them to secrecy, that's when you went back to the park to look for your medal. You didn't find it, but you picked up Lucy's body and brought it here. You know, it would be one thing if you did it just to hide the body and save your own skin. But you had something even nastier in mind. You knew that if the other kids were scared that someone had seen them, they'd keep their mouths shut. You held it over their heads for forty-five whole years. And you knew you were safe because you're the one who knew about the plastering the next day. I'm not much when it comes to construction, but let me guess . . ." I moved closer and took a look. "That's a heating duct or an air vent or something. You knew once the walls were finished, nobody would ever find Lucy. And that was that. Until the city swooped in and scooped up your building. That's why you fought so hard to keep it from being torn down. You knew what they were going to find when they started demolition."

Andrews must have come right from the office. His suit

coat was off and thrown over a nearby three-legged chair. His white business shirt glowed eerily in the half-light. "You really are a ridiculous young lady, and I don't know why you're spouting all this nonsense. You don't think if you tell the authorities, they'll actually believe you, do you?"

I grinned because, let's face it, another piece of the puzzle chunked into place and I was feeling damned proud of myself. "That's why you killed Janice and never bothered with Will. Once you liquored him up again, you figured you were safe. If Will said anything to anyone about what happened that night, nobody would listen. He's just a crazy drunk, after all. But Janice . . ."

I remembered the portrait that hung in the lobby of the tony real estate building.

"They would have listened to Janice. She was an intelligent, successful woman. And she wasn't stupid. Let me guess, she called and told you Will came to see her to tell her I was asking about Lucy. She wanted money to keep her mouth shut. You don't have to confirm or deny," I added, though I wasn't sure he was going to do either. "From what I know about her, that sounds like Janice."

"Well, that certainly is an interesting story you've concocted." Andrews took a step toward me. Don't worry, I hadn't forgotten he was holding that shovel. When I saw his hand tighten around the handle, I stepped back, and gauged the distance to the doorway.

Sure, I was hopped up on adrenaline. But I wasn't stupid.

I can't say for sure because it happened pretty fast, but I think I'd already made a move toward the door when I slammed into something.

I should say *someone*.

Someone short and skinny who was wearing jeans just

like mine and a cami that hugged her bought-and-paid-for curves.

"Ariel, what the hell are you doing here?" I wailed.

It only took me a second, but it was one second too long, and Darren wasn't stupid, either. He knew a skinny little kid was an easier target than a tall, imposing woman.

Before I could warn her or push her away, Darren had an arm around Ariel. He dragged her away from me, back toward the wall, and when she saw the skeleton arm dangling there, Ariel panicked. The more she screamed and squirmed, the tighter he hung on.

"Shut up." Andrews gave her a shake.

Ariel shut up, all right. I'd like to think it was because I was signaling her to keep her cool, not because the creep was threatening her.

"Your friend and I here . . ." He gave her another shake, just for good measure, and Ariel's head snapped back. I didn't like the look of that, and I sprang forward, but I didn't dare get too close. Especially when he dragged her too close for comfort to the gaping holes left by the missing windows.

I put on the brakes.

"Your friend and I here were just discussing what we were going to do about this surprising discovery I've made," Andrews told Ariel. She wasn't listening. Her eyes goggled out of her head and tears streamed down her cheeks when she slid a look toward the missing window and the seven stories of nothing between her and the ground.

I had to tell myself to ignore her, or I'd end up crying, too, and then where would we be?

"I was going to call the police," Andrews purred. "But then you showed up."

Was Ariel canny or incredibly stupid? I can't say, but I'll

give the kid credit, she worked past her fear. "I'm a detective," she said. "Just like Pepper. That's why I followed her here tonight. I heard everything about the medal and the trunk and the blanket. I know you killed Lucy."

"I said, shut up!" This time when Andrews shook her, he lifted Ariel's tiny body clear off the floor. I would have been alarmed if I'd had the chance.

But then, when Ella and Will raced into the room, I was a little taken aback.

"You let her go right now, Darren!" Oh, yeah. That was Ella, all right, except that in all the time I had known her, I'd never seen her like this. Her chin firm, her gaze steady, and her eyes spitting brimstone, she stalked into the office like a lioness.

"That is my daughter," Ella said, her voice iron. "If you so much as harm one hair on her head—"

"If any of you get one step closer . . ." Andrews twirled around. His hand was still clamped on Ariel's shoulders and he swung her closer to the window. Ella let out a gasp. Behind me, I heard Will curse.

"We're all getting a little overemotional." Pepper Martin, the voice of reason. It wasn't exactly an everyday occurrence, and I had to remind myself that this one time, I had to play it for all it was worth. Ariel's life depended on it.

"What we need to do is just talk this out." I took my eyes off Darren just long enough to glance at Ella and Will, just so Darren didn't feel singled out. "All of us."

"Sure, let's talk. Just like the old friends we are." Darren threw back his head and laughed. "What would you like to talk about, Will? How about which whiskey's your favorite?"

Will scuffed his shoes against the floor.

And yeah, I'd been talking the talk about staying calm. But walking the walk was something I'm not very good at.

"Darren Andrews, you son of a . . ." I growled at him and dared to take a step nearer. If I could just get close enough to grab Ariel's arm . . .

"How dare you ridicule Will," I said. "It's your fault he's the way he is. Your fault that Bobby killed himself. Tell him, Darren. Tell Will how Lucy didn't die because you kids did something wrong. Tell him how you wanted to shut her up. Tell him how you said you were going around to the back of the car to let her out, but you really held a blanket over her face. You smothered her to death."

At my side, I heard Will take in a long, stuttering breath. "Is it true?"

Darren's only response was a smile.

"This piece of crap has been holding it over all of you for forty-five years," I said. "Just to make sure you kept quiet."

In the silence of the decrepit building, Will's moan sounded like the howl of a banshee. "I had a life," he wailed. "I had a life, and you took it away from me."

Will moved fast for an old guy, but Andrews was in better shape. He dropped the shovel and got a two-handed hold on Ariel. He lifted her up and dangled her over the side of the building.

"I'll drop her," he said. "I swear I'll drop her if you come any closer."

"Mom!" Ariel cried.

And maybe it's the whole motherly instinct thing. It was all Ella could take.

I knew what she was going to do even before she moved, so I was ready. When Ella and Will darted forward, grasping for Ariel, I moved, too. I had that shovel in my hands in an instant.

Darren Andrews was out cold before he ever knew what hit him.

It was the first I dared take my cell phone off of where it was clipped to the waistband of my jeans.

My hands were shaking, but I think my voice was pretty calm when I said, "So what do you think, Len, did you hear all that pretty well?"

On the other end of the phone, Len Cranston chuckled. "All I can hear now is that noise in the background. Is that laughing or crying? No, don't even bother to try to explain. I'm not sure where Quinn found you, Pepper, or how you do what you do . . ." I heard him whistle under his breath. "I can only say I'm glad you asked me to do you this favor and sit down here on the street so I could monitor what you were up to. Stay put. I'll be right up there."

We waited for him, Will hugging Ella, who was hugging Ariel and me, keeping an eye on Darren to make sure he didn't come to and decide to make a break for it.

While I was at it, I took a closer look at the Saint Andrew's medal and the delicate skeleton hand of the woman who held it.

And I thought about how right Quinn was.

The dead really do talk, and it looked like Lucy Pasternak still had a lot to say.

19

"It was a nice funeral, wasn't it?"

Since the look in her eyes was far, far away, I wasn't sure if Ella was talking to me, or herself.

I answered, anyway. It beat sitting there on the rapid watching Ella stare out the window.

"It was perfect," I told her. "You did a great job of planning everything."

"It was the least I could do." Her smile was more relaxed than any I'd seen from her in the days since Darren Andrews had been arrested for a forty-five-year-old murder. But then, she'd almost seen her youngest daughter thrown out a window. I guess I was willing to cut Ella some slack.

"I still don't see what Lucy's funeral at Garden View had to do with taking a ride on the rapid," she said. "But that's OK." She patted my knee. "After all you've done for us . . ." Her eyes gleamed with tears, but I knew they were happy ones. "Ariel's decided she doesn't want to be a detective anymore. She told you that, didn't she? As a matter of fact, before she left for school today, she told me she'd decided to become a librarian."

"She's good at research, and she actually enjoys it." I nodded. It made sense. In a sick and twisted way. "She'll be a great librarian."

"And Will's going to be OK, too." I knew this part of the story, of course, but Ella never got tired of talking about it. "His attorney's sure he'll get probation, provided he goes into rehab and stays there. It's the best thing that could have happened to him. Maybe now he'll be able to put all the sadness behind him."

"Will you?"

She tipped her head, thinking. "I'll never forget Lucy, or all that was taken from her. The world would be a better place if she was part of it. But I'm at peace now." She drew in a breath and let it out slowly, then looked at me out of the corner of her eye. "Are you?"

"Me?" In the great scheme of things, I was the one who was least affected by all that had gone on in the previous weeks. Except for—

"Oh, you're talking about Quinn."

Ella chuckled. "Of course that's what I'm talking about. You went to the hospital again to see him, didn't you? What's that handsome detective of yours have to say for himself?"

Since he wasn't *my* detective, I suppose I wasn't officially obligated to answer. I did, anyway. "Quinn and I have a lot to talk about." Understatement! Though we'd discussed the medications he was taking, the physical therapy he would eventually have to go through, and every other subject under the sun including the poor quality of hospital food, we had yet to get down to brass tacks and talk about what we should have been talking about—that little visit he'd paid me in those few minutes when he was dead.

"We're taking it slow," I told her and reminded myself. "Maybe one of these days—"

"Of course you're going to get back together!" Ella sounded so sure of herself. I didn't know if this was good news, or bad. "Everything is going to work out perfectly. I just wish . . ."

Her voice trailed off, while her gaze wandered away. I knew Quinn's and my relationship wasn't the only thing that would take some time to work through. Ella didn't have the guilt to carry around, not like the other kids did, but she had memories. And regrets.

"I know I can't change anything," she said. "But if I could . . ." She giggled, uncomfortable with the thought of playing fast and loose with the past. "If I could change one thing . . . I mean one thing other than Lucy getting murdered . . . I would . . . well, it's going to sound crazy . . ."

Again she glanced my way, and when I didn't jump right in and agree with her, she went on. "I wish I would have said good-bye to Lucy that night. We were right here. On a rapid car a lot like this one." She glanced all around. Since it was the middle of the afternoon, the train was just about empty. Ella looked back over her shoulder. "I was sitting right about here, too. About this close to the door. And Lucy was next to me. And when I got up to get off the train, she wanted to come along. I wish I would have let her. I wish I would have stopped long enough to say good-bye. I wish—"

I wasn't surprised to see the golden shimmer in the aisle next to Ella. I was surprised, though, to realize that she must have seen it. And pleased, too. After all, this was the chance

I was hoping for when I insisted we take a train ride after the funeral.

When Lucy appeared out of nowhere, Ella's mouth dropped open and she clutched a hand to her throat.

"Hey, Little One, you're the best sister anybody could ever have," Lucy told her. "And you don't have to worry about saying good-bye. You've been doing that all these years. If it wasn't for you, I wouldn't be at peace now." The rapid pulled into a station, the doors slid open, and sparkling, Lucy got off.

When I looked at Ella again, there were tears on her cheeks.

"What is it?" I asked, because let's face it, if I didn't, she might suspect I'd seen what had just gone on, and I couldn't let that happen.

A grin like the spring sunshine outside split her face. "Oh, Pepper," she said. "You wouldn't believe me if I told you!"

By the next week, life had settled down into the old familiar routine. Summer was right around the corner and there was lots to do at Garden View. As always, I wasn't exactly looking forward to any of it, but hey, I was feeling pretty mellow. The bad guys were in jail where bad guys belonged, and though it was a long shot, the real-life CSI-types were taking apart that classic car of Darren's, looking for traces of Lucy in the trunk. Between what they might find there, the Saint Andrew's medal, and the evidence they were testing and retesting from Janice's office, it looked like ol' Darren had bigger things to worry about than just that building of his coming down.

But that wasn't the end of the good news. I told Lucy's

family that I thought there might be an original copy of "Girl at Dawn" in with all the old things of hers they'd kept, and they were busy sorting through things. Patrick Monroe was about to be exposed.

I mean, in a good way.

Will was getting much-needed help, Quinn was on the mend, Ariel was no longer dogging my steps, and Ella was as sparkly as those crazy beaded earrings she always wore.

Life was good, and I intended to celebrate it by hiding out in my office and drinking a diet iced tea before I plunged into preparing for a tour I had scheduled for the next day.

Which explains why I was a little perplexed when I walked into my office and found Ella already in there. She was crying.

My good mood dissolved in a flash. "Now what?" I asked, even though I wasn't sure I wanted to hear it. "Don't tell me somebody else has been murdered."

"Oh, no. It's nothing like that." Ella was the only person I knew who still carried around those old-fashioned cloth handkerchiefs. She pulled one out of her pocket—it was purple with pink flowers—and dabbed it to her eyes. "Oh, Pepper!" she wailed.

I knew better than to try to get anything out of her when she was this upset, so I sat down behind my desk, sipped my tea, and waited while she dabbed and sniffed.

"You know I think of you as one of my own girls," she said. "You're smart and you're clever, and honest to goodness, I don't know how or why it always happens, but you've got a way of getting involved in puzzles and figuring them out, too. You're wonderful, Pepper."

There didn't seem to be much else to say besides, "Thank you."

"And you know I don't want to be doing this. In fact, Jim

wanted to tell you, but I insisted. I mean, not like I want to tell you or anything, but . . ." A fresh cascade of tears erupted, and this time, a little dabbing wasn't enough. She wiped and blew her nose.

"You know we've been involved in some cost-cutting measures, right? And I know you've done your part and—"

"If this means pulling more staples out of old newsletters, I'm your man!" I wasn't, of course. In fact, I fully intended to do all I could to avoid the job, but at least if I agreed, Ella might stop crying.

"It's not that," she said. She pulled herself to her feet. "It's just that . . . well, really, Pepper, I'm not sure how to say it so I'm just going to say it. You know I love you and I admire you and—"

"And?" I couldn't stand it anymore. "Ella, what is it?"

"Pepper," she sniffled, "We've got to cut costs, and you're our only full-time tour guide, and . . . and . . . Pepper, I hate to be the one to have to tell you this, but you're fired."

SIXTH IN THE PEPPER MARTIN
MYSTERIES FROM

CASEY DANIELS

TOMB WITH A VIEW

**Cemeteries come alive for amateur sleuth
and reluctant medium Pepper Martin.**

Cleveland's Garden View Cemetery is hosting a James
A. Garfield commemoration. For Pepper Martin, this
means that she'll surely be hearing from the dead president himself. And when she's assigned to help plan the
event with know-it-all volunteer and Garfield fanatic
Marjorie Klinker, she'll wish Marjorie were dead . . .
too bad someone beats Pepper to it.

penguin.com

"[Features a] spunky heroine and sparkling wit."
—Kerrelyn Sparks,
New York Times bestselling author

FIFTH IN THE PEPPER MARTIN MYSTERIES

DEAD MAN TALKING

CASEY DANIELS
Author of *Tomb with a View*

Heiress-turned-cemetery-tour-guide Pepper Martin is not happy to discover that a local reality TV show, *Cemetery Survivor*, will be filmed at Cleveland's Monroe Street Cemetery—and she has to be a part of it. To make matters worse, the ghost of a wrongly convicted killer needs Pepper's help to clear his name. But digging for the truth could put her in grave danger.

M649T0210

DON'T MISS MORE PEPPER MARTIN FROM

Casey Daniels

NIGHT OF THE LOVING DEAD

Pepper Martin, heiress-turned-cemetery-tour-guide, has her hands full with work, two hotties, and the ghosts who won't let her rest— or work, or shop—in peace...

The specter of Madeline—a young woman in a lab coat—wants Pepper's help. Before she died, she worked with the sexy, mysterious doctor who claims Pepper is in danger. Little does Pepper know there's more to the story, including a devious doctor—and an obsessive, crazy love.

"[A] charming...blend of romance, mystery, and nostalgia."
—Publishers Weekly

penguin.com